Jo Thomas worked for many years as a reporter and producer, first for BBC Radio 5, before moving on to Radio 4's *Woman's Hour* and Radio 2's *The Steve Wright Show*.

In 2013 Jo won the RNA Katie Fforde Bursary. Her debut novel, *The Oyster Catcher*, was a runaway best-seller in ebook and was awarded the 2014 RNA Joan Hessayon Award and the 2014 Festival of Romance Best Ebook Award. Jo lives in the Vale of Glamorgan with her husband and three children.

www.penguin.co.uk

Chasing the Italian Dream

Jo Thomas

CORGI BOOKS

TRANSWORLD PUBLISHERS
Penguin Random House, One Embassy Gardens,
8 Viaduct Gardens, London SW11 7BW
www.penguin.co.uk

Transworld is part of the Penguin Random House group of companies
whose addresses can be found at global.penguinrandomhouse.com

First published in Great Britain in 2021 by Corgi
an imprint of Transworld Publishers

A CIP catalogue record for this book
is available from the British Library.

ISBN
9780552176866

Typeset in 11/14pt ITC Giovanni by Jouve (UK), Milton Keynes.
Printed and bound in Great Britain by Clays Ltd, Elcograf S.p.A.

The authorized representative in the EEA is Penguin Random House Ireland,
Morrison Chambers, 32 Nassau Street, Dublin D02 YH68.

Penguin Random House is committed to a sustainable
future for our business, our readers and our planet. This book
is made from Forest Stewardship Council® certified paper.

For the grumpy one at home,
who makes things happen!
Thank you for the adventure.
Love you always.

PROLOGUE

'Shit, shit, shit!' I type like my fingers are on fire.

Outside I can hear the engine of my taxi running. It's been waiting for at least twenty minutes, and when I booked it I knew I was cutting it fine to get to the airport.

I finish the last email in my inbox, press return on my automated out-of-office email, slam down my laptop lid and scoop it into its case and into my big shoulder-bag. I grab my suitcase, which has been sitting by my desk all day – a patient companion – waiting to go.

'Oh, Luce, you leaving already?'

My heart sinks.

My boss, Anthony Gwyn-Jones, comes out of his glass-fronted office.

Jasper, my new young colleague, looks up from his desk, which is next to mine, as if he's surfacing from a pile of work, but I know he's had his eye on the clock for the last hour. He tries to be the last to leave every day and likes Anthony to notice, but staying late and actually getting the job done are two different things. Hopefully he'll learn that one day.

'All done,' I say, slightly out of breath. 'And, yes, I'm off. I have a plane to catch. Annual leave, remember?' I smile.

'Ah, yes, of course.' He nods. 'Back to Italy! The homeland!' He laughs, his cheeks ruddy. Perhaps his long lunch meeting involved a few glasses of red wine.

Jasper joins in, smiling with apparent good nature. But Jasper's smile never meets his eyes. He's ten years my junior, sharply dressed and determined to make his mark in the firm. But not this time. It's not his turn, it's mine. This promotion has been a long time coming.

'Well, I'm not exactly from Italy. I grew up in Wales,' I tell Anthony, for the umpteenth time.

'Yes, but with a name like Rossi, you must be Italian.'

'Anyway,' I say, 'I've done that document you wanted.' I have to stop him before he asks where my family are from again, and I have to do the whole bit about my grandparents moving to Wales from a small town just outside Naples, then going back to take over the family restaurant. My parents stayed here to bring up me and my brother. And I don't want to explain that my full surname is Rossi-Llewellyn – I'd taken my stepfather's surname after Dad died. I certainly don't have time for that.

I'm pulling my case towards the door.

'Already? That was quick.'

'I have a plane to catch. My taxi's waiting!' I say, as politely as I can, but I feel quite stressed now.

'Oh, right, yes. I just sent you another email, but Jasper can deal with that for me.'

I hesitate. 'Well, I could take a look at it at the airport.'

'No, no!' He waves a hand. 'Go and enjoy your holiday. You deserve it.'

Jasper grins at me. 'I'll take care of it. Have a great break.' Something about the way he says it makes me nervous, as if I'm leaving my children with a baby-sitter for the first time. Not that I have children. I never managed to fit it in alongside my work as a business lawyer with one of the biggest firms in Cardiff and London, dividing my time between the two.

'Go, go!' Anthony waves his hands at me. 'Enjoy!'

'Enjoy!' Jasper repeats.

Suddenly I want to turn around, sit down at my desk and turn the computer on again.

'Luce' – the receptionist appears from the front desk – 'your taxi driver says he has another job to go to if you're not coming.'

'She's coming!' Jasper jumps up from his desk, takes

my case from me and leads me to the door, holding it open for me, then into the cloudy August afternoon. Maybe he's not so bad after all. I'm tired. I need time off. I've been working too hard, getting everything finished in time to take my break.

'Now, do as you're told by the boss. Go and have a good time!' he instructs, as I get into the back of the cab. 'Thanks, Driver. Quick as you can, yeah? She'll tip you heavily!'

I'm prickly again. I can speak to my own taxi driver!

'The airport, yeah?' the driver says, listening to Jasper's command.

'Please,' I say. 'And as quick as you can,' I add, but my words have lost their impact as we pull out into the rush-hour traffic.

I tip him heavily, yank my case from the back seat next to me, run up the escalator, stripping my bracelets from my wrists and whipping my iPad out of its case. As I reach the security conveyor belt, I toss my shoes into the plastic box with the rest of my belongings, reclaim them on the other side, then sprint towards the departures gate. As usual, I wish I was made for sprinting and that my boobs didn't feel like balls bouncing in a net shopping bag as I run.

I make it to the end of the queue just in time. Red, hot and out of breath. I slip my shoes back on and straighten.

The air stewardess smiles at me. 'Just made it!' she says, as I flash my boarding card on my phone and try to recover my composure.

I find my seat, put my case into the overhead locker and wait for the man next to me to let me in. 'Thank you,' I say, and sit down. He rests his leg against mine. I look down at it, then back at him sternly. He adjusts his sitting position and moves his leg. I take a deep breath and pull out my phone to check my messages. I made it. Got the report in and made the plane. I smile to myself. I did it.

All I have to do is sit back and wait. I've done everything I can to get this promotion. And when I do, everything will change. I pull up a picture on my phone of the apartment for which I've put in an offer and smile. A home of my own. Finally. This is where I belong. A kitchen in which I can enjoy cooking, relaxing and spending time with friends and family. I look at the clean lines of the brand-new building. Mostly I look at the kitchen, and the dining area. The coffee machine, and the dinner parties I'll hold there . . .

'Phones turned off, please,' says the attendant, sharply. I disconnect mine and slide it into my bag.

I lay my head against the headrest, shut my eyes and make a list of people to invite to my first dinner party. Mum, of course, and my stepdad. My brother and his family, although he's so busy running his own business, in swimming-pool tiling, that I barely see him these days. Who else? My boss and his wife? Not Jasper. Well, maybe Jasper. I could throw a house-warming party, look up some old friends from college I've lost touch with.

The plane accelerates down the runway, and all I can think about is the kitchen in the new flat, my cookbooks lined up, and having the time to use them. I'm determined to make time for myself when I get this promotion, instead of doing the partners' work for them as well as my own. Everything will change and I'll make sure it does.

As we take off, my thoughts turn to Italy and my grandparents' kitchen. Breathe, I think, smiling . . .

ONE

The scent of the tangy tomato sauce hits my nostrils, head and heart before I even taste it. My nostrils tingle, my head practically pops with joy, and my heart is so full it feels like it might explode.

I don't rush it. I take a moment to savour the joy it brings me. I breathe in deeply, the rich, garlicky sauce, the aroma of peppery olive oil, shut my eyes and let my world recentre itself. I open my eyes and twist tagliatelle, smothered in the familiar sauce, onto my fork. I put it into my mouth, and it's like coming home to the comfort of the hug that awaits me every year.

'You look like you never eat!'

'Oh, Nonna, of course I do. It's just that nothing tastes like your cooking.' It's true. I never have time to cook. I barely notice what I'm eating. It's all pop in the microwave and ping. Nothing tastes as good as this.

She puts down the pan she's drying, comes over and kisses the top of my head. 'And nothing feels like having the ones we love here to cook for.' She beams, puts a finger under my chin and lifts it. And although I'm turning thirty-three and it makes me feel like a child again, I love it.

'You look tired. You're working too hard,' she tells me, letting go of my chin.

'I know, I know. But when I get this promotion it'll be worth it, Nonna. It's what I've worked for. I've dreamt of partnership since I started college. Business law is what I love to do. I want to help people set up their business, live their dreams. Be a part of their goals and the lives they make for themselves.' Mind you, with the rate at which I've been working lately, I wouldn't say I love it at the moment. But once I get the partnership, I'll feel all the hard work has been worthwhile. Or, at least, that it's been recognized. I've invested as much of myself as my clients have. Given up any social life.

I spin my fork again in the pasta, scoop it up and let the flavours reach into the corners of my mind. It's as if I'm reacquainting myself with my family home. I'm back. I sigh and smile. I'm back.

'Where's Nonno? I thought he'd be here, resting. Did the doctor say it was okay for him to be up and about?'

Nonna puts more bread into the basket in front of me

and tops up my glass with red wine as I sit at the same kitchen table I've sat at every summer since I was a child. No matter how many people are in the house, it accommodates us all. It's not a fancy kitchen, with the same tiles on the wall that have always been there, the worn work surface, and the huge bottle of olive oil from the few hectares of land where Nonno cares for his olive trees and used to grow vegetables. On Sundays we often went out to the olive grove to picnic, or Nonna would cook on the old *forno*, the outside oven, among the olive and walnut trees. I loved those Sundays. There's a big jar of olives on the side too: we ladle them into a bowl at *aperitivo* time when we sit on the balcony overlooking the street, the café and the apartments opposite. Caged birds get a daily outing on the balconies, and washing hangs like bunting from the sides.

Outside on the street I can hear children playing in the late-evening sunlight, just as we did. Parents are calling them in, but they're pleading to stay out a little longer. I remember not wanting the day to end until the sun finally went to bed. I know, too, that teenagers will be in the square, hanging around the *bocce* pitch. And Nonno will tut at the rubbish they leave when he goes there to play. I remember being one of those teenagers and not wanting our evening to end. Especially not when I had a boyfriend. I wanted it to go on and on, and in some ways it did, for years. But that seems a lifetime ago. And the older groups of young people will be gathering in the cafés around the square, drinking coffee and talking until the heat has gone from the day. I remember wanting to be a bilingual businesswoman, spending my time between here and London, the best of both worlds. That was when I thought anything was possible. Before I discovered it wasn't.

'He's at the restaurant,' Nonna says, putting the big pan away, ready for it to come out in the morning. Everything in its place, as it always has been. The pans hanging by the big oven. The chipped jug beside it with wooden spoons and ladles.

'At the restaurant? What's he doing there?' I stop eating, fork held in mid-air, tagliatelle and sauce dripping from it.

'He had a few customers tonight. He didn't want to let them down. Old customers.' She looks up at the clock on the wall and I can see she's worrying.

'Eat, eat,' she tells me, patting my shoulder.

I put my fork into my mouth, chew and swallow. 'But surely he shouldn't be working. He's only been out of hospital for a week or so.'

She shrugs. 'But you know what Nonno is like. That restaurant is his lifeblood. He hates to shut it. Besides, he is doing much better. Even playing *bocce* again!'

'*Bocce!*' I can see him now, with the same group of friends he's been playing with for as long as I can remember. Under the big olive tree in the square, with the metal bench under it, in front of the entrance to the narrow cobbled street where the restaurant is. A big round sign, 'Pizzeria Nonno', hangs out from the old stone wall over the metal gates leading into the restaurant courtyard. He likes playing *bocce* in the town square so he can keep an eye on his domain just down the street.

'Have they agreed which rules to play by yet?' I ask, still smiling.

'No,' says Nonna matter-of-factly. 'I don't think they ever will!'

I scoop up another mouthful. 'I'll go down to the restaurant and help him finish up,' I say.

Nonna stops what she's doing, a little misty-eyed.

'Nonna, are you okay?'

'Yes, yes.' She waves a tea towel and looks at me. 'You're a good girl, Lucia.' She cups my face and kisses me, like only a grandmother can, with pure love, leaving her lips on my forehead long enough for me to know how she feels. Those kisses say everything.

I take a big sip of wine.

'Don't rush. Finish your food,' she instructs. 'There's more if you want it.' She points to the pot on the big old cooker. Then she sighs. 'The stove is getting old, like me and Nonno.'

'You're not old, Nonna.' I laugh but there's a hint of sadness in her eyes. 'You never change. Never any older.' And it's true. I don't remember her ever looking

11

any different. Nothing here changes, and that's why I love it. Just the way it is.

She laughs, her chest wobbling with her chins. 'But it would be nice if I had a cooker that worked better!'

I finish my pasta, wipe out the inside of the bowl, noting its familiar worn pattern, with a piece of ciabatta and pop it into my mouth. I'm so full I can barely move, and happy, really happy. I can feel my shoulders dropping and the tension easing in my neck.

'I'll go and meet Nonno,' I say, standing and picking up my bowl.

Nonna takes it from me. 'He'll love that,' she says, turning back to the sink, where I think she has probably stood all her married life. 'Just be careful walking through the square. Those youngsters can be boisterous. And walk back with Nonno.'

'I'll be fine, Nonna,' I say, kissing her again and grabbing my bag.

I leave the apartment and cross the piazza, the town square, and walk towards the cobbled street leading off it. The piazza has stone arches all the way around it, under which people sit and eat in the more expensive tourist restaurants. Not that Castel Madrisante is teeming with tourists, but those who arrive in Naples and are looking for some countryside often head out here in search of a rural idyll. Well, it may have been rural once, but it's not now. More and more people moved out of Naples for the countryside and it's grown into a busy little town, with apartments built up around the main piazza. The ones above the arched terraces go for huge amounts of money these days, mostly to city people wanting a weekend retreat.

'Nonno!' I call, as I open the gates to the courtyard at the front of the restaurant. It's a sight I will never tire of, with the lemon trees in the pergola and fairy lights. I see him on the covered terrace to the side of the courtyard. A terracotta roof, on whitewashed pillars, stands over a worn terracotta-tiled floor, leading into the restaurant and the kitchen beyond. He's holding two empty plates and talking to a couple of customers. Candles are flickering on the tables, giving the terrace an orange glow. The air smells of citrus from the lemon trees, with a hint of woodsmoke. Nonno looks up, his face suddenly full of delight. It's just him working and the one table of customers. Very quiet.

'Lucia!' he calls. 'You remember my granddaughter!' he says excitedly, to the couple at the table, holding out a welcoming arm to me.

'Sì, your Welsh granddaughter! Of course!' They turn to smile at me.

'Ciao, Lucia! We haven't seen you for a long time. You've grown!'

I wonder how to take that. I'm a thirty-three-year-old woman. Do they mean I've put on weight?

'Ciao, ciao.' I smile at them both. It feels good to be speaking the language again.

'Come here, let me see you! Come and hug Nonno!'
He turns and puts down the plates on an empty table
as I run over the courtyard to the terrace, as if I'm
twelve years old again. I fall into his arms, squeezing
my eyes tight shut, breathing in the smell of
woodsmoke from his chef's whites.

Eventually I pull away.

'You look tired,' we say at the same time, taking in
each other, and laugh.

'I'm fine,' we say, and the customers laugh with us.

'Here, I've come to help. You sit down. I'll finish up.'
He starts to protest.

'Join us, Enzo,' say the customers, offering him a
glass of wine.

'Well . . .' Nonno looks at me, and I know he's
tempted.

'*Va bene* Nonno! It's fine. I know where everything
goes, unless you've had a sudden changearound while
I've been away.'

He chortles. 'Well, it's been a long time. Too long!'
he scolds, wagging a finger. 'A whole year.'

'I know, I know, but I'm here now. *Siedeti!* Sit down.'
I put my hand on his shoulder and push him gently
into a chair.

'But no changes.' He smiles up at me, his eyes crink-
ling in his round face. His grey hair is nearly all white
now.

'*Bene!* Good, now stay there,' I tell him.

14

'Maybe just for a while, and a little wine,' he concedes, and picks up the glass.

'Er, are you allowed? Did the doctor say it was okay?' I say, concerned.

'Lucia, this is Italy you are in now, not Wales!' he reminds me, as his customers pour him a glassful and congratulate him on their fabulous pizza.

I pick up the plates and walk into the cool white-washed restaurant, where the tables are set with red and white checked cloths and the lights are low. On the walls I see photographs of Nonno and his father before him, holding the pizza peel, the flat paddle, standing in the courtyard in front of the old *forno*, long since retired.

I push open the swing door, between the tables and the high, dark-wood bar, with my backside as I loved to do as a child, and walk into the kitchen. Immediately I can feel the heat of the wood-fired oven, the embers glowing in its big pot belly. And I can see the meat he has put in, so as not to waste the heat overnight. A piece of *porchetta*, slow-cooked pork, clearly for a special pizza tomorrow. The smell of the crisping skin, the garlic and rosemary remind me of Sundays when we weren't at the olive grove. Sunday lunch, with slow-cooked pork like this. Sundays were always a family time whether in Italy or at home in Wales.

I wash up the plates and clear up the kitchen, turning off the lights. As I return to the terrace, the customers are wishing Nonno goodnight and thanking him for a wonderful meal as always. Nonno walks them from the terrace, across the courtyard to the gates and sees them out, waves, then pulls the bolt across the gates.

'Right, we should get you home,' I say. 'Nonna is worrying about you. You mustn't do too much too soon.'

'I know, I know. Now, *siedeti*. Sit!' He walks back under the pergola and returns to the terrace, pointing towards the table where the candles are burning low and the empty glasses are still sitting there. 'Let me enjoy some time with my granddaughter.' He goes inside the dark restaurant and returns with two clean glasses and a bottle of grappa. 'Here,' he says, pouring a glass for me and one for him. Then he raises his to toast me.

'Now, could you manage some *gelato*? You could always manage some *gelato*. I have a new flavour I want you to try.'

'A new flavour?'

He nods. 'You see? Some things do change around here,' he says, laughs and coughs.

'Perhaps tomorrow, Nonno.' I take a sip of the burning clear liquid, my eyes smarting as it goes down. We sit in silence with our thoughts, listening to young people in the piazza.

'So, tomorrow's special? *Porchetta*?'

'Hmmm.' He nods. 'With mushrooms.'

'Pork and mushrooms. Wild mushrooms cooked in white wine to give them a bit of zing, and fontina-style cheese?' I think about the semi-soft, nutty cow's milk cheese, that originally came from the Alps, but Nonno has a friend who makes something similar locally. Everything at Nonno's restaurant is produced locally.

He nods again and smiles widely.

'One of your extra specials,' I say, my mouth watering, even though I'm full of Nonna's pasta. Food is never far from this family's minds and that's how I know I'm Italian. Whatever else is going on, the next meal is always what's on Nonno's mind. And mine too. I just wish I had more time to enjoy it at home.

Once I get my promotion and buy the flat, with its fabulous kitchen, I intend to cook more. I've been so busy working towards the promotion, making sure Anthony Gwyn-Jones knows exactly how much I want it, that I'd forgotten everything else. I eat most of my meals at my desk and I can't remember the last time I opened a fridge and took time to decide what to make. Once the promotion is sorted and I'm in the new flat, I'll cook every day.

'It's good to have you here, Lucia.' He smiles and gazes out over the courtyard. 'The nights are warm, maybe too warm.'

'It's always like this at this time of year, Nonno. It's the same every time I come back.' And it is. I come for the same two weeks every year, the first fortnight of August.

'It's good to be here, Nonno. *Semplicemente bellissimo.*' A wave of contentment floods over me.

He smiles.

'*Casa dolce casa.* Home sweet home!'

And as we sit in the darkening courtyard, I can make out the outlines of the gates at its far side and the buildings beyond in the narrow street, just as they've always been. It is so good to be here.

TWO

I wake to the sound of singing, loud and joyous. I smile. It's not birdsong. It's opera from the café below. Angelo the waiter trained in opera but runs his parents' café now. He sings every morning. It lets me know I'm back.

My bed seems moulded to my body shape but I toss back the thin duvet, walk over the cool tiled floor towards the window and push open the shutters, enjoying the warm morning sun on my skin. I reach for my phone, but stop and smile at the singing, the sun on the yellow-painted walls opposite and the sounds of the town waking up.

The smell of coffee is winding its way up from the balcony below my window.

'*Buon giorno.*' Nonna is pegging washing to the line that hangs over the balcony.

'*Buon giorno!*' I say. '*Caffè!* Pour me a cup! I'm coming down.'

'Lucia! Great to see you back!' Angelo looks up from serving coffee in the ground-floor café.

'*Ciao*, Angelo. How's things? Still singing?'

'Always!' He breaks into song again.

I grab a T-shirt and shorts, and rummage for my phone charger. I can't see it in my case or my handbag. I slap my forehead. Must have left it on my desk in my hurry to leave the office. I'll deal with it later. I know I won't hear anything about the promotion until Monday at the earliest. Right now, I want to be sitting in the sun with my coffee. I hurry downstairs, leaving my phone by my bed. My tired brain and body are craving Nonna's coffee. Two weeks here was exactly what I needed. I'm so glad I came. I can see for myself that Nonno is doing well and I'm glad I didn't put off coming just because the promotion will be announced next week. It'll make no difference that I'm away, Anthony said, and insisted I take my annual two weeks' leave.

'Come, sit, tell me more about life back in Wales,' says Nonna, as I kiss her and Nonno, then sit down and let the sun do its job, massaging my tight shoulders. I can feel them loosening as I hold my face up to its warmth.

'How is your work?' asks Nonno.

'What he really means is, have you found a young man yet?' Nonna laughs.

I laugh too. It's one of their first questions every time I speak to them, and no matter how they try to wrap it up or hold off asking, it's never far behind.

'No boyfriends. Nothing serious anyway.' Actually nothing at all, but I don't say that. 'There's never time, really. Maybe once I get this promotion.' I remember my phone upstairs. I'll need to buy a charger. But after I'd messaged Mum last night to say I'd arrived, I'd promised her I'd switch it off and not look at it, at least until Monday, and have some proper time off. And that is what I intend to do. Have some proper time off.

'I can come into the restaurant and help out today,' I say, as Nonna puts down a basket of bread, a dish of butter and a pot of homemade orange marmalade.

'I'd like that.' Nonno smiles. I can't help but notice he looks tired again today. 'But only if you want. You're on holiday, remember!'

The smell hits me before the plate arrives at the table. '*Sfogliatelle!*' I exclaim. 'My favourite!'

'That's why I sent Nonno out early to get them. Now, eat,' Nonna commands.

I help myself to one of the shell-shaped flaky pastries. 'You can stay here and rest if you like,' I offer, sinking my teeth into the pastry and reaching the creamy ricotta filling. Oh, heaven! 'I've missed these,' I say, reaching for the thick, black coffee Nonna has poured for me. 'It's *soooo* good to be back!'

Nonno chuckles.

'So, you can stay here and I can work the restaurant this evening, if you like,' I suggest to Nonno, who's watching me with a smile.

'It's a lovely idea, but I need to be in the kitchen to serve my customers.'

'Nonno, I can do that. I've been helping you in the kitchen and watching you cook pizza for as long as I can remember. Why not let me take over today? You could play *bocce* with your friends.' I take another glorious bite of pastry. The crumbs tumble over my front, my plate and the table.

'It's a kind offer. If you'd like to help me, and you're sure there's nothing you'd rather be doing, I'd like that very much.'

'Of course I'd like to help. What else would I be doing?' I smile. 'If you're certain you don't want me to open up for you.'

He shakes his head.

Nonna heads back to the kitchen.

'I wish I'd been here when you were in hospital,' I say, looking back at how busy the last few weeks have been at work.

'It's fine. I closed for a while.' He shrugs.

Nonno never closes, and I know it must have hurt him to do so. 'I just wish I could have run the place for you then.'

'But you're here now, and that's what counts.' He pats my arm.

The scent of tomato sauce drifts to me from the kitchen, and I know Nonna has been up early, too early, cooking for our family meal later.

'And your brother. He's well? I spoke to him this week,' says Nonno, not catching my eye.

'He's fine. We barely see each other, to be honest. You know how busy things are. He has his business and the family now.' I really must make an effort to see them, I think, when I get back. When I have the new apartment, I'll invite them over. They can be the first people I cook for.

Nonno nods thoughtfully as if he's miles away. 'He'll be out here with the family soon, I'm sure,' he says. 'It would be nice for us all to be here together.'

'I'd like that.' I hope with my promotion I'll be able to plan my work a little more easily and not be picking up Anthony's as well, maybe work from home some days . . . 'Perhaps I should come out for longer next time. Work from here. People do. Remote working.' Maybe, with the promotion, I could do that. With my laptop and my phone it might be possible. I feel excited all over again at the prospect of being promoted and how it could change my life.

Nonno stands stiffly. 'I'm going to the restaurant.' I pick up my cup to finish my coffee and leave with him. 'Sit, enjoy your breakfast and the sun. Take your time. We are not on city-lawyer timings here! Help your grandmother. Meet me at the restaurant when you're ready. You can help me make the pizza dough for tomorrow.'

'*Come sempre!* Just like always!'

'Just like always.' He smiles.

He looks exactly the same, but the stiffness and tiredness were never there before. I must make sure I help as much as I can while I'm here so that when I leave he'll be back to his sprightly self. 'Don't worry, Nonno. I'm here to help. You'll be back to your old self in no time. The restaurant won't know what's hit it. Everything will be just the way it was.'

He smiles again. 'Meet me at the restaurant, Lucia. There is something I want to discuss with you,' he says, and I suddenly feel it's something serious.

I glance round for Nonna. 'Ha!' I try to laugh. 'As long as you're not going to tell me you're planning to do something crazy like retiring!' I laugh loudly and wait for Nonno to join in. He doesn't. 'Nonno?' Again, I look for Nonna, who's standing by the door now. She's not laughing either.

Nonno nods. 'It's time, Lucia. It's time to retire.'

And my whole world rocks on its axis.

THREE

'But retiring!' I stand up, away from the work surface in the restaurant, flour and dough on my hands. 'You? Retiring?'

'Keep kneading,' Nonno says. 'Don't leave the dough.' He carries on working it, just as I've watched him for years, focused and concentrated on each ball he rolls and kneads.

'It's time, lovely,' he says again, not looking up from the table. Nonno still has Welsh expressions, which he uses even though he hasn't lived in or visited Wales for more than thirty years.

'But, Nonno, the doctor said you were fine. A little more rest . . .' I roll the ball, then stand and look at him again.

'Careful with that dough!' he says. 'Start it again. You must treat it with respect. Firm but consistent.'

The dough had been rolled out into a long line and cut into pieces ready for my arrival. Now all we have to do is knead it into balls and let it rest. But I'm feeling far from restful.

'But, Nonno!'

'I know, I know.' He holds up a floury hand. 'We never thought this day would come either. But' – he looks straight at me – 'it's time.' His eyes fill with tears and so do mine.

'Can't you just get in more staff to help?' I say, rerolling the dough in my hand and then on the worn, flawed surface, just as I have for years, from when I first stood on a chair beside Nonno, was given a piece of dough and helped to make my first tiny pizza. I remember the glee I felt watching it cook, then eating the misshapen base, heavily loaded with all the toppings I liked: Nonna's sauce, cheese and prosciutto. But never pineapple. You never mention pineapple on pizza when Nonno is in the kitchen. I smile at the memory.

'Now roll it and push it, roll it and push it,' he says, as if I'm learning from scratch, and I can tell he's trying to keep his thoughts under control, as well as mine.

We focus on the balls of dough in front of us.

'So, let me get this right,' I say slowly, rolling the dough and pushing it, rolling and pushing rhythmically, with the heel of my hand. 'You *want* to retire? I mean, the doctor hasn't told you you should?'

He shakes his head.

'You want to?'

He nods. 'Yes,' he says. 'It's time.'

I take a deep breath, and once the shock starts to pass, I can see it makes sense. It's just I never see my grandparents getting any older. Not before this trip anyway. They always seem the same. A few more grey hairs for Nonna maybe, and in Nonno's case white ones, but otherwise just the same.

'Are you sure you don't feel you just need a bit more time off? Maybe you came back to work too soon.' I'm hoping this might be a hiccup.

He shakes his head. 'It's time to hand it on,' he says, sadly but firmly. 'I'm getting older and, much as I hate to admit it, it's getting harder. I want to pass the legacy on while I'm still alive to see it.'

'You're not going to sell it, are you?' Again, I stop what I'm doing. It had never occurred to me that Nonno's restaurant might be sold one day.

He stops kneading. 'I hope not, lovely. I hope it won't come to that. I hope I'll be able to hand it on to someone who really wants it,' he says reassuringly, with an encouraging smile. 'Someone who wants it and will carry on doing what I've been doing here, your great-grandfather before me.'

'Well, that's something at least.' We carry on kneading in silence, until we've dealt with all of the dough.

Then Nonno lines up the finished balls on the

floured work surface and, again not looking at me, says, 'I contacted your brother, and spoke to him in the week.' He's still turned away from me, tweaking the balls of dough in their lines with pride, giving them just enough room to grow and prove when he puts them into the walk-in refrigerator.

'And?' I ask impatiently. 'Is he thinking about it?'

Nonno shakes his head. 'He has too much on, what with his own business and family. He's never really had the interest in taking over here. It's a long way from his home. Home to him is Wales now, like you. Not here.' He gives me a loving smile, which says he misses us, the family, being together, and touches my cheek. I miss it too. I love it when we're together. But the last time was my brother's wedding. I'm hoping the next won't be a funeral.

'So, he won't take on the business?' I ask. In my heart of hearts, I knew he couldn't. He's worked hard for what he has. He may have the same Italian traits as me – thick, dark hair, short, rounded body, a love of food – but cooking isn't one of them. Much as he loves to eat, he's never had the desire to cook. Unless it's a barbecue. Even then, I end up taking over as he cremates everything.

I take a deep breath and pick at the clumps of floury dough stuck to my hands. 'So now what? Does that mean you'll sell after all?' I can't bear to think of this place not being Nonno's.

Nonno shrugs. 'There is no one else. Here, it is tradition. We pass on the tradition of the pizza-maker, father to son. *Pizzaiolo* to *pizzaiolo*. Like my father did to me. But with your brother not interested . . .' His eyes fill again with little tears, like diamonds, and I know he's thinking of my father and how different things would have been if he was still alive.

'Won't you think about taking on more staff, see how you feel in six months?' But I know that's not the answer. His mind is made up. I can see that. And it's for the best really. I know. The restaurant, though, is imprinted in my brain. It's my happy place when work gets tough. What will happen now, then, if they sell?

'It will stay a restaurant, won't it? If you sell it? You could write a clause into the contract that you want it to stay the same. I could arrange that for you.'

He smiles at me fondly and shakes his head. 'It wouldn't be fair to ask that of someone,' he says. 'And, besides, who would want to have to keep things just the way they are because that's how I've done them and my parents before me?' He swallows. 'Unless I can hand the business on to someone, this is where the legacy will end.'

I rack my brains, 'Let me speak to my brother, see if he has any thoughts.' I know he's not into cooking, but maybe he could run the place and employ a chef. I'm trying to find a solution to the problem. After all, isn't that what I do, work out the problem and find solutions, get the deals signed and sealed? I think of my phone, the office and Monday. My stomach flips with excitement. But, right now, getting my phone charged can wait. There won't be any news until Monday and I have to find a way of sorting out my grandparents and the future of the family business. I'm a business lawyer: I need to think with my head, so why is my heart doing all the shouting?

'No, it's not for him,' Nonno says. 'I understand. Besides, he doesn't have the knowledge. He didn't grow up with it. You always loved being here in the kitchen.'

'Then I'll do it!' I say suddenly, with all my heart.

He laughs and touches my face.

'I mean it! I could do the paperwork and rotas from home. The ordering. Keep an eye on the books. You have Dante working as a waiter and Carlo your sous-chef. They know all the ropes. Dante has been here for ever! We just employ a chef. Maybe another kitchen hand.' I'm putting together a plan in my head.

'It's a lovely idea, but you have your job, a city lawyer. I'm proud of you! You don't have time to eat, let alone run this place. Besides . . .'

He stops.

I cock my head to one side and frown. 'Besides what?'

'I think I may just have the answer.' A smile tugs at

the corners of his mouth. His shiny round face looks happier.

'Really?' I smile back. 'But that's great! What is it?'

He smiles even wider. 'I think I may have found the person to hand the business on to. Like I say, your brother wouldn't want to take it on and I needed to think who else there might be. And I've thought about this hard. But now I have the answer,' he says. 'I've explored all the options.'

There's something mysterious in his voice.

'So, who is it?' I ask eagerly.

'That, lovely, you will have to wait and see in the morning,' he says, walking towards the stove where the pot of tomato sauce is waiting to be stirred. He's still smiling to himself. 'Let's just say I think it could be perfect!' He turns back to me, as if he's trying to read my reaction. 'This place will continue to have a *pizzaiolo*, a master pizza-maker, making pizzas here. Like I say, the best thing you can do is hand on a legacy while you're still alive, and that is what I plan to do. To pass on my father's legacy to the next generation.' He steps out of the back door and comes back in with a pile of wood. He lays the fire in the pizza oven, ready to light before service later.

'When can I meet them?' I ask. 'And why can't you tell me about them?' I frown, keen now to have every bit of information on the person taking over my family's business.

31

'Tomorrow. All will be revealed tomorrow. I will invite them to the apartment to talk things through. You can meet then,' he says.

Well, I think, at least I won't have to leave here worrying about him and Nonna. It looks as if he's got everything in hand and this place will go on being 'Nonno's'. As long as it stays as it is, I'll be happy, very happy indeed. I can't think why he seemed so worried about telling me.

FOUR

The following morning I wake to Angelo's singing, as he serves customers in the café below, the scent of coffee and pastries floating up from the street. I can hear the town stirring, feel the sun's warmth rising above the apartments opposite and smell my first meal of the day. Just the same as yesterday, and every morning for as long as I can remember coming to stay in my grandparents' apartment. Why do we never take time to sit and have breakfast before we go to work? I'm at my desk with a cereal bar by seven thirty. We make time for the gym, exercising inside on machines. Why don't we sit, smell the coffee, enjoy the sunlight on our faces? It makes me feel better than the gym.

I remember asking Angelo why he sang every morning. He said he had to do it to bring in the customers from the piazza, away from the overpriced cafés and into the side streets. Nonno's place is in a side street on the other side of the square. But it's Nonno's reputation and word of mouth that bring the customers, new and old. To bring in customers, Angelo said, and because singing makes him feel alive. He may not sing on stage any more, but singing is who he is. The day he stops singing is the day we'll all have to worry.

I smile to myself as I climb out of bed in my cotton pyjamas, stroll over to the window and look out at the yellow-painted apartments opposite, and the cream arches over communal doorways on the street below. I've slept late. Nonna is laying out coffee, pastries and milk-bread rolls in a basket on the table on the balcony below. And I know she will have been up early baking and preparing the family lunch. We always eat at the apartment at lunchtime, once everything is ready at the restaurant. Afterwards Nonno has a siesta and goes to the restaurant to light the *forno* ready for service in the evening. He doesn't open during the day: it's too hot to cook in front of the *forno*. People round here like to eat out in the evening when it's cooler. Nonno often brings back members of staff to eat with us at lunchtime. It's how it's always been. But it's Sunday, and Sunday lunch is always special with Nonno and Nonna, and I can't wait to hear what she's cooking today, maybe guess from the smell from the kitchen.

The sound of the buzzer makes me jump. I can hear

Nonno's voice. He's greeting someone at the front door. I realize it must be whoever he has in mind to take over the restaurant. He said I'd meet them today. I feel a little leap of excitement in my tummy.

I wash and dress, tie up my hair loosely with a scrunchie and hurry down the stairs to where I can hear muffled greetings, polite conversation and laughter. I get a jolt of recognition. That laugh. There's something familiar about it. I'm excited to find out who Nonno has in mind to take over. I stand at the bottom of the stairs by the kitchen and look through the living room to the balcony beyond, where I can see Nonno shaking hands with a figure in the shadows.

'*Buon giorno*, Lucia,' says my grandmother, appearing from the kitchen where she has cooked family meals all her adult life, however many there are of us visiting. She's holding a cafetière in one hand and a plate of perfectly formed miniature cakes in the other. She must have bought them from the expensive bakery on the piazza. It must be a special guest. I'm sure I recognize the laugh. It scratches at the back of my brain. Someone I used to know? I've been so busy with work over the last few years that I've hardly kept in touch with anyone out here. In fact, no one. I used to have a big group of friends here and in the neighbouring town, but these days, I just arrive and decompress with Nonno and Nonna before flying back, wishing my annual holiday was twice as long.

I kiss her on both cheeks. '*Buon giorno*, Nonna,' I say, with one eye on the balcony, where the sunshine is pouring in. '*Chi è qui?* Who is it? Who's here?' I whisper.

'Go and see,' she says, staring at me, as if she's trying to read a reaction that hasn't happened yet. I frown. She holds out the coffee and cakes for me to take out to the balcony and nods.

'We are very lucky,' she says, and I'm intrigued. But if this person is going to take on the business and keep things as they are, I have to be pleased for them too. At least I won't be trying to run it from Wales, like I suggested to Nonno. And I'll be able to return home, not worrying about them, knowing the restaurant is in good hands. I take the coffee and cakes, and smile as I walk out onto the balcony.

'*Buon giorno!*' I say.

'Ah, Lucia!' says Nonno. 'Come, come,' he beckons, 'and say hello. It's been ages since you two have seen each other.'

The visitor stands up with his back to me. Even before he's turned, I recognize him. My whole body jolts and I think I may stop breathing too. I'd know those shoulders, that outline, that frame any time. That laugh. It's been a long time since I've heard it, but I thought I knew it. He turns to me, and as I look up at him, his soft white linen shirt billowing at the edges in the breeze, his dark hair parted in the middle, falling over his face, I recognize everything about him only too well. I'm frozen to the spot. And Angelo stops singing, just as my whole world stops too.

'Lucia.' He nods as if we're practically strangers. 'Good to see you again,' he says formally, as if we're old friends. Then he steps forward, leaning in to kiss me, but I move back. We're not strangers and we're definitely not old friends.

'Giac!' My heart is racing. I'm breathing again, but shallowly. The mid-morning sun is getting high in the sky now, making me hot, and I'm shielding my eyes, trying to focus on his silhouette. I feel really hot now. I wasn't expecting this, not at all. He's the last person I'd expected to see standing on my grandparents' balcony. 'What are you doing here?' My heart is thundering while my head pounds and feels light at the same time. Why now, after all this time? Why come here now?

'Um . . . we have a guest on their way. Now's not a good time,' I say uncomfortably. 'Nonno and Nonna have someone very important coming to talk business with them.'

He looks at me, then between me and Nonno.

'About that,' says Nonno, studying the floor.

'I've come to speak with your grandparents,' Giacomo says, Nonno and Nonna looking suitably sheepish. 'Haven't they told you?' Nonna's eyes flick from me to Giacomo. Nonno attempts a tentative smile. 'About me looking at taking over the restaurant?' he says.

My knees give a little.

'We thought it would be a surprise.' Nonna forces a smile.

'It's certainly that.' I grab a glass of water from the table and down it in one.

FIVE

'Y-you?' I stutter. I don't mean it to sound rude but it just falls out of my mouth. I try to find my lawyer's face but it's deserted me. 'This is who you're planning to hand the business on to?'

Nonno raises his shoulders and holds out his palms. 'It makes perfect sense,' he says calmly.

Giacomo shrugs, a little too confidently for my liking. He's looking well. Fit. Time has been good to him, I find myself thinking.

'It makes sense. I'm here, looking for premises,' he says casually, as if this is perfectly normal, and my feelings really don't count.

'I'll get my jacket,' says Nonno, heading into the hall at the bottom of the stairs. Nonna disappears into the kitchen, leaving us alone, staring at each other like two territorial alley cats, wondering which is going to swipe first.

'Why here?' My legal face returns. The mask I can hide behind, a barrier between me and the client, me and the world.

'I grew up here. This is my home,' he says calmly, with infuriating charm. As if that gives him the right to my family's business.

'But you have a business,' I persist. 'Your family has their own in the next town!'

'They do. We are all professional *pizzaiolos*. Which is why your grandparents have asked me to consider taking over the pizzeria.'

'Over my dead body!' I say, through gritted teeth, just as Nonno reappears, pulling on his lightweight jacket, despite the hot sunshine hitting the streets below.

'Ready to go to the restaurant?' he says to Giacomo.

'Sì, of course,' he says, with a tight smile. 'It was good to see you again, Lucia. You look . . . well.'

I feel furious. How dare he tell me I look well? He knows nothing about me and whether I'm well or not. He knows nothing about my life now. And I feel as if he's wading back into it like a tsunami. It's no thanks to him I look well. When we last spoke, my wellbeing couldn't have been further from his mind. I'm not going to let him come in and take over. No way. Nonno may be taken in by his charming ways, but I'm not.

'Wait – I'll come with you!' I say quickly. I want to hear whatever is discussed.

'Of course. It is good for you two to get to know each other again,' says Nonna, coming out of the kitchen. 'You were so close at one time.'

'Nonna!' I hiss, as Giacomo and Nonno make their way out of the front door. 'We were married! In fact, we're still married on paper! I don't think you can get any closer!' Then I'm cross with myself for being short with Nonna. And cross with myself that I haven't sorted out our divorce. It's one of those things that keeps getting put to the bottom of the pile on my desk. To start with, I was avoiding it. I didn't want to look at the paperwork. It reminded me of everything I'd lost, and made my heart ache with an almost physical pain that I thought would never ease. Why would you put your hand in the fire if you knew it was going to hurt? So I buried the paperwork deeper and deeper, until it wasn't the first thing I thought about when I looked at my desk. Until I stopped thinking about it altogether. It's been so long I'd forgotten it still had to be done.

'Giacomo is still practically family!' She beams, blatantly ignoring my frustration. 'It will be good for you to be reacquainted.'

The last thing I want is to be reacquainted with Giacomo, or for him to have anything to do with my family. I have to put a stop to this. I should have sorted those divorce papers ages ago and this wouldn't have happened. It's my fault that Nonno and Nonna think he's still part of the family. I can hardly believe I've been so lax! And me, a near partner in a law firm. I'm furious with myself. How could I have made such a fundamental error? It's the first thing I'd tell a client to get in place when I was sorting out their business and life. Talk about the shoemaker's children! Just like the old expression, the shoemaker is so busy making shoes for everybody else, his own children end up going barefoot!

'I'll see you later, Nonna.' I kiss her soft, round cheek, and see her chew the corner of her bottom lip as she turns back to the stove to stir a sauce. My heartstrings tug. I love her, both of them, dearly. But I have no idea why either of them thinks this is a good idea.

I follow Nonno and Giacomo along the main hall of the apartment block to the front door, experiencing déjà vu at seeing them walk and talk together. They have always enjoyed each other's company and have so much in common. At the main door onto the street, Giacomo turns to me and I'm catapulted out of the past and into the present: he has suddenly appeared back in my life, wanting to make himself a permanent feature in my family's business. I won't be able to go to the restaurant because he'll be there, all the time, when I visit.

'You're coming with us to the restaurant?' he asks, as if surprised.

'Yes,' I say firmly. I have every right to be there. I'm not letting him walk in and take over.

'Right. Well, you might want to—'

I put my hands on my hips. 'What?' I snap. 'Stay away? Let you get on with it? No, I'll join you. This is my grandparents' business.'

Nonno is greeting the postman.

'Like I said, over my dead body!' I say, in a hushed whisper.

'Um, no. I just meant you might want to get rid of the toothpaste,' he points to the corner of my mouth, 'and change from your slippers . . .' He looks at my feet.

I want to scream. As my cheeks burn with embarrassment, my frustration rises. The sooner I get Nonno to see sense, and that Giacomo isn't the right person to take over the business, the better.

SIX

'Nonno, *davvero*? Really? You can't be serious about handing the restaurant on to . . .' I swallow, barely able to say his name '. . . Giacomo.' There, I've said it. A name I haven't spoken for the best part of seven years, and voiced only in frustration, anger and grief as my marriage disintegrated before that.

We're standing in the courtyard at Nonno's restaurant. My favourite place, apart from the kitchen. You can smell the lemons in the pergola and the wisteria over the arched gateway and the faint scent of woodsmoke from the *forno*. A pile of dried wood is delivered regularly, stacked and never allowed to run low.

Giacomo is exploring the kitchen and Nonno is leaving him to it. I feel invaded! It's like he's riffling through my drawers, and it's been a very long time since he and I were in a bedroom together. I remember the bedroom

44

we shared in his family's home, while there was talk of the house he and his father would build for us. When we finally had a place, an apartment above a barn on their agritourism smallholding, it never felt like our own because his mother had a key. She would let herself in with supper she had cooked for us.

When Giacomo and I first married, I couldn't have been happier, our whole lives in front of us. I finished my degree, as we had agreed I would, then moved out here with dreams of working bilingually, helping English-speaking clients set up businesses. As the eldest son of a *pizzaiolo*, Giacomo aimed to take on his family business but he wanted to bring in new ideas. He and his father were always butting heads on it. And it wasn't long before I realized my Italian was nowhere near good enough for a career here in business law. In any case there were very few local English-speaking clients. My in-laws couldn't have been more delighted: it meant I would spend more time at home, learning to be a good wife, supporting their son and his career. Just thinking of that time, I can feel the pressure. My shoulders are heavy, weighed down.

'Nonno?'

'Serious? Of course I'm serious,' Nonno says, as we hear Giacomo opening and closing cupboard doors. He's like a security guard at the airport, sorting through my luggage, my most intimate belongings.

'But he's – he's—'

'He's practically family,' Nonno confirms. He smiles. 'I've known his father all my life. We grew up together. Went to school together. And we're family by marriage.'

I was there. And we should have finalized our divorce years ago. What kind of a lawyer can't organize her own affairs? But I'm good at my job. The promotion pops into my head and a vision of the office, next to Anthony Gwyn-Jones's, that I've worked so hard for. It's a world away from the summers I spent with Giacomo's family: long meals when as children we'd wander off between courses, and as teenagers, later, the long summer holidays we spent in the woods making plans. Our first kiss there and, later, our plans to marry, then for me to work and keep us while he worked to build his name in the pizza world, dreaming of competitions and the titles he would win. I would work in law, here and in the UK, while he would work on his skills. And how every night after work we would cook and eat and talk about our day. And one day, in the future, maybe a family of our own. A girl and a boy, perhaps two of each. But not yet. Not for at least ten years. We wanted to live first, enjoy being with each other, friends and family, and making a life for ourselves. We made plans, lots of plans. And finally, seven years ago, all those plans went up in smoke.

'But, Nonno, Giac and I . . . we have history.'

'Exactly! You have history. He's part of the family.

That's what makes this arrangement so perfect. I know I can trust him.' He beams, then looks sad. 'We all had such high hopes. Such a shame you went your separate ways.'

'I know.' It was like something or someone had died. The old me and maybe the old him too. The dreams and plans died when I returned to the UK and our lives took different paths. 'But we did. So you must be able to see why this, well, it wouldn't be right.' I look across the courtyard and the open doorway into the restaurant, towards the circle of clear glass in the frosted-glass window of the kitchen door.

'But, lovely, Giacomo is looking for a new project. He wants to expand out of his family business. His father is still there, a master pizza-maker. His brother and nephews, too, are now on the brink of following in their father's and grandfather's footsteps to become *pizzaiolo*s too. He is very talented. He needs somewhere he can make a name for himself. There isn't room for them all at the restaurant on the farm. His work is getting very well known. Restaurant critics want to see more from him. He has built a reputation in competitive pizza-making and needs somewhere people will come to see him.'

So he'd entered the competitions. He'd made a name for himself. He'd done it without me and our plans. 'And,' Nonno continues, 'you and he, well' – he shrugs – 'as you say, it was a long time ago.'

'But, Nonno . . .'

He holds up a hand to stop me. I look at him, his familiar kind face, and take in the tired shadows under his eyes, the extra lines that have appeared around his eyes, the white hair now practically covering his head.

'I have no choice, lovely,' he says quietly. 'Your nonna and I are not getting any younger, and with your father gone, your brother not interested in taking over the business' – he swallows the emotion I can see rising in his throat – 'this is a good option. This way it will stay a pizzeria and not become part of a chain of restaurants or, God forbid, a holiday home for people wanting to fly in and out of Naples.'

I swallow too. 'And he's going to keep it as it is?' I ask slowly.

'It will stay a pizza restaurant, he assures me.'

'And the name?'

'Stays.'

I nod and chew my top lip.

'It's the best option, lovely,' he says. 'This way, I can pass it on to someone I know has the passion for pizza. Someone who respects the tradition, the terrain where the ingredients come from, and understands the craft.'

I have heard my grandfather talk about these things over the years, sharing his passion for his craft as a master pizza-maker. I was never happier than when I was in the kitchen watching him cook and hearing him tell me why his methods are important, why the ingredients matter and where they come from, and why this tradition mustn't be lost to one of the fast-food chains popping up across the world.

I reach out my hand and take his. He puts the other over mine, patting it. 'If there was another way, I'd take it. But there isn't. This is the best.'

He's right. If only there was another way, but there isn't. I couldn't run it as well as my career back home, especially with the extra responsibility my new role will bring. I'd have no time at all to enjoy that new kitchen. I may not want to have anything to do with Giacomo. I may not want this place to change. But who else is going to take it over?

'It all looks as I remember.' Giacomo appears in the doorway from the restaurant, filling it. His soft linen shirt is half tucked in, and his shoulders lean against the door frame.

Yes, it all looks as I remember too. And that's the thing. I don't want to remember. Being here with Giacomo is not what I want to remember when I think of this place. I have spent so long trying to erase those memories, avoiding friends from the past or, I suppose, anyone who had a connection with him. I like this place without him in it.

'Good,' says Nonno to Giacomo, and pats my hand reassuringly once more, then lets it go. 'So, I'll see you here tonight? You can work the service with me. I'll be on hand if you need to ask anything and after that' – he looks at me, then back at Giacomo – 'if you agree, the place will be yours to run as your own.'

'Excellent,' Giacomo says. He puts out his hand to Nonno, pulls him into a big hug and slaps his back.

'Take care of the place,' Nonno says, with a choke in his voice.

'Wait!' I say, with a crack in my voice, unable to stop myself. This seems to be happening way too quickly. I need time to get used to the idea. We all do! And this time, I have to make sure the *is* are dotted and the *t*s crossed. I mustn't let Nonno down. I must prove I'm the lawyer he can be proud of, who deserves that promotion. Not one who's failed to put her personal life in order. I have to make sure this is all legal and above board. 'You need . . . You need a cooling-off period. What if you're not happy and change your mind, Nonno? If you feel better and decide you want to stay in charge. Or, Giac' – I swallow – 'maybe it's not for you. You may have bigger ambitions, a move to Naples. Nonno tells me you're making quite a name for yourself. Maybe this town will seem too small for you and you'll want to move on to the bigger stage.' I'm warming to my theme.

'Ever the lawyer.' Nonno smiles proudly. 'Well, that seems a very sensible suggestion. What do you say, Giacomo? A trial period, see if you're happy with the arrangement,' he suggests. 'Just so you're sure.'

Giacomo shrugs and nods agreeably. 'Sounds good to me. When shall we say?'

'What about a month's trial? Four weeks from now?' I propose.

Nonno looks at him and me. 'The thirtieth of August! An auspicious date,' he says.

'Really?' I ask.

Nonno and Giacomo nod in agreement.

'The annual *bocce* tournament between our towns. You remember?' asks Giacomo, and I do. 'Between Castel Madrisante and Campo Verde where we lived . . . I live. My family lives.' His usual composure is ruffled just for a second or two. 'Papa is already in training.' He laughs gently, brushing over the reference to our former life together.

At the mention of *bocce* training, I see Nonno's jaw twitch. Honour and pride are at stake at the annual tournament.

'So, we agree? The *bocce* tournament will take place here, as always. After that, you can decide if you want to go ahead, Giacomo, or whether, after all, we sell.' I set out the terms of the agreement. That, at least, sounds like a well-laid-out plan. I nod at Nonno and he nods to Giacomo.

'Right, I'll write up the terms,' I say. I need to make my new position clear to Giacomo. Just as he has succeeded in going where he wanted, so have I. I made it on my own. And I'm proud of that. I managed to pick up the pieces of my life and make them into something. And now I'm practically a partner. I look at Giacomo, and wonder if he cut out family time, meals, rising early and falling into bed with exhaustion and think, probably not. He may have worked hard, but he lives to work, while I work to live. I think again of the new apartment and the kitchen I plan to make time to use. That's why I've worked as I have, to give me the life I want.

'So, everyone is happy?' Nonno throws out his arms and smiles. I'd hardly call myself happy but it's certainly a workable solution. And at least I can go home knowing that Nonno and Nonna have a way out of this if it isn't working. As long as I don't have to be in contact with him before I go back.

'Will you join us for lunch, Giac? Nonna will be cooking.'

My heart lurches, then plummets, hoping he'll turn Nonno down.

'*Grazie*. Thank you . . .'

I hold my breath.

'. . . but I had better get back,' he says regretfully. 'I would have loved to, though. Another time maybe. Nonna's cooking was always wonderful.' He looks at me as if checking for my reaction.

I breathe a sigh of relief.

'I think it would be best for you to have family time, without me.' Giacomo looks at me again. 'I want to take some time to talk to my family, too. And Lucia has seen enough of me for one day. She needs time to adjust to the idea.'

'Come soon to the apartment. Nonna will cook. It will be like old times!' Nonno ignores his comment about me.

I have this weird feeling that my old and new lives are clashing together, making me shudder. I shake it off. He has his life and I have mine.

At least Giacomo and I are in agreement on one thing. The less time we have to spend together, the better.

SEVEN

The following morning, I wake up to the smell of coffee, dogs barking, people getting ready to go to work, and the market setting up in the square at the end of the street. That tells me it's Monday. My stomach flips. Today's the day. Today I find out about the promotion. I'm filled with nerves, then excitement, listening to all the sounds from the street, excited as a child on their birthday, in anticipation of what the day will bring.

Something's different. It takes me a moment or two to realize there's no singing.

I get up and walk over to look out of my window. The tables are in the street below at the café, as normal, but no singing. Odd, I think. My stomach leaps again at the prospect of the news today. I get dressed quickly, grab my dead phone from the bedside table and make my way downstairs, drawn by the smell of garlic, olive oil and tomatoes from the pot of sauce that is always on the go in Nonna's kitchen. She will have been up cooking it from five.

'Ah, there you are, Lucia,' says Nonna, picking up her basket from the back of the door. 'I was just going out. I've run out of radishes. I don't know where my brain is these days. I've already been to the market.' She tuts crossly.

'I can go, Nonna,' I say. 'I need to get a charger for my phone.' I take the basket from her. It goes everywhere, even if it's only for one thing. I'll have to get a basket for my new kitchen back home, I think, and hug myself. I'll look for one in the market.

I grab a quick coffee that Nonna pours for me. I breathe it in and feel it fortify me for the day ahead and settle my nerves. Then Nonna tells me off for not sitting and eating breakfast properly, but I head out of the apartment door and down the wide stairs. I need a charger urgently.

As I push open the heavy door of the apartment block and go out into the street, I see Angelo, in his white shirt and dark trousers, a small apron around his waist for a notebook and pen. He's holding a round silver tray on the palm of his hand.

'Hey, Angelo. *Buon giorno!*' I call, and wave. He looks downcast, but raises his free hand. 'No singing this morning?' I ask. 'Are you okay? *Stai bene?* You're not ill, are you?'

He shakes his head. 'There's been a complaint.' He points to the apartments opposite, the first floor. 'New people moving into the neighbourhood. Everything is changing around here. The town may be attracting new residents, "professionals", but what about the old ones, eh? Isn't that why they liked it here in the first place? Everyone wants to change things!' He tuts and clears the table. 'Next we'll be welcoming burger chains and drinking coffee from disposable cups.' He tuts again. 'No one will take time to enjoy their breakfast. Everyone will be too busy changing what's around them to notice life.' He gestures towards the market.

How long will it stay if people want to grab a coffee to go, get to their desks and stay there until way after home time? I get a flash of my life back at the office, then remember my urgency for a phone charger.

I nod in agreement with Angelo and look up at the apartment opposite, its smart patio furniture and potted olive trees, no washing. And now no Angelo singing. The town is certainly changing and it worries me. What will it be like this time next year when I come back? Will there still be a restaurant with Nonno's name over the door? Or will Giacomo have given up, run out on it with a better offer somewhere else, a bigger restaurant, in a more prominent position?

'*Ciao!*'

I wave goodbye to Angelo and chew my bottom lip as I hurry down the street towards the busy market, determined to avoid the pizzeria. I have an errand to run for Nonna and a charger to buy. I have my future to find out about.

I walk through the bustling market. Lots of the same stalls are where I remember, and I wave as I pass, but there are some new ones too. I head straight to Giuseppe's fruit and veg shop, with a stall outside that blends with the market. Nonno always gets his produce for the restaurant there.

'Hey, Lucia!' Giuseppe says, as soon as he sees me. 'How is our girl from Wales? Back for a holiday? How is your Enzo? He's looking well? Getting better?' He fires questions at me while serving customers. At least nothing changes at Giuseppe's. 'And how is life as a top lawyer?' He finishes serving a customer and leans around the stall, bulging with brightly coloured tomatoes, oranges, and melons that I can smell are ripe and delicious. 'Little Lucia!' he says, just like he does every year.

'I'm thirty-three, Giuseppe!' I laugh.

'Thirty-three and still no family of your own?' He looks at my stomach and I suck it in as he shakes his head.

I bristle. 'Marriage isn't for everyone!' I tell him firmly. And definitely not for me, I want to say, but don't, I tried it once, remember?

'Nonna sent me to pick up some radishes.' I move the conversation away from my reproductive organs, reminding me of everything I didn't enjoy about being newly married in Castel Madrisante. Everything I came to resent about being here. The constant pressure to conceive and give the family nephews, nieces and grandchildren.

'I have some beauties, just for your *nonna*.' I shake myself back into the here and now. He picks up a bunch, drops it into a paper bag and hands it to me. 'I'll put it on the account, *sì*?'

'Great. Thanks, Giuseppe.' I know he doesn't mean any harm but, still, I feel ruffled. His comments have taken me back to when I left here. I needed to get away, breathe, have some space. Go somewhere where my monthly reproductive cycle wasn't the focus of so much attention. *'Ciao!'* I attempt to smile at him. It's just how things are around here, I tell myself. It doesn't change. And maybe I don't want it to. I look out on the market, feeling the sun on my face, smelling coffee in the air. Maybe if I hadn't let the comments get to me, the spotlight, the pressure it put on Giacomo and me, would I have left?

Once again I shake myself back into the here and now. I have a whole new life to look forward to, and the sooner I find a new charger the better.

'Ciao, bella, our little *pomodoro*!' Giuseppe calls.

He's referring to my glowing cheeks, already tinged pink by the sun. They always do that when I first arrive, eventually turning light brown. Back home, people always comment on my lovely tan. Here, I stand out like a sore thumb for the first few days as my skin turns pink.

'Oh, Lucia, can you take this to the restaurant? It got left off the order this morning. I had to get it in especially.' Giuseppe waves a bag at me.

'Oh! I – I wasn't going to the restaurant,' I say, not keen to see Giacomo standing in the kitchen in place of Nonno. He's holding a bunch of rhubarb. Rhubarb? 'I didn't know Nonno was doing a rhubarb dessert.'

'Not a dessert!' Giuseppe shakes his head. 'For the pizza!'

'The pizza? Are you sure it's for the restaurant?' I point.

'Yes, some new ingredients were added over the weekend. Apparently, goes well with basil and barbecue sauce!' Giuseppe shrugs. 'It's for Giacomo. But no worries. I'll take it later.' He puts it to one side.

So, Giacomo is making changes to the menu already. Rhubarb! Barbecue sauce! My hackles rise. So much for keeping things the same. What's going to be next? Bananas on pizza? An overhaul of the interior? God forbid, a name change? Is he actually going to stick to his word and keep it as 'Nonno's'?

'It's okay! I'll take it if you like,' I say. 'No problem!' Suddenly I'm very keen to get to the restaurant and see what Giacomo is doing. Picking up the order from Giuseppe and taking it to Nonno at the restaurant was always one of my jobs in the holidays. I loved the responsibility, the smell of the kitchen when I arrived, Nonno teaching me how each tomato should look, smell and feel: never compromise on the core ingredients.

'Okay. Tell Giacomo I'm sorry I left these off when he picked up the order earlier. I can get whatever he wants, though. He just has to give me notice. And it's good to see him in these parts. So, you and he back together?'

'No, definitely not,' I say. That name again. Giacomo. My ex-husband. The summer after I graduated, I stayed on here, we got engaged and then married. I was twenty-four. Two years later, my marriage was in tatters, my dreams of having a career and living in Italy dead in the water. The pressure from his family, the community, to be the perfect stay-at-home wife and mother, created cracks in our relationship that were just too big to repair. If only he could have told me how he felt, not just retreated into himself, watching our dreams crash and burn, claiming we were on a break when we both knew I wasn't coming back. I moved back to Wales and threw myself into my work, as I have for the past seven years. To say it was a shock seeing him here is an understatement. After all this time. I feel as if the lid has been lifted off a box I'd shut tightly and not looked in for years.

'If it's a problem, I can take it to him in a bit.' Giuseppe has read my face.

'No, it's fine,' I say, and take the paper bag. 'I can deliver it.' It was seven years ago, Luce, I tell myself. We were young. Life has moved on. I put the bag into my basket. *'Ciao!'*

'Ciao, Pomodoro!' Giuseppe smiles affectionately and goes back to serving the line of customers, knowing them all by name and asking them how they are.

As I walk out from the shade, onto the sunny street, heat hitting the walls around the piazza, I pull down my sunglasses from the top of my head. A group of young men on the corner heard Giuseppe's farewell to me. 'Hey, Pomodoro!' one calls. The others laugh and join in.

'Pomodoro!'

'Tomato cheeks!' Another laughs. I laugh with them.

Giuseppe looks up from his customers, scowling at the young men. 'Hey!' he calls. 'On your way! I know your fathers.'

The group reluctantly moves on and I don't give it another thought, just lads being boisterous. The only thing on my mind is Giacomo and the restaurant, his change in the menu. Rhubarb! Barbecue sauce! I move quickly through the market towards the restaurant. Much as I want to stay as far away from him as possible, I can't. I have to see what he's doing. I can't let him come in and change everything. Instead of staying away from the restaurant, as I'd planned, I walk across the piazza, past the stallholders and the people having coffee in the cafés under the arches, past the *bocce* pitch, where the group of young men have reconvened and smile at me as I pass. I ignore them. I have somewhere I need to be.

EIGHT

'Rhubarb!' I call, as I let myself in through the wrought-iron gate. A tendril of wisteria drops down and whips at my head. That needs tying back, I think, as I dodge it, close the gate and walk into the old courtyard.

'*Buon giorno?* Hello?' I can't quite bring myself to call his name. I feel as if I'm returning to a house I grew up in, after my family had moved out, yet all the photos and treasured possessions are still on the walls. Like the one of Nonno and Nonna's wedding reception, which took place here at the restaurant. Newspaper reviews that Nonno has cherished over the years. His father's pizza peel, which rests above the fireplace. I take it all in again as I walk across the courtyard and the terracotta-tiled terrace, then go into the restaurant, with its off-white walls telling the story of Nonno, his life here, his parents before that, and our life during family get-togethers and holidays. I head into the kitchen at the back and hear swearing.

I stand on tiptoe and look through the clear-glass circle in the frosted glass on the big swing door. Then I take a deep breath, push it and stand holding it open with my foot. Even though I'm expecting to see him there, my heart still lurches at the sight of his familiar shoulders hunched over the drawers, searching through them, clearly, and not unusually, frustrated that he can't find what he's looking for.

'*Che cosa stai cercando?* What are you looking for?' I ask. I'll need to reorganize the drawers, I think.

He swings round in surprise. 'The dough cutter.'

'It's in the drawer, over there, on the right.' I point, not moving, not wanting to feel we're in a room together, just me and him.

He walks the length of the kitchen, clearly not impressed with the way things have been set up. 'Right,' he says, reaches in and pulls out the dough cutter. He holds it up.

'It was my great-grandmother's,' I say, aware of his critical eye.

He raises his eyebrows, giving it an it'll-have-to-do look, and I bristle.

'Shouldn't you have your sauce going by now? Nonno always does his . . .'

He holds up a hand. 'Lucia.' It's odd hearing him say

my name: a strange familiarity that reminds me of good times and bad. 'Your grandfather has given me free rein to run the place for four weeks. Until the end of the month. To do things my way. Please. I'll find my way around. I'll work it out.'

'Fine!' I sniff, feeling snubbed, and turn to leave, the door swinging behind me. Then I turn back, pushing the heavy door open again. 'You forgot your rhubarb,' I say, holding it up, then putting it firmly on the wooden table in the middle of the kitchen, and begin to stalk out, my head high.

'Oh, and the dough cutter? It only works if you use the left side at an angle,' I call over my shoulder, thinking of the much better dough cutter I could have pointed him towards. 'But I'm sure you'll work it out!'

I walk across the terrace to the courtyard, breathing in the familiar scent of lemons and wisteria, listening to the buzz of the bees, vans making deliveries and people calling to be careful on the narrow streets. I look around the courtyard at the wrought-iron chairs, the cushions and the matching red and white tablecloths that I would usually be helping to spread, and feel the sun on my face, massaging it, like it's feeding my soul.

'A hidden gem': the restaurant has been described as such on Tripadvisor. And they're not wrong. I smile as I reach the gate, put my hand on it and stop to look back. I lift my chin and hold it up, not letting any hot, angry tears fall, feeling as if my home is being demolished. I take a deep breath, pull back the gate, shut it behind me, and walk home through the market, now packing up for lunch, towards the apartment where I can see Nonna hanging washing on the line over the balcony. I wave and smile, and she waves back, as do her large aprons in the warm wind.

'Hey, Lucia, Luce!' I hear my name and spin round, delighted to see a familiar face. This time a friendly one from the past.

'Sofia!' We fall into a hug, despite the two children pulling at her clothes, clearly bored by markets and meeting people.

'*Come stai?* How are you?' we ask at the same time and laugh. She looks tired, thinner, and as if she has the weight of the world on her shoulders. The children continue to pull at her, bickering and testing her patience.

'I haven't seen you for ages!' I say, and feel guilty that I made the conscious decision to distance myself from my friends here, once Giacomo and I had split for good.

'No,' she says. 'I – I haven't been out much.'

'The two weeks I'm here each year seem to go so quickly. I always plan to come out more and make time to see people . . . It's true: I have meant to pick up my old friends. '. . . but I never seem to get round to it. By the time I feel I'm relaxing, it's time to go again!' I smile. 'I'm determined to change that,' I say, and I am, once the promotion is in the bag. I feel for my phone. 'What about you? How come you've been staying in? Work?' I try to read her expression.

She shakes her head and looks at the children.

'Gosh, I know people say it, but how they've grown! They were babies when I saw them last. Talk about time flying.'

'Here, go and buy some *gelato*,' she says to them, pointing to the ice-cream parlour under the shade of the arches. She pulls out her purse and gives one of them a ten-euro note. They squabble over who's going to carry it as they run to the open-sided shop.

'So.' She looks up at me as she puts away her purse, then smiles. 'It's so good to see you.'

Sofia and I grew up playing together in the streets round here. Every year we'd count the weeks, days and hours until I'd be back for the summer holidays. And then, as teenagers, we hung out, drank bottles of wine pilfered from our families' cupboards, tried smoking and hated it. Then we started dating, me and Giacomo, her and Paolo. We'd picnic in the woods, cook over open fires there. Make our plans.

Then, in our twenties, came our weddings, except Sofia stayed married and had children while I went back to Wales. We drifted apart and lost contact, as I separated myself from everything that reminded me of Giacomo and our life out here.

'How are you?' she asks again, and I can't help but frown at how tired she looks.

'I'm fine!' I say. 'You know, working.' I can't think what else to say about my life back home.

'Are you with anyone?'

I shake my head. 'No,' I say, and stare at the tiled floor for a moment. 'What about you?' I look up at the children. 'I can't believe how big they're getting!' They're clambering about to see the different flavours behind the glass at the ice-cream stall. 'I can't believe you stopped at two.' Sofia loved having children. I just wasn't ready back then. Giacomo understood, but no one else did.

She looks down, then up at me. Tears fill her eyes as the market stallholders pack up and shout to each other, clearing away their boxes of whatever fruit and vegetables are left and disassembling their stalls. Suddenly it seems very noisy.

'Sofia?' I say, concerned, and touch her elbow.

'Paolo died, Lucia. A year ago. Very sudden. A stroke,' she says, as if she's giving me the information as neatly and precisely as she can, and in as few painful words as possible. Each one causes her more pain than she can bear by the look of it.

'Oh, God! Sofia!'

'I didn't know if you'd heard or not. I should have contacted you, but life seems to have taken us down different paths and I had so much to think about.

Then I heard that Enzo had been taken ill and didn't want to give you any more worry. I tried to get in touch on Facebook, but didn't hear anything back.'

I haven't looked at Facebook in an age. All those people with their happy lives. I just kept my head down and worked.

'Oh, Sofia,' I say again. I wrap my arms around her and hold her tightly. When I release her a stallholder is trying to get past us with his boxes – a van is backing up towards us.

I take Sofia's elbow and guide her out the way. We walk slowly, in step with each other, in the direction of the children, trying to catch up with what's happened before we reach them. They turn, holding big cones with homemade *gelato* piled on top, their smiles as big as the ice-creams.

'How . . . I mean, how are you?'

'I'm okay,' she says. What else can she say?

'The children keep me busy. Well, to be honest . . .'

'Yes?'

'I wish I was busier.'

'Busier?'

'You know how things are here.' She stops walking. 'Paolo's parents . . .' She looks at me for understanding and I nod slowly. '. . . they want to do everything for me. They want to look after the children so I'm not too tired. She cooks. He works. I offered to work in the bakery, but he won't hear of it. Says it's their job to look after me and the children, now Paolo is gone! The little ones miss him, but they love being with their grandparents, both sets.

'I just wish . . .' she lets out a long sigh '. . . I just wish I could, well, work out what I'm supposed to do.'

The children come over with their ice-creams, happy now, and hand Sofia her change. She thanks them and smiles back.

'I have to go,' she says. 'Nonna will have lunch ready and you'd better eat it!' She waves a finger at the children. 'It was so good to see you again,' she says to me. 'Perhaps we could have coffee. I have plenty of time when the *nonna*s have the children.'

'I'd love that!' I say, and hug her again. 'My phone is dead.' I pull it out of my bag. 'I need to buy a charger.' It seems so unimportant now. But I suddenly feel its loss, the focus it gives me, my career, which has guided me when I had no idea what else to do with my life. I need to get back, charge it and let it help me get some control back in my life.

'Don't worry. You know where I am – at Paolo's parents'. Come over. They'd love to see you.'

'I will. *Ciao.*' I say goodbye to the children, rubbing their beautiful dark heads, before we head off in different directions.

Poor Sofia, I think, wiping tears from my eyes. I must definitely make time to see her. When I get back, when I start the new job, I must stay in touch with old friends. I head for the phone stall, catching him just before he packs away.

Inside the apartment I know exactly what's for lunch as soon as I open the door. Nonna has been slow-cooking the rich tomato sauce since the early hours of this morning. Fried pizza. *Pizza fritta.* There is none of the dough stretching or tossing that I've watched my grandfather do over the years in the pizzeria: she is working swiftly and nimbly to seal small parcels that fit into the palm of her hand, filled with ricotta and leftover pork from the *porchetta* Nonno cooked in the *forno.* This isn't the luxury of Margherita pizza, with mozzarella. This is home cooking, by Nonna, and it fills me with joy. I feel my spirits lift, the smell giving me the hug I need. Reassuring me.

'Did you get what you wanted?' she asks, handing me the cutlery to lay the table just beyond the archway from the kitchen, leading to the living room and the balcony doors beyond. There are small tumblers in different colours catching the light – I remember them so well from my childhood. The jug of water and the patterned plates. I feel the same as I did as a young girl, then a young woman, a sense of home.

'Yes, I got your radishes, and a new charger for my phone in the market. And I saw Sofia.'

'Oh, Sofia. So sad about Paolo,' says Nonna.

'I didn't know,' I say.

'Nonno was going to tell you when you got here. It must have slipped his mind, with everything going on at the restaurant. I'm so sorry you had to hear it from her first.'

I don't know what to say. I keep thinking about Sofia, at home, grieving for her young husband. I wish I could do something for her. I know that keeping busy can help when your world is disintegrating. I threw myself into work when I left Italy and Giacomo. When I realized it wasn't just 'a break', we had that stilted conversation on the phone when neither of us knew what to say. Finally I said, 'This isn't working, is it?'

'*No*,' he replied, and I had wished he could have said something else, come up with some solution. But he didn't. Neither of us was happy. So that was it, the end. As we finished the call, our marriage was over. It didn't end with a bang, just fizzled out. I worked even harder. It helped somehow.

'Oh, and I delivered the rhubarb to the restaurant. Giacomo had already picked up the order, but his rhubarb got left behind.' Even saying his name out loud still feels strange after all this time.

'Rhubarb?' says Nonna.

I nod and tut.

'Giacomo wanted rhubarb?' She hands me a knife and points towards the salad bowl for me to start chopping. She doesn't need to tell me, I just know. It's how it's always been in her kitchen. We all just get stuck in, apart from Nonno. It's always been the same. I expect it will stay the same when he hands over the restaurant, except his days will be filled with trips to the café and *bocce* with his friends. If he does hand over the restaurant, that is, and I still have everything crossed that he won't. I still can't believe he'll go through with it. He lives and breathes that restaurant. He says he wants to hand on the legacy while he's still alive to see it, and I'd like him to take things easy, but not hand it over to – to Giacomo! I just hope I can come up with something else in the meantime.

'The rhubarb was for dessert, no?'

'No. For pizza!'

'*Pizza?*'

'Do you think he'll go through with it, Nonna?' I say, and stop slicing a cucumber. 'Do you think Nonno is going to hand over the restaurant?'

We're standing side by side in the galley kitchen with the archway that opens into the dining and living area, where the family has always gathered.

She shrugs as she stands over the pot of oil, her apron faded and stretched, but clean and bleached by the sun. 'I don't know.' She sighs. 'And what will I do with him under my feet all day long when he does hand it on?' She tries to joke, but I can tell she's worried about him. 'His recent little turn has made us realize we're not getting any younger. And he wants to see the tradition carried on, the legacy passed to someone who will keep it going. He doesn't want it to leave the family, and this is his only option at the moment.' She's watching the little pizza parcels frying in the bubbling oil.

'But to Giacomo?' I say, unable to stop myself. 'Of all people.' I resume slicing the cucumber with speed and maybe a little more force than necessary. It smells so fresh.

'He is the closest we have to family, someone who wants to take over and has the skills.'

'I wouldn't be so sure of that, not from what I saw in the kitchen. Couldn't find his way around it. Had to find him a dough cutter! I pointed him towards Great-grandmother's!' I say, and smile naughtily at Nonna.

Nonna's eyebrows lift just a little. Her eyes twinkle. 'He doesn't know his way around, not like you do.' She lifts the crispy parcels out of the pan and onto a plate.

'What are you saying?' I frown a little. If Nonna says something, there's always a reason behind it.

'I'm just saying . . . let's eat!' She puts the last parcel onto the plate as if she's feeding the town, not just us. 'Nonno is at a check-up with the doctor. He'll join us in a bit.' She carries the plate of fried pizzas to the table and I follow with the salad. I pour the water, and she pours two small glasses of red wine. As always.

I help myself to salad and drizzle it with olive oil from the decanter on the table. Then I take a pizza – only when my plate is full will she sit and serve herself. I cut into it and its fragrance rises up to me, like a rush of love from an old friend.

I bite into it. Heaven! I shut my eyes and listen to the street below. 'It's odd not hearing Angelo sing, isn't it?' I say, after I've swallowed my mouthful.

Nonna sighs. She looks sad, which isn't like her. Her beautiful round face is always smiling. 'It is,' she agrees. 'Everything is changing . . . So, you say Giacomo wasn't coping too well in the kitchen?' she says, her eyes twinkling again.

I take another bite, chew and swallow. 'Not that well. As I said, he didn't know where anything was.'

'Maybe . . .' she sips her wine and places the glass carefully on the table '. . . maybe you should help.'

'*What?*'

I put some salad into my mouth.

'Well, he's not used to the kitchen. You know it like it's your own backyard.'

I swig some wine. 'The last thing he wants is me in that kitchen helping him.'

'Hmm,' she says thoughtfully. 'Maybe.'

'Definitely.' I eat some more salad.

'But what is important is that the restaurant stays the same, serving up Nonno's dishes. Keeping the customers your grandfather has looked after all these years happy. No one wants to see it go under.' She looks at me, and adds, 'You have helped your grandfather all your life in the kitchen. Maybe you should help Giacomo now.'

'He doesn't need my help.' I stab at the salad on my plate more forcefully than I need to. 'I'm the last person he'd want in that kitchen with him.' I push the leaves into my mouth. Nonna is staring at me with interest and those sparkling eyes. I crunch the salad, with its peppery olive-oil dressing, then chase a lettuce leaf around my plate. 'Really, Nonna. It's not worth thinking about. The last thing Giac wants is me in the kitchen. And I certainly don't want to be in there helping him.'

'But you always help in the kitchen,' she says, with unusual frustration.

'But things have changed.' I put down my knife and fork more noisily than I meant to.

'Not yet they haven't,' she says quietly.

I can't help but feel there's something she's not saying so I'm not sure what she means.

'He's putting rhubarb on his pizzas,' she says.

'Exactly! We'd never get on!'

'The one thing Nonno wants is for that place to be a reminder of what his parents started and he carried on. Giacomo is a brilliant pizza-maker, a *pizzaiolo*, a craftsman, but we all do things differently. Different families have different methods and recipes. It might be good if you helped Giacomo, just while he gets settled and you're still here.'

'But we'd kill each other! He doesn't want me there and I don't want to be there with him! We haven't spoken in seven years! And the last time we did, I could have throttled him. I just wanted him to . . . *phffff* . . . not end it like that. To fight for us, not let me go, like he did.'

She's still staring at me, and I'm sure now that something else lies behind her words. Is she worried that Giacomo will change things – like with the rhubarb? That Nonno's legacy will be lost? I sip my wine.

The front door opens and Nonno returns from his doctor's appointment. 'Ah, my two favourite ladies!' he announces, clearly having stopped for *un caffè* on the way back, and smiling broadly. He looks happy. Maybe retirement is exactly what he needs. And if that's the case, maybe I have to accept that Giacomo is taking over, but make sure he does it Nonno's way.

'You know what they say, keep your friends close, and your enemies closer,' Nonna murmurs, just before Nonno pulls up a chair at the table. He pours himself a glass of wine and she offers him a fried pizza. She's on her feet again, never still unless everyone is eating.

Nonno holds the jug of red wine over my glass and tops it up. 'It's so good to have you here, lovely. And now Giacomo is in the restaurant, my worries are over and we can spend some proper time together. I've started growing vegetables again, on our bit of land out of town. I could do with a hand. What do you say?' He beams. It's clear that that's of some relief to Nonna:

at least he doesn't plan to be under her feet all day long.

But what if Nonna is right? What if Giacomo does plan changes? What would that do to Nonno?

'What news of work and this promotion?' he says, tucking into Nonna's fried pizza.

My phone! With everything that's going on, I haven't charged it. I excuse myself, plug it in and feel the flip of excitement as it comes to life. I scroll my messages with shaking hands, but nothing . . . yet.

'Hmm. *Buonissimo!* As always!' Nonno says, finishing his pizza and beaming at Nonna as I return to the table. He takes her hand and kisses it. She brushes him off playfully. It's so good to see them like this and I wouldn't want that to change. Like how Nonno likes Nonna's food the way it is, especially her fried pizzas! Why change what isn't broken?

I've never seen rhubarb on a pizza. What next? Nouvelle cuisine or, worse, takeaway pizzas?

'More wine?' Nonno asks.

'Not for me, Nonno.' I put my hand over my glass and pick up my plate, empty apart from the one green leaf that got away. 'There's somewhere I have to be.' I need to take my mind off my phone and checking my emails.

'Really? Where?' He looks up at me, surprised.

'The restaurant. To help! Isn't that what I always do when I'm here? Help in the kitchen?' I try to sound as if that was exactly what I'd been expecting to do even with Nonno out of the picture.

'Ah, to see Giacomo!' He grins. And Nonna's eyes twinkle, but perhaps not for the same reason.

The less I see of Giacomo the better. But I'm determined to make sure that he doesn't change the restaurant, that everything should run just as it always has and that it stays Nonno's. I grab my short denim jacket and dash out. As I pass the café I see Angelo: '*Canta*, Angelo! Keep singing!' I call. 'Don't change for anybody!'

He breaks into a wide smile, waves and begins his version of 'Nessun Dorma', as he pours coffee from the jug. I can hear the neighbours opposite complaining over their balcony, but he ignores them and continues. My world tilts back into place. Everything is as it should be, I think, with a satisfied smile, as Angelo's customers clap, as do some residents from their balconies above, and the complainers are silenced. Now to make sure that the same happens at Nonno's.

I need to see exactly what Giacomo is up to, and if that means keeping an eye on him and Nonno's while I'm here, I will.

NINE

'Er, hey! *Ciao?* Can I help?' I hear Giacomo's voice behind me. I've been waiting for it, of course, but it makes me jump and bristle. I get to my feet from where I've been tidying the cupboards in the kitchen at the back of Nonno's restaurant, putting everything back into its place. I take a deep breath, straighten myself and turn slowly, giving him my full business-lawyer gravitas. While Giacomo was at lunch and then siesta, I'd let myself in with the key from under the rock in the courtyard.

'It's more that I'm here to help you,' I say evenly, even though every bit of me wants him to be out of here. It feels so odd looking at the Giacomo I knew and loved yet he's a total stranger now. I take a deep breath and even attempt a smile.

He frowns. 'What exactly do you mean, help me?'

He folds an arm across his chest and taps his lips with his forefinger as I remember him doing when he was unsure.

'Exactly that,' I reply, with another smile – fake it until you make it. I use this technique in meetings. And I seem to have a good poker face. 'I always help Nonno here in the kitchen when I'm staying. You should remember that!' My heart twists. 'And, well, seeing as you're new to the restaurant, I thought I could help. I mean, I know you've worked kitchens, of course, just not this one. So, I've done the cupboards and I can show you where everything is and the menu, if you like.'

He holds up a hand. 'It's good of you, Luce, but, really, there's no need. I've been making pizza all my life and I'm capable of finding my way around a kitchen. Besides, Carlo the sous-chef will be in soon. He can help me. And Dante, the waiter. We'll work it out. We'll be fine. But thank you. *Grazie.*' He steps away from the door for me to leave.

I hold my ground and his stare. This is a polite battle of wills. 'No, really, I don't mind. Like I say, I always help Nonno. And it's this or take up *bocce* with him or help him plant a vegetable plot. I was never one for ball games or gardening.' I waggle my fingers at him. 'Butterfingers and certainly not green ones, that's me!' I say, a little too high-pitched. I'm sure I see a tiny smile pull at the corners of his mouth as he looks to the floor, then runs his fingers through his thick, dark hair, looks at me, and his hair falls right back to where it was, this way and that, as it always did. His shirt has broken loose from his trousers on one side and flaps around his hip.

'It's fine. I can manage. But thank you,' he says kindly but firmly, pushing the door wider.

'No need to thank me,' I say just as firmly, turning my back to him. 'I'm here and happy to help. It's my family's restaurant, after all. Hey, Dante, *ciao*!' I say, as my grandfather's head waiter swings in through the back door. Dante is about my age. He's good-looking and knows it.

'Lucia! Is it that time of year again?' He kisses me on both cheeks. 'Your grandfather said you were coming. And that changes were taking place in the kitchen.'

'*Ciao*, Giac!' Dante waves to Giacomo, then puts out a hand to shake.

'Dante! I haven't seen you in years. How's the family?' Giacomo asks.

'*Bene, bene*, good, good,' Dante says, glancing around. 'And you're taking over from Nonno, from Enzo? He said it was time to hand the business on.'

'I'll be here for four weeks, see how we both like it. In the meantime, everything as normal,' says Giacomo. 'Just a few tweaks to the menu.'

'Yup, no big changes around here,' I say, and start laying out the dough balls from the fridge, just as

Nonno always likes them. Giacomo lets out a long breath.

'You going to let me take you out this time, Lucia? Dinner, after work one evening maybe.' Dante runs his hand over his neatly cut hair. 'You never accept my invitations.'

'Oh, I don't know, I have a lot on,' I say, although I'm flattered he's still asking.

'Maybe this time you'll say *sì*!' he says.

Giacomo's face is set.

Maybe I will, I think. Now, that would please Nonno!

'Since you're here then, Lucia, and don't look to be going anywhere for the time being, perhaps you can help Dante out front.'

'Oh, no, it's fine. He doesn't need me. Don't forget the basil – Nonno always likes to use plenty. It's in the window box by the back door.'

Giacomo sighs.

I'm going to make sure this place runs exactly as it always has done and that he doesn't change a thing.

TEN

'That went well,' I say, finishing the washing-up in the sink at the back of the kitchen, rinsing away the mountain of bubbles after the end of a fairly busy service. Lots of regulars came in, wanting to know how Nonno was. They'd heard I was here for my holiday and also wanted to say hello. It felt good to be there, even if Giacomo was taking centre stage, talking to customers when he'd finished cooking and telling them to come back and try his new recipes.

'Good job I was here, really,' I say, and I mean it. I don't think he would have coped. He has no idea how Nonno does things, and as they've been like that for years, the place runs smoothly. And with Carlo, the sous-chef, phoning in sick, it was lucky I was here.

I rearranged the orders when they came in from Dante, so it was an easier system than Giacomo's and made sure the sauce never boiled. I even helped out at the pass as Carlo would have done, although from the look on Giacomo's face you'd think he would have been happier if I hadn't been there at all.

Giacomo throws a tea towel onto the wiped-down work surface. 'Well, that's great,' he says, taking off his apron. 'And thanks for helping and showing me around. But I'll be fine from here.' He's re-wiping the clean work surface.

'Oh, it's okay. I can be here tomorrow too,' I tell him, taking off my apron.

He holds up his hand and I stop what I'm doing. 'No need,' he says. 'I'll be fine. Really.'

'No,' I insist, standing my ground. 'As I say, I like to do it when I'm here.'

He takes a deep breath. 'Luce . . . this isn't going to work.' I remember those words. Suddenly I'm right back there, with that phone call and me saying, 'This isn't working, is it?' That was it: the end of our marriage. I remember feeling as if the rug had been pulled from under my feet, lightheaded, like I was free-falling, not knowing where I'd land or if I'd survive. But I did. I lift my chin to him. I won't let it happen again. I'm older now. I have my own life, one I should get back to – I need to check my phone. But I'm not going anywhere until I know this place is going to stay exactly as it has always been.

'What isn't going to work?' I feign innocence, using my poker face again. And this time I'm not agreeing with him, like I did all those years ago, wishing one of us had the guts to fight harder for what we'd lost. But I didn't want to fight for it if he didn't want it . . . want me. And that was how it had felt: he just didn't want me.

'You and me, here together.' He holds his hands in front of himself, like bookends.

I'm suddenly brought up short, trying to push away the memories that are rushing in on me, remembering when there was a 'you and me together'. When life was very different. Before he became a total pillock. I can't imagine what I saw in him. Apart from his obvious dark good looks and the way his food made me smile when he cooked for me. And I'd been ready to spend the rest of my life with him! He did me a favour by ending it – I had such a lucky escape, I tell myself.

At the end, we barely spoke. The silence was like a chasm between us, getting wider all the time, neither of us knowing how to fix what was going wrong. I couldn't work: my dream of English-speaking clients was dead before it had started. There just weren't the clients. And then his mother teaching me how to cook his favourite meals and iron his underpants, the constant talk of 'when the babies arrive'. Giacomo's brother was married and his wife was pregnant almost immediately, then again. The family celebrated and I was pushed aside. Giacomo was busy butting heads with his father about the direction of the business. Neither of us was happy. I became more resentful about being there and he retreated into his world of pizza and recipes. There was no more talk about plans for 'us'. I take a deep breath and look straight into the dark eyes I used to love.

'Like I say,' I say, barely a waver in my voice, though I know it's almost there, 'this is my family's restaurant, Giac. I'm helping because I want to. I want my grand-father's legacy to be passed on and his name to stay above that door. You might not like me being here and I don't like being here with you. But I'm here to help get things running smoothly before I leave for home. I want to know that this place will be exactly the same as it is now when I come back next year.'

His face hardens, as do his eyes.

'You see, that's the thing, Luce.' It feels strange, him calling me Luce. He called me by my British name. He knew the Italian me and the Welsh me. I wish now he didn't. And I wish with all my heart that he wasn't having this effect on me, all the familiar sensations: my stomach fizzing, my knees giving, my heart quick-ening. His very presence and that look can do this to me, and I hate it. I have to find a way to make it stop.

'The thing is, Luce' – he's still staring at me and I can't not look at him – 'nothing stays the same. There is always change.'

I let what he says sit with me, trying to take in what he means. Is he talking about the restaurant, I wonder, or about us? Then, or here and now?

'Like I say, I'm grateful for your help. But I don't need it. I'm doing things my way. Your grandfather asked me to take over, to keep it as a pizza restaurant. And I will. But I will do it my way. Actually, I have already made plans.'

'What plans?'

And something tells me that, no matter how much I'm here in the kitchen, things are not going to be the same at all. Not for any of us.

ELEVEN

'An electric oven! Are you serious?' I throw up the apron in my hand in utter disbelief. I didn't see that coming. When he said, 'Everything changes', I expected him to tell me about the rhubarb pizza, but not this. It's dark outside now. Everyone has left for the evening. It's just us in the kitchen. And I'm wishing it wasn't.

'Entirely,' he says evenly, watching me as I turn away, then back to him, trying to make sense of what he's saying.

'But – but you can't make an authentic Margherita unless it's in a wood-fired oven!' I splutter. 'It's what it is!' I hold my head.

'Maybe it isn't authentic' – he nods, seemingly listening – 'but people are taking the authentic pizza and pushing the boundaries now. There is even the deconstructed Margherita! Like I say, everything changes.

For us master pizza-makers, we must try new ways of doing things. I have a top-of-the-range electric oven coming to be fitted here, at the weekend. A company making them are keen to sponsor me, we have a deal, for the oven to be seen. In the courtyard, I'm creating an outdoor kitchen area. And the new oven will be the centrepiece, cooking the dough to perfection.'

My mouth opens and closes. This is exactly what I was afraid of. There is no way I can let this happen. 'No way, Giac!'

'Sorry, Luce, but I'm the one here. And will still be here when you've gone home. This is my plan.'

I glare at him and he holds my gaze. I can feel the heat between us, fiery passion crackling for this restaurant and what it means to us. We're at different sides of the chasm widening between us. I have no idea how to respond – I'm rarely lost for words, but right now, I am. Furious, I grab my jacket and bag and storm out of the back door, where the woodpile is kept, rather than have to pass him to go out through the courtyard. I swing open the back gate and run straight into someone coming the other way.

'*Scusi,*' I say, holding up a hand.

'*Scusi,*' she echoes, as we rebound off each other. We apologize profusely, and then she steps past me, her jacket pulled tightly around her. The car she's just got out of speeds away as her high-heeled boots clip, clip, clip down the dark side street. I wonder where she's going. Home, or is her work still not done for the night? I sigh and march towards the piazza, thinking of work. As Giacomo said, I'm the one going home. I have my own life to get back to. But, still, I can't believe Nonno is going to be happy about an electric oven. I need to speak to him as soon as possible.

He shrugs and sighs.

'But, Nonno, you can't really think this is a good idea. An electric oven? At Nonno's?'

He shrugs again, sitting in his chair by the open windows, breathing in the warm night air. 'Lucia, it is a changing world. *Pizzaiolo*s are doing all sorts of crazy things, these days. I mean, who ever heard of a "deconstructed Margherita"?' He stands, pours me some grappa and hands it to me. Nonna is in bed, he tells me, on the condition that he waited up until I was in. I can hear her snoring from the bedroom. But she'll be up early, just as she is every morning. Preparing the breakfast, the coffee, the sauce, and making pasta for lunch later that day. Every day. I don't know how she feels about it, really. Will she take it easier when Nonno retires, let him help out in the kitchen? Now it's only going to be the two of them at lunchtimes, not the staff from the restaurant as well, whom Nonno often brought home, it should be easier. Nonna never likes to be without a meal ready to serve to whoever comes through the door.

'But surely you can't want him to do that at Non-no's,' I say, a little too loudly. I hear Nonna snuffle and worry I've woken her. We listen and wait for her to fall back into a rhythmic snore.

I sit down next to Nonno, holding the grappa.

'*Grazie*,' I say and sip. It makes me wince as it burns my throat.

'Lucia, don't worry.' Nonno sits back in his chair with the moonlight reaching out a silvery strand, lighting his face. 'I want that place to stay a pizzeria. I want the work your great-grandparents and I've put in to survive, live on and evolve. If this is evolution, so be it. I'm happy that Giacomo wants to be there and it won't just close down and be sold.'

'But an electric oven! What about tradition? Isn't that what it's all about?'

Nonno nods slowly. 'It is, but it's also about handing over the reins. From father to son. That's tradition too.'

I look out of the window onto the street below, wondering how different things might have been if my father had still been alive. He loved life. He loved *this* life. He might have worked as a taxi driver by day, but by night, he was king in his own kitchen, with dreams of returning to Italy one day. A massive heart attack put paid to that. And even though Mum is remarried and happy, he's left a hole in our lives and in the kitchen where he should be. I'm not prepared to let

Nonno work himself to death and leave another hole in our lives. If Giacomo really is his only option, then maybe I have to accept it, electric oven and all. We stare down onto the street. I can see the woman I ran into earlier, walking up and down. But it's quiet tonight. And, by the look of it, business is quiet for her, too, as she eventually gives up waving at passing cars, slips off her high heels and heads for home, barefoot. I feel a certain amount of relief.

She looks up as she passes and smiles at Nonno and me sitting there in the warm night air. I raise a hand. She does the same.

'Buona notte,' she says quietly, and sashays down the street, no doubt towards her apartment. Once again I find myself counting my blessings. At least I have a job and career to go back to. And Nonno is happy to go along with the idea of the business 'evolving'.

'Buona notte, Nonno. Goodnight,' I say, stand up, then bend to kiss him.

'Buona notte, lovely,' he says, holding my hand. 'It's wonderful having you here.'

'It's wonderful being here!' and I mean it. I always love being here and will hate it when I have to leave again in just over ten days' time.

I walk up to my bedroom, listen to Nonna's robust snoring and smile. From my room I look down onto the street, leading to the piazza. As I do, I see Giacomo passing, his jacket slung over his shoulder, heading to the car park on the outskirts of the piazza, lifting his head to the night air. He turns suddenly to look up at the apartment and I step quickly back from the window, my heart racing – I have no idea why. Is it that I'm still furious with him for being here, back in our lives? I hope he hasn't seen me. He's right: I'm going home. Soon I won't have to see him at all. I have my own life to sort out. I sit on my bed, and pick up my phone, pressing the on button. To my relief, it comes to life before my tired, sore eyes. I watch as it loads, my stomach suddenly tight with nerves as I shakily scroll through my new messages. Giacomo will be here. Nonno seems happy enough, and I have my life back home to focus on right now.

I scroll the messages as they arrive in my inbox, until I see one that catches my eye. No matter how tired I am, I know I won't sleep until I've read it. This is the one I've been waiting for. Now, everything really will change. From Anthony Gwyn-Jones. Subject: Promotion. And I open it.

TWELVE

My eyes are wide open as I listen for singing. I've slept barely a wink, the words of the email replaying in my head. Fury is still surging around my body, making my eyeballs burn and pumping my blood. 'I'm sorry to say . . . not this time . . . but we're very grateful for your loyalty and hope your turn will come . . . We hope you don't feel too disappointed . . .'

Overlooked. Again! I couldn't feel more disappointed if I tried. I sit up. Actually, it's not disappointment, it's anger. Overlooked and angry is how I'm feeling right now. Stuff Anthony Gwyn-Jones and Partners! Stuff their job, and their gratitude for my loyalty!

I should never have looked at Jasper's Facebook page announcing his promotion within the firm. I can't believe it! He doesn't work nearly as hard as I do and hasn't been there half as long.

I can hear Nonna in the kitchen. Brushing away the furious tears in my eyes, I get dressed quickly and go downstairs, kiss her and sit down as she hands me some coffee. 'Everything okay, Lucia?' she asks, sliding a plate of freshly baked pastries towards me.

I wrap my hands around the mug and breathe in the comforting aroma, thinking about the hours I had put in at the office before everyone else arrived and late into the night to try to get recognition for my work. But for what? Why had I bothered, all those early starts? Why did I feel I needed the recognition of the partnership? Without that, it felt like wasted time. I felt worthless.

'Nonna, why do you do this?'

'Do what?'

'Cook every day. Why do you get up at five to cook the sauce and make the pasta?'

She looks at me as if it's the most unusual question, as if doing what she does is the most natural thing in the world.

I take one of her freshly baked milk-bread rolls, spoon some of her homemade jam onto it and bite. It tastes of my great-grandmother's kitchen early in the morning. Their home out of town, when they were still alive. This taste is in my memory bank and my DNA.

'Because I love it. I do it because I want to. I do it for love. To feed the ones I love. It makes me who I am. It's not always easy, getting up, but without it, well, where would I be?'

Does being a business lawyer make me who I am? Do I wake at five and dive to my desk because I love it and the people I work for? Or have I been doing it all this time to earn more money, to try for the promotion so I can have an apartment I want, with a kitchen where I can cook for people I love?

I look at Nonna.

'I love to cook, and I love to cook for the ones I love,' she says simply, her eyes soft.

'Didn't you ever want to do more with it?' I ask, picking at crumbs from the soft bread.

She laughs. I love to hear Nonna laugh. 'What? Like run a restaurant?' She's still laughing and her boobs wobble like jelly.

'Yes,' I say, helping myself to more of the jam she's made with fruit from Giuseppe's.

She shakes her head and shrugs. 'It wasn't how things were when I got married,' she says matter-of-factly. 'Nonno took over the restaurant and I ran the home.'

I'm finishing my bread and jam when she joins me at the table with her pasta board between us and her long rolling pin. I help her make the pasta shapes, just like I've always done, ready for lunch later in the day. I find the repetitive rolling and cutting therapeutic as my thoughts whirl – what will my life be like when I return to the UK, back to the office, to the same desk, with a new partner sitting beside me? My hands shake and I have to start the pasta shape again.

'I didn't get the promotion, Nonna,' I say.

She stops for a moment. My eyes fill with tears, and so do hers, and she pats my hand, her soft, plump one on mine.

'Overlooked again,' I say.

'Maybe,' says Nonna, 'you are searching in the wrong place for your place in the world.' Then she laughs gently, with a sniff, looking at my uneven pasta shapes. 'No, no, not like that, like this!' she says, correcting my attempts. 'How will I find you a husband again if you can't make good pasta?' She laughs.

'Maybe it's not a husband I want, Nonna,' I say, as my thoughts slowly start to take a new path in my head.

Nonna's eyes twinkle. 'Maybe not yet. Maybe you don't know what you want yet. But you will. You just have to listen to what's in your heart. Now, let me show you again. You do it.' And I watch, listen and learn, as I always have, and feel I'm just where I want to be. Something inside me shifts, then seems to re-settle and slot right into place with a satisfying click.

THIRTEEN

'Impossible!' Nonno says.

'Nonno, I do. I want to run the restaurant.'

I've thought of nothing else, waiting for him to get back from his trip to his olive grove and vegetable patch in the countryside.

Nonno seems to be wondering if I'm joking. Then his face breaks into a smile and he laughs again. 'Ah, wouldn't that be a lovely idea?' he says, taking off his hat and easing himself into his chair at the lunch table after a morning of digging, then coffee with friends in the town, planning tactics for the *bocce* tournament. 'But we talked about this. It wouldn't work, you running the restaurant from Wales. It would be too tricky. Better to have Giac who is here and hands-on. But it was a nice idea.'

'No, Nonno, not just an idea, I'm serious.'

I'd lain awake all night and thought of nothing else. This is what I want to do. It's where I want to be. It was never about the promotion. I realize that now. It was about what it could give me. And it's not what I want. Not a shiny new kitchen, with barely anyone to cook for at the end of another busy week when I barely have time to microwave a TV dinner, let alone go late-night shopping and cook. When I learned I'd been overlooked again, I was furious with my boss and humiliated, and the more I thought about it, the more frustrated and angry I felt. That was when I realized I wanted to be in the kitchen, at the restaurant, serving the evening pizzas, with the smell of the woodsmoke, wisteria and lemons, chopping fresh basil and tearing apart the soft mozzarella. It's my happy place, where I want to be. My safe place.

'I want to stay here, take it on, run the kitchen myself.'

Nonno's face falls. 'But you can't be serious.' He leans over and pours the wine. Outside in the street, Angelo is singing. Someone calls for him to be quiet, but he sings anyway, louder this time, making me smile and all the more determined.

'I am, Nonno. You don't need Giacomo to move in with his electric oven. I can run the restaurant just the way it's always been. Just as if Dad had been alive to take it over. I'm here, and I can do it! I know I need to be hands-on, but I've been watching you for years.'

He stares at me, his eyes sparkling with little tears. He sniffs, shakes his head and smiles, even laughs a little. 'It's a lovely idea. But you have your own life back in Wales. You are a lawyer, with a promotion on the way.' He puts his hand over mine. 'I can't let you walk away from your career to run the restaurant. You have trained hard, worked hard. I can't let you give that up. But thank you.' He pats my hand. 'It was a lovely gesture.'

He starts to serve himself from the bowl of pasta in front of us, then hands me the spoons to do the same.

I take a deep breath. 'There is no promotion, Nonno.'

He stops what he's doing and looks at me. 'No promotion?'

Nonna stops by the table, puts down a basket of bread and looks at me.

'What do you mean, no promotion?' he says. 'I thought it was all arranged. In the bag.' His accent and expressions make me smile, despite my upset.

Phhhhfffff! I blow out and take a quick run at saying it. 'Lost out . . . again.' I pick up a piece of bread and rip it in half.

'Who to?'

I toss a piece of bread into my mouth.

'A guy in our office, Jasper.'' I chew and swallow. 'Hasn't even been there that long.' I rip at another piece of the crusty bread with my teeth.

Nonna reaches over and piles a mountain of pasta onto my plate, the size of Vesuvius.

'Eat, eat!' she tells us both, gesticulating.

Nonno starts on his pasta, which is covered with thick, rich tomato sauce, as Nonna grates flakes of Parmesan over it for him. They fall like snow on the mountains. I'd love to be here for the winter and see it, I think, knowing that this is exactly where I want to be. It's just Nonno I have to convince.

'Your time will come,' he says. 'And you will make us all very proud.' He pats my hand again. 'You are wonderful at what you do. They are stupid not to see it.'

I doubt Nonno really knows what I do, and I love him for that. But my mind is set and I've never felt more determined about anything. Out of all the legal cases and businesses I've fought for, the businesses I've helped set up and support, this is the one that means the most. This is personal.

'It's not what I want to do, Nonno. Not any more. I realize that now.' I put down the bread and lay my hands on his forearm. 'I've spent my life helping others get into business and stay there. Now I know it's me who should be in business. I just needed this to understand it.'

'But . . .' He stops stabbing at pasta with his fork and puts it down, my hands on his arm still. 'You're just angry. You've trained and worked hard for years. You must use that passion. Show them what you're made of. Show your passion for what is inside you and what you love.'

'Exactly, Nonno. And it's not the law. It's not hours

on end in an office, dreaming of what I want to be cooking that night for dinner, then being too tired to get to the shops and going home to an empty flat. I know what I want to do. I wake up every morning, dreaming of what I'd like to cook that night. I've been waiting for time to cook, hoping I'd get more of it with this promotion. I really wanted that promotion, but I realize it's about the buzz, the excitement of getting other people into business, to follow their dreams. Now it's my turn to be brave. Do what I love. I need to live to work, not the other way round. I need to see that what I'm doing means something. I need to feel I'm invested, not just turning up every day, giving myself to the company but never feeling a part of the business. I need to belong. And here, this place, the food, this is what's inside me.' I put my other hand to my chest. 'The food I've grown up with. This place!' I jut my chin towards the open doors onto the balcony where the sun is pouring through. I can hear Angelo, against the backdrop of moped engines and friends calling to each other, a dog yapping, and smell the lunchtime pasta. 'It's what I love. Just like you and your father before you. I want to make pizza. I want to take over the restaurant.'

'But . . .'

'I saw Sofia in the market. She told me about Paolo and it made me think—'

'Oh yes, Paolo. I'm so sorry, we should have told you

sooner. Such a tragedy. So young. Like your father.' He shakes his head, as if Paolo's death has brought back all the memories of losing his own son too young.

'But it made me see that life's too short not to do the thing you love. Not to follow your heart, to feel like you belong. You said it yourself.' I'm on a roll, delivering my persuasive argument to the opposition. 'It's about the passion, what you love. I love pizza, and I love being in the restaurant. I love everything about that place. It's in here.' I touch my chest again. 'I want to take it on, keep the tradition alive.'

Nonno stares up at Nonna as if searching for help. She shrugs, sits down at the end of the table and serves herself some pasta without looking at him.

'Nonna, explain . . .' he says, raising his shoulders, holding out his hands palms up to Nonna and then to me.

Nonna ignores his pleas.

'Why not, Nonno? It's perfect! I'll hand in my notice. With all the holiday I'm due, it'll have immediate effect.' The idea appeals more and more to me. 'Then they'll find out who does most of the work in that office – and it's not their new partner. Just because he stays later than anyone else, always the last to leave, even if it's two minutes after me, it doesn't mean he does more work.' I let the thought sit, then let it go, like a balloon I've filled with air. It's gone. I'm not going back. I've decided. It's not what I want. I want to feel I'm part of a business, a community. All this time, I needed to be brave enough to work at something I loved, instead of for other people so they could do just that. What I want is right in front of me.

I look at Nonno, who is lost for words. I know he thinks I'm doing this because I didn't get the promotion. But I'm not. It's just made me understand what I do want. And I want the restaurant. I want to make pizza and become a master pizza-maker like him.

'But . . .' He gives Nonna another look, but she shrugs, letting him know he's on his own.

'Yes?' I wait. We all wait.

'You can't take over the restaurant,' Nonno finally says.

'Why not? I've been in that kitchen at your side for as long as I can remember. I know the dough recipe by heart, and how to prove it. And you can teach me as I go. Hand over the reins to me . . . or the pizza peel!' I smile at my little joke. It's a perfect plan.

Nonno drops his head sadly and shakes it. 'I know, I know,' he says, looking up at the ceiling, as if asking someone up there for help. 'It's not that. You do. And one day you will make someone a wonderful wife and cook for your family.'

'But that's not what I want right now, Nonno! I want to do more than that. I want to make cooking my career. I want to be a master pizza-maker like you! A *pizzaiola*!'

He holds up his hands in frustration. 'But you can't!' he says.

'Why?'

'Because you are a woman! There are no *pizzaiola*s!' he splutters out.

There is silence in the room. Even the singing outside has stopped.

'That's not true,' I say quietly, with steel in my voice. I have no idea where it comes from.

'A few, maybe, in Naples . . . but not here. It would never work. They will never accept a *pizzaiola*! I'm sorry, Lucia. I wish it was different. But it isn't. You know this place! You have lived here. You know how set in their ways they are. Your own in-laws couldn't accept you wanted a career before having children. They are stuck in the past. The women cook in the home and the men in the businesses. It's how it's always been. We have had people try and fail. Customers won't go to the restaurants! They believe the best chefs are men. Like *bocce* players.' He shrugs. 'The women who have made it have so many obstacles to face, so much stupid prejudice. It's how it's always been. It is considered such a masculine profession. You have to be strong. You have to be hungry to compete in this world. I would love you to take over but if the locals knew, it would be so hard for you. I do not want to see you judged in that way. I won't have it! But it is just . . . They are set in their ways. That's why there are no *pizzaiola*s here.'

I look at Nonna, who stares straight back at me, clearly finding the words as hard to hear as I am. And what Nonno has said may indeed be the case. But I do know one thing: I may not succeed, but I'm determined to try to change his mind.

'Until now . . .' I say, with that steel again, and I swear Nonna does a small fist pump into her chubby side.

FOURTEEN

'No, no way!' Nonno is still insistent the following morning as we walk through the few ancient olive trees on his parcel of land, outside town, surrounded by old stone walls, separating it from neighbouring plots, to where he's been digging and planting vegetables again. It's early morning. There is a smell in the air of dew on the ground and trees, and the earthy scent of the few tomato plants he's growing. Cobwebs sparkle in the rising sun.

He walks and talks as he gathers rakes from the old stone building there, turns on the hose and hands it to me, waving at the tomatoes and peppers that need watering. I take the hose and do as I'm told as he rakes over more of the earth around them.

'Now, put the restaurant out of your mind. Relax and enjoy the rest of your holiday.' He hands me a rake and points to the dug-over, now damp earth that needs attention. 'Put it out of your mind. Come this time next year, and you can see how well my plants are doing,' he says. 'This place will be full to bursting with fresh vegetables. Straight from the ground to the table,' he says, picks a tomato and hands it to me. It's a beautiful red, and has the peppery smell you get from really tasty tomatoes on the vines. He picks one for himself, bites into it and watches me.

I smell the tomato again, and it brings back memories of my being here as a child, with my great-grandparents. This place, the sun on my face, my feet in the soil. It makes me feel alive, as if I could grow like the plants here. I bite into the tomato. Its juice rushes to the corners of my mouth, sweet and full of flavour. I shut my eyes. This is what here is all about, the tastes and traditions.

I feel even more determined as I open my eyes and look at my smiling *nonno*. 'You're happy to accept an electric oven, but not me in the kitchen as the pizza chef,' I say, frustrated. 'It's like replacing fresh tomatoes with tinned! It's fake. It's not what Nonno's is about.' Inside I'm furious all over again. Furious that Jasper has blagged his way to the promotion and that Anthony Gwyn-Jones allowed himself to be hoodwinked. And now Nonno will let Giacomo in but not me. This isn't right. Determination and fury build in me from the ground upwards.

'I've told you, Lucia. It's not my choice. I'd love to hand it on to you, if that's what you want.'

'But it is what I want! I know that now!'

'But it just won't work,' he says more softly. 'I love you. I don't want to see you hurt.'

'But there are *pizzaiola*s in Naples!' I try to reason with him again.

'But not here. Here is different from Napoli. I don't want you to have to be the one to try to break the mould. It would be too hard. Too painful. Like I say, people are very set in their ways and I don't want you hurt trying to change that. It's my job to protect you, with your father not here, and I want to see you happy. Now, let's hear no more about it. Focus on what you know. The law. I'm proud of you, Lucia.'

I don't want law. It was just . . . an escape route. When I needed to stick my head in the sand and forget what had gone wrong in my own life, I could lose myself in law and other people's lives. Along the way, I forgot to have one of my own. But I'm here now. I'm back, and my old life, with Giacomo, is standing in the middle of my family kitchen in my way, messing with my life now. And I want to reclaim it.

'Come on. Let's get back and have coffee, perhaps a pastry, too,' he says, putting away the tools. We drive through the lanes, brushing past the overgrowth and barely skimming the stone walls as we arrive in the town and park the car.

At the apartment, I greet Nonna.

'How was it?' she asks. 'Did you bring me anything?'

'It was . . . amazing,' I say. 'Just amazing.' I still have the taste of the tomato in my mouth, the memory of the smell filling my head and my soul. It's all about the traditions and the terrain, the land the food comes from.

Nonno hands her a basket of tomatoes he picked before we left. We travelled back in silence, lost in our thoughts, as the sun crept up into the sky, getting hotter all the time. I had the window down, the warm breeze on my face, and the scent of the earth filling my head. There is nowhere else I'd rather be. Jasper is welcome to the promotion, welcome to the long hours, never seeing the light of day. I want to be here. I want to be a part of it.

I grab my bag and one of Nonno's baseball caps from the hook by the front door to shield my eyes from the sun and stop my cheeks turning quite so pink. I kiss Nonna and tell her I'll be back later.

'You can't go out until you've eaten!' says Nonna, holding a basket of bread.

'I'll eat out,' I call back. 'Love you!' and I leave the apartment.

Angelo is singing softly and I stop to listen to him. As I do, he raises his voice to reach the balcony opposite, where the doors are firmly shut.

'You're still singing, then?' I smile.

'Sometimes in life you have to do what's right for

you. Singing makes me happy. My customers like it. If they don't, they'll go somewhere else.' He hands me a *cornetto* from his tray. 'You just have to be you in life. If it's not hurting anyone and is making people happy,' he shrugs, 'if it's what you really want, and who you are, nothing can stop you. It is other people's loss if they choose not to let you into their lives.' He looks up again at the doors, closed to the morning sunshine. An apartment in the dark.

I smile and bite into the flaky *cornetto*. '*Grazie*, Angelo.' I lean in, kiss him briefly on the cheek, then walk off in the direction of the piazza, in the warm morning sunshine. It's heating the worn, cream flagstones, where so many people have walked, making their mark on this part of the world. And that is exactly what I intend to do.

'Luce, you're back!' Giacomo turns to me with surprise and perhaps a hint of irritation. I ignore it.

'I brought the greengrocery order from the veg shop.' I carry the box into the restaurant kitchen.

'I was just on my way to get it.'

'It's no trouble. I was up and about early with Nonno.' I even surprised Giuseppe by arriving as he was still making up the boxes. Mind you, I didn't expect Giacomo to be at the restaurant so early.

I put down the box on the table in the kitchen and take a deep breath. 'I saw you made a few changes to the order again, so I set it right and brought what Nonno

111

usually gets.' My heart is pounding. I know I shouldn't have, but I couldn't help myself. Some of his order was just . . . Well, it's not what Nonno's does. My palms are sweating. I want to turn and run, but seeing Giacomo in the kitchen, the cupboards emptied and rearranged, everything turned upside down again, I just can't.

Out in the courtyard a builder is creating a work-space for Giacomo's outside oven and kitchen. I stand on tiptoe to look out through the clear glass circle in the door. He steps in front of me and the door, his shoulders obliterating my view, infuriatingly.

'Look, Luce, thanks for trying to help but, really, there's no need.' My heart is pounding even harder at his use of the name I'm known by at home in Wales. Here, I'm Lucia. I glare at him. It seems to help keep my nerves at bay. I may not have run a restaurant on my own before, but I'm going to try. I'm not going to let him stand in my way.

'No need to thank me. I'm happy to be here.' I start to pull on my apron, hanging next to Nonno's chef's whites. Nonna puts clean ones out for him every day. I take off the baseball cap and hang it up. Not some-thing I'd wear back home, but back home I'm a professional in suits every day. Here, I'm a holiday-maker not used to the sun.

'But, you see, I don't need you here to help.' He stares back at me, just as determinedly. 'Carlo will be here today. I'm working up my new ideas and my kitchen is being sorted.'

I bristle and step around him to look out at the bricklaying. Then I turn slowly and look directly at him. 'Oh,' I say evenly. 'I'm not here to help.'

'You're not?' He smiles. 'Well, good. Thank you for being so understanding. And for bringing the green-grocery, of course.' He points to the box.

'No, I'm not here to help you. In fact, quite the op-posite.' I'm shaking inside but I can't back out now. 'I was hoping you could help me. I'm here to run the place.'

'What?' He throws up his hands, and I copy him.

'What what?' Two can play at the Italian drama game.

'You cannot run this place!' He holds his hands on his head and his shirt lifts, as it always does, showing the top of his jeans and the dark olive skin.

'Why not?' I raise my chin to him.

He says nothing.

'Because I'm a woman? Is that why?' I challenge him.

Again he says nothing.

'Or maybe you just don't want me to. Maybe you want to ruin my life some more!'

He throws up his arms again and spins away. I wish I could think he feels just a tad guilty for the hell he put me through when he called time on our marriage.

'And maybe you just want to punish me,' he says quietly, turning back to me.

We stare at each other, and I can feel the hatred and hurt ricocheting between us. Just like it was seven years ago. As raw as ever. It wasn't what he said so much as what he didn't say. The more unhappy we both became, the more he clammed up. I couldn't work, but he was out most of the day and evening working. I was at home without a role. And the more lost I felt, the more I felt he was leaving me adrift. I didn't feel I belonged anywhere. Not here, not in Wales. And Giacomo could see I was unhappy. We were making each other unhappy. And now, like then, I want my chance to work and prove myself. Prove I'm capable. Just like I was at Anthony Gwyn-Jones and Partners.

I swallow and say slowly, 'I'm here to work.'

He throws out his hands and laughs hollowly.

'What? Because I'm a woman, you don't think I can do this? Well, watch me!' I say, pulling my apron tight. I'm not going to let the fact that I'm a woman stand in my way. What was the difference between me and Jasper getting that promotion? I was more experienced, harder-working, and a woman. Was that it? Well, my sex is not an excuse to deny me an opportunity. Not back in the office and not here.

'It's not that.' He turns away, his palm to his forehead, then back to me. 'Luce, you're not even Italian!' He holds out his arms. 'This is not your world!'

I'm dumbstruck, speechless, thrown off my stride just for a moment, then right myself. 'Of course I am!'

'You grew up in Wales! You just visit here. It's not the same!'

Phhhffffffff! I turn away so he doesn't see the angry tears filling my eyes. This man infuriates me.

'Luce, you could bankrupt the place! That's not what you want, is it? That's not what your grandfather needs right now. He needs to know this place is in safe hands, that it'll keep bringing in an income. It's not the time to take that kind of risk, Luce!'

I rip off the apron, toss it onto the table, slam out of the wooden door into the restaurant, and head out to the sunny courtyard, where the workman greets me with a smile. I walk out of the metal gate and march up the street, then across the square, ignoring the group of young men gathering there, calling out to me again. 'Pomodoro! Pomodoro!' They make me feel every bit of what Giacomo just said to me. I'm a visitor. I stand out like a sore thumb. I march through the piazza with its familiar archways, past the expensive tourist restaurants – you pay for the view rather than the quality of the food. Everyone knows that, I think crossly, as I stalk back to the apartment. Only once I'm inside do I let out all my frustrations. I tear up the stairs to my room, like a proud teenager, and then the tears flow.

FIFTEEN

'Sit, sit,' says Nonna, ushering me downstairs, waving a tea towel behind me, to the kitchen table, a place of safety, warmth, tears and celebrations. 'Here.' She pushes coffee, bread and jam towards me. Also a plate of Parma ham and bright orange melon – its perfume wraps itself around me. Then, as I sob, she pours me grappa and insists I drink it, despite the early hour. Surprisingly, it helps.

'Who am I, Nonna? I mean, what am I doing here?' I cry, and feel like a snotty teenager all over again. Or the wrung-out twenty-something I was when I realized Giacomo's and my marriage was coming to an end. The more I tried to make it work, the more he distanced himself from me. I tried to fit in, but I was lost. I had no purpose other than to have grandchildren for his parents, and there was no way I could do that until I had found out what I was going to do. I couldn't work here as a lawyer. All I did was clean, count our wine glasses, and look for furniture to buy for our home. But it never felt like our home. It was always Giacomo's family's and I was just living there.

When I was at school, I'd always thought I'd do law. I was fairly bright and my teachers guided me that way. Mum and my grandparents had been delighted when it was suggested at parents' evenings. Mum thought law would suit me, because I'd always hated injustice – like when my brother was picked on in the playground for 'not being Welsh', being told to 'Speak *italiano!*' Sometimes the bullies pretended not to understand him when he spoke, all because of his surname. Well, I wasn't having that. I confronted his form teacher, outraged, and went on to give a talk in assembly about the history of Italian immigrants to Wales, and how proud we should be of our heritage, no matter where we come from. It earned me house points, a place on the debating team and an endorsement from teachers that law would be my chosen career. Chosen by whom? I talked about what I cared about, what I was passionate about. About celebrating our heritage, our mixed heritage, never about law!

I did what everyone expected me to. I worked hard. And when I returned to Wales, I worked hard for the people who were making their own dreams come true. Now it's my time. I worked hard for Anthony

Gwyn-Jones and Partners and was overlooked for promotion. Now I'm being told I can't take over the restaurant because tradition means that *pizzaiolo*s are men. 'Tradition handed down from father to son!'

I'm not going to be overlooked again.

'I can't let it happen again, Nonna. I can't! I ...' I stumble, then say what I know I've been hiding from for many years. 'I'm not a lawyer. I don't want to be. It's not who I am in here!' I hold my hand to my chest. 'It's what people expected me to be.' Just like Giacomo's parents expected me to produce children, stay at home and be a 'good wife'. Where am I in all of this? Where is Lucia? 'When I'm at home in Wales, everyone thinks I'm Italian. When I'm here everyone thinks I'm Welsh. Nonno and Giacomo think it wouldn't work if I took on the restaurant, yet it's what I want more than anything! I just don't know where I fit in!' I hold my head, tears still burning my cheeks. Anger at Anthony Gwyn-Jones and Partners for promoting a less-experienced male over me. And anger because, no matter what I want to do, a man is always standing in the way. This time, it's Giacomo.

'Have I taught you nothing, Lucia?' Nonna says gently, taking my hands. 'Look at me,' she says, and I gaze up at her. 'The way to a man's heart is through his stomach.'

'I told you, Nonna, it's not a husband I'm looking for.' I despair. This feels more like the 1960s than the twenty-first century.

'I know, you said. And I said, the way to a man's heart is through his stomach.'

I frown.

'You want to convince Nonno to let you take on the restaurant, right?'

'Yes. I really do. I know it's what I want.' I swipe at any loose tears that might still be falling and feel better for having let them all out.

'Then show him.' She smiles, her eyes twinkling in the usual mischievous way. 'Show them all.'

'I tried! I can't even get into the kitchen. Giac was there, with a builder, waiting for his fancy new oven to arrive and rearranging the cupboards. He has Carlo coming in to help work out a new menu. I feel like a cuckoo in the nest!'

Nonna looks at me steadily, still holding my hands. 'If you really want this, you'll have to find another way of getting it. You have to prove yourself.'

'How?'

'By cooking. What do they say? Keep calm and carry on cooking!' She beams. 'It's helped me through the good times and the bad.' She's talking about my father: when he died, Nonna found cooking was her map through grief. Talking about the evening meal, the ingredients, and feeding the family was how she got through it. Maybe still is. 'Now, come on, let's get started,' she says.

'But I told you,' I sigh, 'I can't get into the restaurant. And, like Giac said, not only am I a woman, I'm not even

Italian. Who would come to eat my food? It could ruin the restaurant!' I throw up my hands and cover my face with them, furious all over again that he is probably right. Who would trust a *pizzaiola* who's only half Italian? Well, Italian parents, but growing up in Wales. Gah!

'But that's not who you need to convince right now. Not Giacomo or the customers or even yourself. Right now, the only person who matters is Nonno. He's the one you need to convince. If he believes you can do it, that's all that counts. Because I believe you can. Now, come on, let's cook.'

At 1 p.m., as usual, Nonno arrives back from *bocce* and coffee.

'Ah, that Alfonso, he makes up the rules as he goes along!' he says, stripping off his hat and sitting himself at the table in front of the open doors onto the balcony. 'Makes them up to suit himself. Telling me we've always played that way. Just because he played those rules in the town up the road. We don't! We never have! He makes it up!' he repeats, caught up in replaying to us the whole match, how it came down to the final decision and Alfonso altering the rules to suit himself, while Nonno stuck to what he knew because that gave him the outcome that suited him.

Nonna shoos me out of the kitchen, where I do a last check to see that everything is ready, and to the table to sit with Nonno.

'Pour him wine,' she says, in a loud whisper. 'Make it a nice bottle.'

I go to the rack and look through them. 'Here we go, Nonno. How about a glass of this to take the edge off the *bocce* game?' I hold up the bottle. He looks at it, nods and smiles.

'That could do the trick,' he says. I open it and smell the cork, then pour him a drop to sniff, swirl and taste.

'Very good,' he says appreciatively.

'Excellent,' I say, sitting next to him, as Nonna and I have arranged, feeling nervous, like I'm going for a job interview.

Suddenly there is a knock at the door. 'Ah, just in time!' says Nonno.

Nonna and I look at each other.

'I invited Giac to join us. He has work going on in the restaurant and I said he should eat with us.'

My eyes widen. Of all people! My heart starts to thud.

'Well, answer the door, Lucia,' instructs Nonna, with a firm nod.

I get up and open it. Giacomo indeed is standing outside. 'Um, Enzo, your grandfather, invited me,' he says, sounding a little nervous. 'I hope this is okay, Luce.'

'It's fine,' I try to say airily, as I turn towards the living room.

'And, um, look,' he says, catching my elbow. I turn back.

'I just wanted to check you were okay. I mean, what I said back there, I didn't mean to hurt you. I was just being honest.'

'It's fine, Giac,' I repeat, and turn back to the dining table where Nonna has set another place.

'Come in, Giac, there's always plenty to go round.'

'*Grazie*,' he says, sits at the table, accepting wine from Nonno in a short stubby glass, and pours himself water in one of the coloured ones.

There is bread on the table, marinated olives, mozzarella balls, sundried tomatoes, and Nonno insists that Giacomo helps himself, which he does, as if it's the most natural thing in the world for the four of us to be having lunch together. Only the occasional worried glances at me tell me it's not. Nonno talks about his plans for his olive grove and vegetable patch out of town, and tells the story again of that morning's *bocce* match.

There are fried pasta balls and fried vegetables on a wooden board on the table. When these have been eaten, Nonna brings out a steaming hot dish held between two tea towels and places it on the table.

'*Parmigiana di melanzane!*' Nonno exclaims. 'My favourite!' And dives for a piece of bread ready to mop up the juices.

Nonna looks at me and winks.

I serve up the deep-fried aubergines, dark skins and light flesh, layered with soft, creamy mozzarella and rich tomato sauce, then baked.

There is little talking as we eat until the plates are wiped clean with the rest of the bread from the basket. Nonno sits back, rubs his full stomach, after a third helping, and sips his wine, Giacomo too.

'*Magnifico!*' he announces. 'Lunch was wonderful.' He picks up Nonna's hand and kisses it.

'*Sì*, really, really good!' says Giacomo. 'You were always a fantastic cook,' he tells her, charming as ever. 'It's lovely to be eating your food again.' And it was that charm I'd fallen for. He was always kind and generous, no matter what he was really thinking, and that was the thing: in the end, I didn't know what he was thinking. I didn't see it coming at all.

'She always has been. A better cook than me!' Nonno laughs and tops up all our glasses with the last of the bottle.

'Actually,' says Nonna, lifting her glass, 'I didn't cook it.' She looks at me.

'I did,' I say, lifting my glass to the same height. 'I cooked it.'

Nonno and Giacomo turn to me, and I give Nonna a little smile. 'Just like Nonna makes, with tradition, respect for the terrain, the ingredients and the skills.'

Nonno looks at Giacomo, who, I'm hoping, will finish his meal by eating his words.

Nonno lets out a long sigh. 'You are a good cook, Lucia. But not a *pizzaiola*!'

'Not yet – but I could be. I can learn, just like Giac has. Just like I cook the dishes I've learnt from Nonna over the years.'

Giacomo says nothing.

Nonno lets out another long sigh.

'Lucia is just as good a cook as me,' says Nonna. 'You've tasted her food. She deserves a chance to prove herself in the restaurant.'

Nonno puts his hands on the table and leans back in his chair. 'Okay,' he says thoughtfully, and my heart starts thundering. 'Meet me at the restaurant tomorrow morning, both of you. And I'll let you know what I decide.'

Giacomo declines coffee. He leaves to check the progress on his outside kitchen and the delivery of the oven. 'See you tomorrow,' I say, seeing him out.

'Yes,' he says, neither of us giving away what we're thinking.

SIXTEEN

The sun shines even brighter than it has done in previous days and it's hot already in the town, as we sit at a table in the shade in the courtyard at the front of the restaurant. Giacomo has insisted on making the coffee and serving us, as if the restaurant is his already. And, for all I know, it may be. I have no idea what Nonno is thinking or what he's planning to say or do now he's called us together.

I sit and look around the covered courtyard, the big yellow lemons in the pergola, which is covered with fairy lights. I love this place on warm sunny evenings. I peer inside at the cool white walls and the blackened fireplace beyond the open-sided terracotta-tiled terrace, the beautiful purple wisteria. This may be off the beaten track, away from the tourist restaurants in the square, but to me it's Paradise.

It's where we enjoyed all our family celebrations growing up, even those I want to forget. I glance at Giacomo and try to push out the memory of the dinner we shared here with friends and family to celebrate getting engaged. He had it all mapped out. Where we would live. Our life together. I would work as a lawyer, he would develop his pizza skills and take over his father's business with my support. When we had our careers sorted, we'd have a family, when we felt the time was right, when our home was ready. We had plans, until they changed. And I still have no idea why they did.

Just before I returned to the UK, I got a job with Anthony Gwyn-Jones and Partners and determinedly clawed my way up to where I thought I wanted to be. Now I realize it was a distraction. I just wanted to forget. Now I want to go back to what I've always wanted, where I wanted to be seven years ago, but this time without Giacomo, to a life that revolves around family and food. At school I had to give up home economics to take options more suited to doing law at university. I thought it was the right thing, the sensible thing. It wasn't. I should have listened to my heart, not my head. Just like I'm doing now, I need to speak up for how I feel, just like I wish Giacomo could have done when we finished. He never told me why he'd distanced himself from me, why he had fallen out of love with me. Perhaps I was no longer the person he'd married, because if I wasn't Lucia the lawyer, I was no one.

He sits down next to me, in front of his new outside kitchen work space. I move my chair away, just enough for him to notice. Then I'm cross with myself for letting him see he still has this effect on me. That I'm still hurt and upset. I'm not. I'm over him. I want to prove that by taking on the restaurant. I've hidden in piles of legal papers for too many years, ignoring what I was running from, and now I know it was him. And I'm not running any more. I'm here to set up the life in Italy I always wanted.

'So,' Nonno says, bringing me back to the here and now. He leans forward and puts his fingertips together. Nonna has joined him and is sitting at his side. 'I've had a sleepless night. My head is telling me one thing, my heart another.'

Giacomo and I are sitting on the edge of our seats. No one is drinking their coffee, although it smells delicious. Nonna gives him a single nod and looks at her hands in her lap, giving nothing away.

'I've talked this through with Nonna, and this is what I've decided.'

I take a quick gulp of air.

'Enzo, I could make this place into a destination restaurant. You know me, my family, what a good *pizzaiolo* I am. This gives me the chance to work up new ideas, to build on what you and your father have made here. You know I will never let you down. It will be a talked-about restaurant in years to come.'

I snap my head round to him, feeling like I'm back at work. Two can play at that game. 'Nonno, I know this place inside out. It's part of me. I'm part of the tradition and its legacy.'

'But, Luce, you—'

Nonno holds up his hand.

'I just want what's best for this place, for your family and you. That's all,' Giacomo finishes quietly.

'It's a bit late for that,' I say, just as quietly, shocked and irritated by his sudden concern for me. But we stop talking, respecting Nonno's wishes.

'I've made a decision.'

I breathe a sigh of relief.

'Giacomo, we agreed to a trial period until the *bocce* tournament, in three weeks and three days.'

I hold my breath again.

'And I intend to respect that. For both of us, Giacomo.'

Phhhhffffff. I let out a long, slow sigh of frustration and disappointment. Giacomo nods.

'But,' he says, 'Lucia . . .'

A glimmer of hope rises in me.

'. . . I understand how you feel. Like I say, it's not usual here for a woman to be a . . .'

I see Nonna give him a swift nudge.

'. . . but I have been persuaded by your food,' he looks at Nonna, 'to listen to my heart as well as my head.'

Giacomo frowns, confused. I'm confused too. He's

128

just said he's going to honour his arrangement with Giacomo.

'I could see both of you taking on the restaurant.'

'Oh, no, I couldn't,' we both say.

He holds up a hand again and we're silent, like children.

'I see benefits in both of you and your vision for the place. So here is what I intend to do.' He takes a deep breath. 'It will be a straightforward competition. Both of you will run the restaurant. Not together!' he says, before we argue.

'One menu, but with two sides, Giacomo's on one, Lucia's on the other.' He holds up the menu to demonstrate. 'Two different kitchens, two menus, on one board. One traditional, Lucia's,' he nods at me, 'one more . . . experimental, Giac's. Whoever sells the most pizzas will win.'

We stare at him, then at each other.

'Agreed?' he asks.

My heart is racing. I'm going to take on part of the restaurant. My menu! Nonno's menu! Excitement bubbles up inside me. And if I outsell Giac and his new ideas, I get the restaurant. It could really be happening! This is my chance and I'm going to take it.

'Agreed!' I say quickly. I look at Giacomo and see in him all the hurt, disappointment and resentment I feel towards my work back home. I'm not going to be overlooked again.

'Giac?' Nonno looks at him.

He nods slowly, as if he can't really believe what he's hearing. 'Yes, okay,' he says. 'I'm happy to do that.' And then, gently, 'If you're sure this is what you want to do, Luce.'

'I do!' I nod.

'*Phffff* . . . you always were stubborn!'

'What's that supposed to mean?'

'You get an idea and . . .' He trails off.

'It's about putting your personality and your passion on the plate!' Nonno butts in, tears of his own passion in his eyes. 'What's in here!' He puts a fist to his chest. 'Which one of you is the most passionate about this place, the terrain, the traditions of pizza?' He looks between us.

'If you're sure this is what you want?' Giacomo says, raising an eyebrow at me.

He thinks I can't do this. 'I am,' I say. All of the frustration and anger about the promotion, about Giacomo, about how I've wasted the past seven years surges up inside me. I want this more than anything right now. I want to prove myself, to Nonno, to Giacomo – but, most of all, to me. I see Nonna give him another nudge.

'Just one thing.' Nonno leans forward. 'No one,' he says slowly, 'no one must know about this.' He raises a finger. 'This is all about the food.' He points to the menu again. Nonna is giving him her sternest look. 'To make this fair, an even playing field, no one is to know that Lucia is cooking. We keep that among ourselves. It mustn't get out that we have a woman making pizza: a *pizzaiola*. You both deserve a fair chance, to be judged on what you put on the table. If word gets out about the competition, that Lucia is cooking, it won't be fair. Also, Giacomo must have a chance to show off his new menu and be judged on his food, not on anything else. If word gets out' – he swallows – 'I will have no alternative but to put the business on the market and sell it to become something else. I won't be able to choose between you fairly so I will be forced to sell.'

I hold my breath. If it gets out that I'm cooking, if it's not a fair competition, Nonno will be forced to sell. The very last thing he wants to do. This has to be fair. I look at Giacomo, who nods.

'Right, let's do this.' Nonno claps his hands together. 'Let's make pizza!'

Suddenly my spirits tumble and bubble and soar through the roof. I stand up, almost giddy with excitement.

'Thank you, Nonno.' I go round the table to hug him. 'Thank Nonna. It was her idea.'

I hug her tightly too.

I have an overwhelming urge to hug Giacomo as well, but I don't. I just beam at him. His face is set. 'Looks like you'd better cancel that new oven,' I say. 'It's not your place yet!'

The challenge is on.

SEVENTEEN

We head towards the restaurant kitchen to prepare for that evening's service. I begin by putting the cupboards back to how they were.

Giacomo tuts and rearranges the ingredients he wants in a different part of the kitchen.

I get the dough from the walk-in fridge and start prepping it. It's always made the day before, in the morning, for the next evening's service. I line up the balls exactly as I've seen Nonno doing it, and that bit, I've got sorted. What I haven't done much is cooking on the peel, the paddle, in the *forno*. I've done it a few times, when we were cooking for ourselves as family, but this will be very different and I'll have to do some practice ones.

Despite the heat of the day and with Giacomo giving me sideways glances, I light the *forno*.

'It's a bit early, isn't it?' he says. I want to tell him to mind his own business, but I don't. 'I'm getting in some practice,' I say, dipping one of the dough balls into a bowl of flour, then pushing it out, then again into a bigger disc. I can feel him watching me as he prepares his pizza toppings for the evening, cutting and chopping and watching me out of the corner of his eye.

I check the oven with the temperature gauge I slide in on the peel. Hot enough. I run my sweating palms over my apron. I just wish Giacomo wasn't watching my every move. I try to ignore him and prep my first pizza, a plain Margherita on the flat paddle end of the peel. The heat from the *forno* makes my eyes sting and water. I push aside the burning embers in the fires, just as I've watched Nonno do.

I give the pizza on the peel one last alteration, so it's looking its best as I lift it to the oven. It's heavier than I was expecting. I'm feeling the heat on my face, and my cheeks are turning red. I attempt to slip it off the peel. It doesn't budge. I try again and still it doesn't move. I'm getting hotter and so is the pizza, still on the peel. I can smell the cheese cooking but the base is still dough. I hear Giacomo behind me and try to ignore him. But I can feel his eyes on me.

'Do you—'

'I'm fine!' I say, my arms aching, and give the pizza a final forceful flick. It flips off the peel onto its topping, fizzing and burning in the embers.

'Bugger!' I mutter, hoping Giacomo hasn't seen but knowing he has. I need to get this right before opening time. If I can't actually cook the pizzas, it's over before it's begun.

'Can I make a suggestion?' he asks, from behind me.

'I said I'm fine. Just rusty!' I lie. 'I just need to practise a few more.' I turn back to the row of dough balls and start teasing out another. I use less topping on this one, hoping for less waste if it ends up in the embers, but I'm determined it won't.

It does. I hear a sigh from behind me. The smell of burning makes me sneeze. I grab my baseball cap and pull it on to try to keep the smoke from my eyes. Then I turn back to the row of dough balls and make another. Barely any topping this time.

I take a deep breath and lift the peel to the oven mouth.

'Here.' Suddenly another pair of hands is on the peel next to mine. I catch my breath. His hands, so familiar, but without the wedding band, so unfamiliar. 'Now lift, push and push again,' he says. The pizza flicks off the end of the peel perfectly and begins to bubble and crisp. We're staring into the hot oven, but I can feel the heat of his body against mine and I can barely breathe. 'Now, in again and turn it.' He covers my hands with his, guides the peel under the pizza, balances it and turns it. We watch it crisp and bubble. Then, 'Now,' he says. 'Pull it out!' He puts his arms around me, thrusts the peel under the pizza and pulls it out. It's perfection! I'm excited, exhilarated, my heart is thumping, I'm hot, out of breath, beaming at the sight of it and how it made me feel.

'Now you do it on your own,' he says. I don't look at him: I just focus on the dough ball, flattening it with my fingers, loading it with the right amount of topping this time, not too much, not too little, and a quick look up at Giacomo, who nods his approval.

I lift the peel again, feeling the pull in my shoulders, biceps and elbows. I push it in and then flick, just as if I'm feeling his hands on mine. I watch the pizza, as does he, in the glowing orange embers, focusing on the bubbling dough, the melting cheese. He turns to me, just as I lean in to slide the peel under and turn it. The smell is of pizza perfection, crispy dough, melting cheese and tangy tomatoes cooking. I lean in, to try to turn it but I can't quite reach.

'Take your time, focus. You can do it,' says Giacomo, and I can feel his shoulder next to mine, his jaw taut. I stand on tiptoe and this time flip the pizza onto the peel and turn it. Giacomo is there, like a co-pilot, moving with me as I do. We watch again. It bubbles and crisps. Then, without a word from him, I push the peel in, lifting my elbow as he did and scoop out the pizza.

We gaze at it. Then I look up at him and we're both smiling.

'A little overdone on the far side, but good job!' he says.

Elated I hold up my hand and he high-fives it, then turns away. I look down at the pizza with all the pride of a doting grandparent. Then I notice Giacomo's shoulders as he returns to the other side of the table. And, pop, like a burst balloon, the moment is gone. I have to do this over and over again tonight, just like this.

'Giac?' I say, still holding the peel with the pizza on it. He turns to me. 'Thank you,' I say. 'I'm not always the . . .' I swallow '. . . easiest person to help. Thank you.'

'I know,' he says, and grins. 'You're welcome. Besides, what kind of a competition would this be if it was over before it's begun?' He smiles wider, just like he used to, and I smile back, just like I used to. For a moment there is a bridge between us and it looks a lot like pizza on a peel.

'Want to try?' I push the peel towards him. He looks at it.

'Sure.' He tears off a piece from the not overcooked side. He chews and nods. 'Good dough. Good sauce.' I take a piece and bite into it. We chew in silence. I watch his jaw, as we both focus on the flavours. Finally he swallows and nods.

'Now, you just need practice. Years of it!' he jokes, but I'm not laughing and the moment is gone. I get to work, practising. Lifting pizza after pizza onto the peel until they're covering the table, some better than others, some overcooked, some needing a little more time in the *forno*, but getting better and better. I place a sprinkling of fragrant basil leaves over one. It's going to be okay, I tell myself. I'm going to check the oven is holding temperature. Just as I've watched Nonno do before service. It'll never work if the heat drops.

I go outside to collect more wood. When I get back, there is a small wooden box in place by the oven, presumably for me to stand on. I look round at Giacomo but he doesn't meet my eye.

'Hey, Dante,' I say, as Dante arrives through the back gate, jacket slung over his shoulder. He follows me into the kitchen, clearly surprised to see me there and then the huge number of pizzas on the table.

'Lucia, *ciao*. I thought you'd be leaving us soon,' he says, putting on his apron. 'Giac.' He shakes his hand. I have never shaken Dante's hand so why would I now?

'So, we have a new member of staff in the kitchen? Is this true? I can't believe we have you here for a little longer.' Dante puts his head to one side, teasing me, and I blush.

'Nonno spoke to you?' I ask.

He nods and laughs. 'He told me! This is a bit of fun!' He rubs his hands together. 'And when you tire of this, you'll go out with me, yes?'

'And you know that no one is to know I'm here as a chef.'

He nods again, clearly enjoying the novelty.

'And that there are two menus,' Giacomo says. 'This is mine, and this is Lucia's. Lucia's is pretty much Nonno's standard menu. Mine is . . . a little different.' He hands Dante the two pieces of paper. His, neatly thought out and printed. Mine, on a notepad usually used for taking orders. But he's had more time to prepare for this than I have.

I've kept things simple. The classic Marinara with *sugo di pomodoro*, the rich tomato sauce, with garlic, freshly picked oregano and thick, green, peppery extra virgin olive oil. Margherita, with *sugo*, mozzarella, basil and olive oil. Diavola with hot and spicy salami. Napoli, with anchovies, capers and black olives. Pizza with mushrooms and cooked ham; and Parma ham and rocket. I'll offer a nightly special when I'm in the swing of things. Perhaps with slow-cooked pork, which Nonno did the other night, or seafood. But, first, I have to deliver on this menu.

Giacomo's menu is ambitious to say the least. He's got his rhubarb pizza, one with four different fish and samphire, then crab, with chilli and rocket, which sounds so good my mouth waters just reading it, beetroot pesto with goat's cheese, and another with goat's cheese, caramelized onion and apple, sweet yet savoury, with thyme. There's spicy sriracha chicken too, grilled peaches and prosciutto, and, if I'm not mistaken, strawberries and balsamic vinegar, which in my opinion have no place on a pizza menu. He was always thinking of new toppings, new flavour combinations, when he wasn't working on his acrobatic skills, learning how to spin and toss the dough base in the air, catch it and put on a show, and this will just be the start of it. I take a deep breath. It's an exciting menu – but some people just want to go out for a Margherita, and at Nonno's, they're the best.

'We need to make a note of who sells what. Could you print the menus on one sheet of paper, with each menu on one side?'

Dante glances between us, smiling, as if someone's going to say, 'Only joking!' When no one does, he picks up the two menus and prepares to put them into the computer. 'And the pizzas?' He indicates my practice efforts, lined up with nowhere to go.

'Um . . . do you have any friends who might like them?' I ask awkwardly.

'Sure, leave it with me.'

He picks them up and heads towards the back gate. 'Hey,' he calls down the alley, and whistles, balancing the gate open with his foot. He hands round the pizzas to the young men out there, and I hear sounds of approval as he comes back in and takes the last out. It's going to be okay, I tell myself again, this time with a smile.

'Order in!' Dante calls in English, it would seem for my benefit. I'd be perfectly happy with it in Italian, as he always calls for Nonno.

Jo Thomas

It's for Giacomo. We're both serving simple starters of antipasti, which Carlo is plating. After checking and calling service for the starters, Giacomo picks up a ball of pizza and begins twirling it round his fist and spinning it out into a disc between his hands. When it's a good size, he goes for a move above his head.

'Order in!' calls Dante.

It's for me and I breathe a sigh of relief. I send out antipasti. Then look around to begin prepping my pizzas. But the big bottle of olive oil with the pouring nozzle isn't where I left it. It's on the other side of the kitchen where Giacomo is working. I hurry to it, and duck under his arm as he passes dough from one hand to the other, high in the air. I'm showered with flour as I pass under it. He heads to the oven, just before me.

It's chaos.

'This is not what the customer ordered.' With a kind, patient smile, Dante is holding a pizza on one of my plates.

'Sorry,' I say.

'Here, give it to me!' says Giacomo, putting out a hand for the dough ball.

'Yes, Giac, if you could . . .' says Dante.

'No, it's not from your menu!'

'But I'll be quicker.' He tosses another pizza base into the air. 'I can take care of this.'

'And you've done great,' says Dante, 'but maybe let Giac take over now.'

140

I glare at Giacomo. 'This is my order!' I say firmly. I start to ease out a ball of dough gently. I need the oil again. I lunge for it, working as fast as I can, just as Giacomo does, and we collide.

'Gah!' I shout.

'*Mamma mia!*' His dough base flies through the air and lands on the floor at Nonno's feet – he has just come in through the back door.

'This isn't going to work!' we both say.

EIGHTEEN

'Okay, you got what you wanted,' says Giacomo, quietly, to me, as Nonno dons his chef's whites and bandanna, then heads to the door into the restaurant to smooth over any mishaps and calm dissatisfied customers. Nonna, who was right behind him as Giacomo's pizza hit the deck, gives Nonno a dusting of flour, as if she's showering him with confetti.

He turns to her and frowns.

'What? It's to make it look authentic!' she says. 'Like you have been cooking!' She gives his face a quick powdering. He leaves the kitchen, clearly thinking this has been a terrible mistake.

'We need to work out a system,' I say, at the same time as Giacomo says, 'We need a work plan.' We stare at each other. And I wonder if he remembers the plans we made for our life together, or if they're as dead to him as the pizza dough that landed at Nonno's feet. I go to put it into the bin.

I turn back to Giacomo with so many unsaid words on the tip of my tongue, but glare at him rather than uttering them. He glares back.

Then he holds up his forefinger. I frown.

He walks towards the big worn work table in the middle of the kitchen, with deep cuts from knives over the years and, somewhere among them, my initials. In the flour on the table he draws a line down the middle. 'This,' he points, 'is your side. And this is mine.' He demonstrates with two hands. 'You keep to your side of the kitchen, I keep to mine.'

'I have a better idea,' I say. 'The new pizza oven.'

'Yes? The one you told me to cancel?'

'Yes. Tell them to bring it. As soon as they can.'

'You want to cook outside? You may find the oven easier to use, but I thought this was all supposed to be a secret.'

'You have outside. A chance to show off your *pizzaiolo* skills. And I'll have inside. That way, people will get to see your pizza skills at work and I'll get the inside space to do mine.'

'Okay,' he says slowly, holding up his hands. 'Who's for working with me outside?' Dante and Carlo move to stand beside him.

He looks at them. 'Carlo, you come outside with me Dante, you'll have to work between Lucia and me until we can get more help.'

Dante doesn't say anything.

'You're sure you're happy with this?' Giacomo wipes the flour off his hands with a tea towel. 'I'll take the outside. What about starters?'

'It's okay. I can manage,' I say. 'I'll be quicker.'

'And your own pizzas. And what about ice-creams?' he asks.

'I'll manage!' I say, but, actually, I have no idea how.

'But you'll need help. Who are you going to get to work for you in the kitchen? You can't do this on your own.'

We both know what he's saying: *who is going to work for a woman pizza chef?*

'I can ask one of the family to come over, give you a hand in here,' he adds. 'A favour to me.'

'What? One of your family? While I have a go at this and fail?' I can hear his mother's disapproving voice: *Let her try to realize it's not possible.*

'I didn't mean . . . *phfffff*!' He throws up his hands. 'I can't talk to you.'

'Clearly!' I say, and bite my tongue. I don't want to rake up the past. And I won't. I'm moving forwards in my life, not going back. 'Giac, I know you mean well, but I said I'll be fine and I will be. Now, go and sort out your outside oven and concentrate on your flipping and spinning. I have . . . clearing up to do by the look of it.'

Giacomo follows Nonno out into the restaurant where the atmosphere sounds full of fun again. Dante looks at me, shakes his head gently, smiles and follows them.

He's right – again! I may have got what I wanted and the chance to prove myself, but there's no way I can do this on my own. And it looks like I have no choice. I'll have to try. I'm not going back to where I was. Just to make sure, I send an email to Anthony Gwyn-Jones, resigning. Somehow I'm going to make this work. I just have to wake up earlier, work harder.

NINETEEN

'What do you mean it's already gone?' I stand in the greengrocer's. I can't help but think of how much has happened since I left Wales and the office a week ago.

Giuseppe shrugs and holds out his palms. 'Giacomo came in, changed the order and said he'd be picking it up from now on, every day.'

Giacomo. *Phhhhffffff!* Of course he's picked up the order and made changes to it! I need to find out what's left for me. There's no way I can tell Giuseppe I want a separate order or order the same things twice. He's bound to think something's up. I can't let on that we have two kitchens and I'm running one. Word'll get out in no time if Giuseppe gets wind of it. He knows everybody and everybody's business. The cat'll be out of the bag.

I hurry out of the shop and across the piazza as quickly as I can on the sunny, shiny cobbles.

At the restaurant, work is taking place in the court-yard to set up the electric oven. Just as I arrive, the electrician switches it on and they all high-five each other. Giacomo glances sideways at me as I hurry through the courtyard towards the kitchen.

I shake my head. That oven could give us a bad name. A very bad name indeed. I have to make sure that people know the pizzas from the kitchen are cooked in the wood-fired *forno*, not an electric oven, as they should be!

In the kitchen I go to see what's cooking in the big pot on the stove. I dip my finger into the dark red sauce. It's not Nonno's usual mixture. There's much more going on in it. More herbs, perhaps even wine, or anchovies.

I hear Giacomo come into the kitchen and I turn, panic rising in me. 'You picked up the order?' I say quickly, and possibly much sharper than I intended.

'*Sì*.' He nods slowly.

'And used everything!' I point to the pot.

'*Sìì*,' he says again. 'I've made my sauce and chopped the vegetables.'

'But that sauce! It's not Nonno's!'

'No, it's my sauce,' he says, as if he doesn't see the problem.

'What am I supposed to do?' I say. I go to the fridge and open it. Empty. The big cupboard. 'Empty!'

'You're welcome to use it,' he says, gesturing to the pot.

'But I'm doing things the way Nonno did. You've used everything from the order.'

'Sorry, Luce, I'm just doing my job. Like I say, we can share,' he says reasonably, which infuriates me even more.

'You should have waited for me!'

He picks up the bowls of chopped toppings and heads for the outside kitchen where a large electric fridge and the oven are now in pride of place. He and the electrician stand and stare at them, like they're things of beauty.

I look around. He's taken everything. Even the bottle of olive oil.

'Gah!' I hold my hands to my face, which is burning with frustration. I take a huge breath and look up to the ceiling, but the tears slide down my cheeks. Who am I trying to kid? This is impossible. Of course I can't do it on my own. I can't even get my hands on the grocery order. Giacomo and the electrician are laughing, talking Italian very quickly. Has he told anyone? Are they laughing at me, the British woman who wanted to be a *pizzaiola*, a master pizza-maker, and follow in her grandfather's footsteps? But he wouldn't. He knows the deal will be off if he tells anyone. But the laughter still rises up from the courtyard, taunting me.

I give up. This was never going to be easy. And I didn't want it to be. I just wanted a fair shot at it. I lean against the wall of the *forno*, still warm from last night, and breathe in the smell of burnt embers. I shut my eyes, finding comfort in it. There's nothing I can do. I suggested he work outside in the other kitchen. I didn't think about the supplies going with him! Now I've ruined everything for myself.

Suddenly the back door opens and bright sunshine floods in. I open my eyes – it's Nonna. When she sees the kitchen is empty she opens the door wider and comes in carrying a big pot. 'Nonna?' I say, wondering what on earth she's doing. She spins round to me, still holding the big metal pot from the apartment. 'What are you doing?'

She puts her forefinger to her lips and the big pot on the stove. I come down the few steps by the *forno* to join her on the terracotta tiles.

'What's that?' I point at the pot.

'*Sugo!* Sauce,' she says simply.

'Sauce?' I frown.

'I made too much today.' A tiny smile tugs at the corners of her mouth.

'You made too much today,' I repeat. 'You always make too much!'

She shrugs. 'It happens.' Her eyes twinkle, like Mrs Tiggy-Winkle's.

'How is it going? Are you ready?' She looks around. 'You aren't!' she says, alarmed.

I put the sauce onto the stove and dip my little finger into it. Perfect! 'But how did you know?'

'I didn't. I just wanted to help a little. What's happening here?'

'Well, I suggested that Giac have his oven and kitchen in the courtyard and I work from here. But I didn't think it through. I've got nothing. Well, I didn't until now.' I point at the sauce. 'I can't ask for another order from Giuseppe – he'll know something's up. And if I go to any of the other shops, he'll find out and be upset. You know what this place is like. It's all about how things have been done and are done. Asking another greengrocer would cause big trouble for Nonno.'

'Oh, I do know!' She purses her lips. 'Which is why I thought I'd help you out a bit.'

I sigh. 'Thank you, Nonna, but maybe Nonno was right. I mean I still have so much to learn . . .' I rub my hand over the worn table.

'Well,' she says, 'we'd better get ready then.'

'But—'

'Come, Lucia. Wipe your tears. Find your strength. It's what we do,' she says, coming over and hugging me. 'After your papa died, I didn't know how I would go on. I didn't think I would breathe again, let alone ever be happy. But I carried on cooking for those around me, because I had to. I still do. It's who I am. Now come . . .' She pats my arm.

'But I haven't got any ingredients. They've all gone outside with Giac.'

'But I have.' She pulls the car keys from her handbag with that twinkle in her eye.

The sun is hitting the windscreen of the little yellow Cinquecento that Nonna and Nonno seem to have had for ever.

'Where are we going?' I ask, as she edges the car into the early-morning traffic on the outskirts of town and joins the roundabout to a blast of horns from other drivers.

'Sometimes in life, when you want something, you have to find a chink and make it happen.' She smiles. 'Feel the fear and do it anyway!' And I'm not sure if she's talking about driving, or me and the restaurant, or something else. She swings off the roundabout, at speed, to more horns blasting, and drives up a pot-holed road towards a small hamlet. 'My friend Nonna Teresa, she has a glut of tomatoes. We will visit her first. I can pick up what we need from her when Nonno has gone to the olive grove or to *bocce.*'

She pulls the car off the road, and cuts the engine. It appears we've parked. I let go of the handle above the door that I seem to have been gripping.

'Come,' she instructs, grabbing her basket off the back seat and directing me up the unfinished drive to the small, single-storey, whitewashed house there, surrounded by greenery. All of the land is taken up with tomato plants, vegetables and fruit. It's amazing.

'Nonna Teresa makes bottled tomato sauce for the winter. Lots of us buy from her,' Nonna tells me, as she greets the woman, no taller than herself. They hold each other's hands and kiss each other's cheeks. Nonna explains quickly that I need tomatoes and hers are the best around. Her brown face lights up and she ushers me into the tomato patch. She plucks one from a vine and holds it out to me, telling me to smell it first. And I do.

'*Mangia!*' she cries. It's the universal cry of *nonna*s. 'Eat!' Then she mimes that I should bite into it, just to make sure I understand.

I bite into the firm skin. It resists, then yields, and the juice flies into the corners of my mouth. There's a taste explosion. I shut my eyes. When I open them, Nonna and Nonna Teresa are smiling.

I have no idea if Nonna Teresa knows why I need so many tomatoes and a constant supply of them. She doesn't ask. I feel as if I've entered into some secret pact where what goes on between *nonna*s stays between them. I insist on paying her there and then, and it seems such a small amount for so much produce. I tell her I'll keep using her tomatoes and her bottled ones in the winter. She seems delighted, holds my hands and smiles, as if she's giving me her blessing, but without words. I feel quite choked.

Nonna Teresa insists we stay for coffee with bread and jam, or maybe lunch. Nonna explains we have to hurry and Nonna Teresa seems to understand, with a nod and the twinkle Nonna has in her eye. She waves us off in the Cinquecento as we set out at speed in a cloud of dust, with a basket of tomatoes strapped to the back seat.

'My friend Nonna Emilia and I were at school together. She is married to a mozzarella farmer. Beautiful creamy mozzarella she makes. Better than the one Nonno buys.' She turns in at the gates to a farm where I see buffalo in the field in front of the farmhouse. We park and, once again, we're met and greeted like family, this time by Nonna Emilia. She and Nonna hug and kiss, and pass a few private words to each other. It seems *nonna*s have a network and honour all of their own. I'm introduced to the buffalo – Italian Mediterranean buffalo, I'm told – lying in the sun on the dusty ground, swishing at flies with their tails. Each has a huge set of ears and horns. Most are chewing the cud lazily, creating white foam on their lips, remnants of their breakfast hay scattered on the ground. Birds peck happily at the hay alongside the dark brown and black beasts. There's a strong smell in the air, but it's not unpleasant. It reminds me of where my food comes from. From the land, from these magnificent animals with their gentle eyes and soft, damp, dark noses. Even if I do keep my distance from those big horns. An inquisitive animal comes to greet us and I rub it between the eyes, as Nonna Emilia shows me.

She guides us towards the farmhouse and the barns, asking if we'll stay for lunch, but Nonna explains we're in a hurry and need to get back. Again, Nonna Emilia nods and understands whatever secret code these women have – maybe just years of experience and a grasp of family matters. She leads us into the milking parlour and a room just off it, where she hands us white coats and blue coverings for our shoes and hair. We put them on. She opens a big fridge, takes out a ball of cheese from a tray and hands it to me.

'*Mangia!*' she says, and I smile. I have learnt that when a *nonna* tells you to eat, you don't argue. They know their food is good. They take pride in what they have put in front of you and they want to see you smile. I hold the porcelain white buffalo mozzarella ball in front of me. The skin is thin when I bite into it and through the soft, creamy, delicately flavoured cheese to the oozing centre, which dribbles down my front, making us all laugh. I shudder with pleasure as the soft, creamy cheese slides down my throat.

'*Mozzarella di bufala,*' the *nonna*s say, as if endorsing its quality.

We leave in the same way we left Nonna Teresa's, this time with mozzarella, and also salami made from buffalo meat with added pork fat. And a smoked mozzarella for a special pizza – Nonna tells me how important it is to go with the ingredients on offer to you and make them work. Oh, and with an invitation to meet Nonna

Teresa's son, recently divorced and very good-looking! He'd make a perfect husband I'm told. I smile and say I'm sure he would. They both seem pleased with that.

Back at the restaurant, Nonna pulls out an apron from her handbag and ties it around her waist. 'We have basil . . .'

I smile as she puts the ingredients on the table. I can't believe this woman. She's incredible. Does nothing faze her? I grab a chalkboard from the cupboard, one I used to play with as a child when I was in this kitchen watching Nonno cook, to put up my smoked mozzarella and salami special. I've been initiated into a tribe, my tribe, and I feel very much at home.

'I can stay and help,' Nonna says.

'But where does Nonno think you are?'

'Making pasta with my friends, of course.' She looks at me. 'Why else would I carry an apron in my handbag?' She winks. 'We women have cooked for our families all our lives. We have always helped each other out in difficult times. We have dedicated ourselves to the kitchen. Now, it's time you show them you can make it your living,' she says. I feel like a phoenix rising from the ashes. Or the flames rising in the *forno* by the back door.

'It's just like feeding the family, the ones we love. It's what we do! We make do with what we have. We make the best of it, with love. Now, let's see what we have.'

I think of all the meals she's cooked over the years, yet it's Nonno who gets the glory. I'm doing this for her as much as me, and all the *nonna*s who have cooked and passed on their skills.

'I thought you'd need these.' She pulls out clean chef's whites from her basket, like Mary Poppins's bag. I run my hand over them, then put them on, admiring the embroidered 'Nonno's'. Then I pick up the bandanna she's laid out and tie it around my head, like a pirate.

'It suits you,' says Nonna, smiling. I roll up the sleeves and study my reflection in the stainless-steel splashback of the sink. This is where I want to be. I always did. I want to be here, taking over where Nonno has left off, and Giacomo isn't going to ruin my future plans all over again. I should have fought harder for what we had and what we lost. I know that now. It wasn't just Giacomo: I needed to fight harder for what I wanted, and this time I intend to.

TWENTY

'Nonna, what are you doing here?' asks Giacomo, as he comes into the kitchen at the end of service and kisses her on both cheeks.

'Oh, just popping in to see Lucia and find out how things went,' she says, stuffing her apron quickly into her basket.

'Pretty good service, I'd say, wouldn't you, Luce?' he says, staring at me.

I realize I still have my bandanna on. I like it so I'm leaving it for now. 'Yes, seemed to go well,' I say, as I finish washing up.

Giacomo walks over to the stove and looks into the sauce pot. 'You got sorted, then?' he says.

'I did,' I say tightly.

'Look, Luce, I didn't mean to monopolize the

greengrocery order. I just didn't think. We can work out what we both need.'

Although he's talking quietly, I know Nonna is listening. She has special powers, I know, after the work she's put in here this evening. 'It's fine. I'm sorted,' I say, drying my hands. 'I have everything I need.'

'Okay,' he says slowly, then leans over the pot on the stove, dips his little finger into it and sucks it. He doesn't turn around and I wonder what he's thinking. Does he know Nonna made it? He nods slowly in approval.

Suddenly the door opens from the restaurant and Dante comes in, his hair freshly slicked back ready for a night out by the look of it.

'I've cashed up and put the receipts and a list of who made what sales in this envelope for Enzo,' he says, waving the envelope.

'I can take that,' says Nonna, plucking the envelope from him. 'Talking of which, I'd better go, he'll be missing me. See you in a bit, Lucia. Be careful walking home.'

'I will, Nonna. And thank you,' I whisper into her ear, as I hug her small, plump body.

'You've got this,' she whispers back. '*Ciao*, Giac!' She waves as she waddles out through the courtyard.

'How about that drink, Lucia?' asks Dante, his smile apparently fixed permanently to his face.

'Not tonight, Dante,' I say, and then, feeling Giacomo staring at me, 'Another time, yes?'

'Okay. I'll hold you to it!'

'You do that! I'm looking forward to it,' I say. Maybe I will go for a drink with him. It might be nice to get out and meet some other people, even if he is a little younger than me. But it's about time I went out. I have a lot of catching up to do.

Dante swings out of the door, leaving me with Giacomo. I'm not sure what to say.

'Well done today, Luce,' he says. 'You did great.'

'Thank you!' I nod graciously.

'See you tomorrow,' Giacomo says, and I'm not sure if it's a question or a statement.

'See you tomorrow, Giac. Goodnight.' I wonder how on earth I'll do it all again tomorrow, from the prepping and kneading of the dough, to the cooking in the hot *forno*. There was a disaster, which I've put outside the back door, hoping he won't see it, and is now being enjoyed by a small street cat. I let out a long sigh as I stand over the sink, watching the water run away. How I'm going to manage tomorrow I have no idea. I need to get help in. I can't rely on Nonna to bail me out every night.

As Giacomo gets his jacket, he hesitates. I hold my breath. I hope he's not going to suggest a drink or anything like that. I pick up a final ball of dough, and toss it into the air.

'Luce, your sauce . . .'

'Good, isn't it?' I say quickly.

'Very good. Now, can I walk you home?'

I shake my head. 'I'm fine. I know my way,' I say. Then add, 'But thank you.'

'Okay. Well, see you tomorrow,' he says again.

'Goodnight, Giac.' I smile.

'Goodnight, Luce.' With that he leaves through the back kitchen door that leads onto the alleyway, closing it behind him. I grin. 'Very good!' I repeat, toss the dough into the air, try to catch it and miss. Stick to what you know, Lucia, I tell myself.

TWENTY-ONE

'So, that was a busy night,' says Giacomo, the following evening, coming in from the outside kitchen at the end of service, heading for his jacket on the hooks by the back door. Dante has put all the information into the envelope for Nonno. And Nonna has slipped it into her bag and left before he misses her after his evening with his *bocce* friends. I'm looking at the mess in the kitchen. It was one thing getting through the service, quite another now I need to clear up.

'Yes, it was busy. That's good,' I say, and begin to fill the sink. My arms are ready to drop off.

Giacomo stops pulling on his coat and throws it onto the stool by the big table where Nonna has sat this evening, ladling sauce onto the pizzas, dressing them, drizzling them with oil, then scattering basil. I watch Giacomo as he rolls up his sleeves.

'Here, move up. One can wash and the other can dry.'

'It's fine. I can finish up here,' I say, suddenly feeling very hot.

'I know you can. I know you can do whatever you put your mind to. And if you can't, you'll die trying.'

I wonder what that means. Is he talking about my failed attempt to set up here as a lawyer? 'But you don't have to. Now let me help. Don't look the gift horse in the mouth!' He grins.

I'm taken off guard. I don't want Giacomo to be nice to me, but I do want to get to my bed. I'm exhausted.

'It's okay . . .' I'm about to say I can manage but stop myself.

He pushes up his sleeves further, showing off his dark, muscular forearms. He tests the water and plunges in his hands, covered with dark hair, and his leather friendship bracelets. I find myself wondering if any of those leather strips were ones I gave him.

The bubbles in the sink rise as his hands go into and come out of the water. I dry and stack on the table, just as I've always done with Nonno at the end of an evening. I like this quiet time when we're closed. It feels like closure on the day.

'You're going to need help. You can't run the kitchen and do all of this at the same time. I've told you I can get help in.'

The last thing I want is one of his family coming in and taking over.

'I agree.'

'You agree? You want my nephew to come?'

'No, no.' I shake my head, so tired I can barely do that. 'I agree I need help. I'll work it out.'

'Well, you need help out here, and quickly. You need stamina as a *pizzaiola*, but you also have to know when and where you need help.'

'I know, I know,' I say. 'And I said I'll sort it.' I know it would make sense for his nephew to be in here helping me, but something stops me saying so. 'And thank you. But I just need to . . .'

'Do this on your own. I know!' He sighs.

'What does that mean?'

'Just that you were always very determined. When you made a decision, you stuck to it. You're set in your ways.'

'Set in my ways?' I frown.

'Yes. It's not a criticism. It's just you have your mind set on something and you don't like that to change. Like this place. You don't want it to change because this is how you remember it.'

'I want this place to stay the same because I want my grandfather remembered.'

'But what if he wanted things to move forward, to change, to take what he's done and adapt, make things better?'

'Like you want. If the plan doesn't work, change the plan. Start a new one.' I raise an eyebrow, remembering when my plan hadn't worked and he'd suggested I stay at home and enjoy it. And when I wasn't enjoying it, when I suggested I went home for a while, he didn't argue, just agreed with the new plan, and although I wanted him to tell me not to go, I stuck to the plan.

'It wasn't like that, Luce,' he says quietly. And I shut my eyes tightly, trying not to think back to then.

'Look, how about a glass of wine and we talk . . . properly talk?'

I open my eyes. He's holding up a bottle and two glasses.

I look at the bottle, the glasses, and back at him, then shake my head. 'I can't, Giac. Not now.' I'm dead on my feet. I can't rake up our relationship and where it all went wrong right now. If I do, I'll end up a blubbering mess. And maybe he knows that. Maybe this is him trying to work his way around me. Trying to lull me into a false sense of security, trying to take over the restaurant, the competition, by getting me drunk and incapable of working. He wants me to give in.

'I can finish up here, Giac. You can go. You probably have . . . someone waiting for you.'

'No.'

He says nothing else. And, in typical Giacomo style, he shuts down any further questions about his love life. Not that I'm interested, of course. It has nothing to do with me. But part of me would love to know. There is a moment of awkward silence.

'Look, thanks for your help, but I'm fine,' I say.

'You're fine. You're always fine. No one can help Lucia!' Giacomo bursts out. He puts down the bottle and throws up his arms. The washing-up water on his shirt is making the soft cloth cling to his chest. I swallow. He certainly won't get me to give in that way. There is nothing he can do to get around me! I won't let him. He's not calling the shots, not this time.

'You need to learn to move on, Lucia. Let life move on!' he says crossly, putting down the wine.

I want to argue, but I can't. The words jumble in my head and don't make it to the end of my tongue. How dare he tell me I need to move on? I moved on. I went back to Wales and started my career. He's the one who's still here. And now I'm moving on again, returning here. It's not going back, it's moving on, I tell myself firmly.

I turn back to the sink and pull out the plug. The water gurgles, splutters and drains away. Then I pick up the broom and hold it in front of myself. 'I can manage here now, Giac. Thank you,' I repeat forcefully. 'See you tomorrow.'

'Okay, okay! Have it your way! You always do!' He holds up his hands, grabs his jacket and slams out of the door.

I breathe a sigh of relief and stop gripping the broom across my body, like it's some kind of armour, protecting me from Giacomo. Or maybe just protecting my heart.

Suddenly the door flies open again, making me jump. 'I suppose if I asked whether you needed walking home you'd tell me you were fine!'

'Yes, yes, I'm fine!' We glare at each other. Then, realizing what it must have taken for him to come back, realizing this is the Giac I used to know and love, a good, kind man, who always put others first, their feelings before his, I say, 'But thank you for asking me.' He nods, and this time when he goes out of the door he shuts it quietly. I may have let down my guard just a little, but it feels okay. Like a little bit of air through a car window.

I finish sweeping and pick up my jacket and bag. I take a last look around the restaurant and smile. I did it. One day at a time. I got today. Thank you, Nonna. I open the back door. I stop and look down at the little street cat. I bend to stroke it but, despite its tiny size, it hisses and spits at me, making me snatch away my hand. I look at it. It wants to be here, I think, but it wants to feel safe. I go back inside, get a bowl, put in some prosciutto and mozzarella, then leave it by the back door. The little cat doesn't move, its eyes shiny, from its dark hiding place behind the bins. It needs time. She – I've decided she's female – needs to do it in her own time. I swing out into the dimly lit lane and straight into someone. Not again! I turn to apologize. Only this time it isn't a friendly face or a polite sorry.

'Hey, hey!'

I recognize them slightly, then realize where from. My heart sinks. It's the two blokes from outside Giuseppe's – they hang around the piazza. Friends of Dante's. 'Hey, English girl!'

'Pomodoro!' says the other.

This time, there's an unpleasant tone in their voices. They're obviously a little worse for wear, sweaty and leering.

'Any more pizza going? I'm hungry!' One looks me up and down.

'Any extras?' The other sniggers.

'*Scusi,*' I say. I go to step round them and head for the piazza, the light there. There's a herby smell to them.

'*Scusi,*' one mimics, and puts his arm against the big stone wall of the restaurant.

'*Scusi.*' The other laughs as he lights a cigarette, the smoke blowing in my face.

My heart quickens. This is not good, I think. Not good at all.

I try to step around them again, but the shorter, stockier one blocks my way.

'So, English girl . . .' He leers again. His teeth are brown, stained from coffee, cigarettes and too much red wine. 'We can be friends, *no?*'

My path is blocked and I don't know what to do. I could back away and let myself into the restaurant, lock the door and stay there. But what if they followed and I was trapped inside with them? I could shout – I open my mouth but, to my fury, my throat tightens and no sound comes out. My heart is pounding. Come on, Luce, you've lived in a city all your life.

I lift my chin and finally remember my self-defence training from college.

'No!' is all I can think of shouting, as the man moves closer to me. I can smell his stale cigarette, cannabis and wine breath. I hold out my hand to his face. He looks at me, surprised, then at my hand and moves forward. I step back and now I'm against the wall. His taller, slightly slimmer friend drags on his cigarette and laughs.

For once, I have no idea what to do. I'll have to make a run for it. My hand is still out in front of me.

'No!' I shout again. 'Get back,' I yell, holding out my hand further, as if it's a truncheon.

'I only want to be your friend. I thought all English girls were friendly.'

'Don't come any closer!' I roar, and push my hand out.

'Just a kiss, please?' he says, and his head moves to-wards mine. I freeze. And he suddenly drops to the ground.

TWENTY-TWO

I stare at the young man now rolling at my feet in pain. His friend drops his cigarette and walks off down the dark street as if he has nothing to do with the other at all.

The man is now on all fours. Clearly the fist hitting the cheek came after a swift kick to the nether regions. But I didn't touch him. Did I? Or was it someone else? I stare at the face coming into focus in the dark. Its owner is rubbing the hand that delivered the punch and stretching out the palm.

'On your way,' says the deep, gravelly voice, with a swear word or two thrown in. The man on his knees doesn't argue. He stumbles to his feet and follows in the direction of his friend, limping and whimpering as he goes.

I turn back to my rescuer. 'Grazie, mille grazie,' I stammer. 'I don't know what would have happened if you hadn't come.' Tears leap to my eyes. I'm shaking. I feel so angry.

'And, by the way, I'm Welsh, not English!' I call after my assailant. 'Got it? And no! I don't ever want to be your friend! Stay away from me, you hear?'

I hear Italian swearing in the distance and think he's got the message.

'Thank you. Thank you so much.' I stare into the dark. Suddenly I turn and unlock the restaurant kitchen door. 'Please come in. Let me look at your hand. Let me get you a drink. God knows I could do with one.'

The face smiles.

'How did you learn to do that?' I ask, pushing open the door and turning on the lights.

'In my line of business, you have to learn to handle yourself against shmucks,' says the woman I saw walking the streets on my first night back. 'It's part of the job description.' She smiles again, still flexing her fist.

'I'm Lucia,' I say.

'Veronica,' she says, in her deep, husky voice.

'Come in, Veronica. And thank you.'

I look down at the bowl by the back door and see the food is gone, as is the little cat. I wonder if she'll be back.

'I thought you were Italian,' Veronica says, as she steps into the warmth of the kitchen where the *forno* is still glowing.

'I did too,' I say. Looks like I still have no idea who I really am. 'I'm going to have to try a lot harder.'

TWENTY-THREE

'Here.' I hand her a tea towel filled with ice. She looks around the kitchen, while sitting on the stool, taking the handmade ice pack from me and holding it to her knuckles. I can see her registering the place, as if it takes her back to somewhere. She looks like she's relaxing, as if here is a safe place.

I remember the bottle of wine and the two glasses on the table. 'Would you like a drink?' I ask, picking up the bottle.

'Well, only if you are,' she says. 'I can leave now, if you prefer.' She looks guarded again and starts to get up.

I hold the bottle. My favourite. I think of Giacomo. Did he pick this especially? But Nonno has always served this wine here. So, coincidence, I think firmly.

'Actually, I'd love a glass. It's been that kind of

night!' I say shakily, as I go to open the bottle, my hands trembling.

'Not helped by those idiots!' Veronica says, taking the bottle from me and opening it.

'Did you know them?' I ask, swallowing bile as I'm reminded of the smell of stale wine and cigarettes.

She shrugs. 'I've seen them around. Just idiots. Like I say, you learn to spot them and deal with them in my line of work.'

She pours the wine, we chink glasses and I sip, trying to push out the memory of drinking this wine here with Giacomo, years ago. If he hadn't produced the bottle tonight, I probably wouldn't be thinking about him at all. And despite my unpleasant experience in the back lane, it's him I'm thinking about, wishing I'd taken up his offer of walking me home.

'So, is it . . . a busy time of year for you, in your line of work?' I find myself asking and stop. 'Oh, God, what am I saying? Sorry! I didn't mean to . . .' I put it down to feeling shaky.

She laughs, a deep, fun laugh. 'It's fine,' she says. 'Erm, do you mind if I . . .' She points to her high-heeled boots.

'No, go ahead,' I say, and she pulls them off, then wiggles her feet and brightly polished red toenails.

'That's better,' she says, and has another sip of her wine.

'Are you hungry?' I ask. 'I can cook us pizza?'

'Really?'

I nod.

'The *forno*'s still hot,' I say, and go to it before she says no. I'm back in my comfort zone, blocking out the incident in the alley. I gently tease out the leftover dough, slowly beginning to breathe normally again. They were just idiots. And they won't be back this way any time soon. Veronica saw to that.

I notice neither of us is talking, just enjoying the quiet of the kitchen, the warmth of the *forno*, and the peppery red wine. Veronica is watching me work, pulling out the dough then stepping onto my wooden crate, putting the pizza into the *forno*, watching it, then turning it, and again. I pull it out. Perfect, I think with a proud smile.

'Wow! You're good!' says Veronica, and I'd practically forgotten she was there, I was concentrating so hard.

'That one went really well!' I beam. 'They don't always.' I cock my head. 'Which I think the little cat outside is grateful for.'

'You cook pizza much?' she asks, as I lay the pizza on a board and cut it into equal segments with my grandfather's wheel cutter.

'Quite a bit, actually,' I say, feeling my way round the situation.

I go to the fridge and bring out the makings of a salad from Nonna's network of *nonna*s, fresh green rocket and plump red tomatoes, and put them in a bowl, with plates on the table, thick, green extra virgin olive oil, again from Nonna's network, and pull up another stool.

'Help yourself. *Buon appetito!*' I say, feeling my world return to normal, whatever normal is, as the smell of the hot dough, rich tomato sauce and soft mozzarella reaches up to me and wraps itself around me. I pick up a slice, after Veronica, and she raises hers to her mouth and smiles. I do the same. This food makes you smile. And I feel such pleasure not only in eating it but in having cooked it. I know this is what I want to do, no matter how hard today was. I take a sip of wine and another bite of the crispy base, with its tangy topping, the fresh basil and black pepper finishing off the flavours at the end.

After a second slice, we sit back and I refill the wine glasses.

'That is magnificent pizza,' says Veronica, pointing a long, painted nail at the board. 'Thank you.'

'It's me who's thanking you, remember? For saving me from the drunken idiots.'

She shrugs it off. 'Like I say, in my line of work you meet men like that all the time. The ones who think they can take what they want and treat you with no respect. I might be doing a job that people don't like, but you don't end up doing it because you want to. You do it because you have to. Because there came a point when there was no other way. But you have to learn how to be respected. How to play some at their own game, but play your own game at the same time. You have to find your dignity and identity in a world that doesn't want you there, that doesn't want to admit they can't do without you either. Not many people do this job out of choice. You have to find out who you are. Just because you don't fit into a mould it doesn't make you any less important. You have to hold your head up and do what's right for you.'

She takes another sip of wine and I can't help but think about me, in the kitchen, wanting to make pizza, trying to find respect in a man's world, an Italian man's world, I shouldn't fit into. I don't. But I feel more determined to prove myself than ever after tonight's incident. I'm doing this for all the other women who have been denied the chance to follow their dreams, to take over the family business. I think of Sofia, not being able to work or even fully look after her children. And the likes of Veronica, who found herself trying to make a living the only way she could. But there is another way!

'And for the record,' says Veronica, 'business is terrible.' She rubs her feet with her manicured hand, the good one. 'Tinder has a lot to answer for.' I'm not sure how to reply, and then she smiles. 'Who needs me when you can hook up with someone for free?'

I have another bite of pizza as an idea starts to grow and take hold in my head. I sip the wine.

'So how come you're here, cooking pizza?' she asks.

'This is my grandfather's place,' I tell her.

'Ah. So you know this kitchen well.'

'I do.' I nod, looking around. And then I don't know what comes over me, maybe the wine, or that this woman saved me from something very scary and I feel close to her. 'Can you keep a secret?'

'Darling, I've been keeping secrets all my working life!'

After I've explained about Nonno wanting to retire, Giacomo, he being my ex, me giving up my job to take on the restaurant and the competition, she says, 'So you are here as a pizza chef?'

'Yes,' I say. 'But no one must know. They may not like me being here, but I'll get them to like my pizzas.'

'And it's a competition. Whoever sells the most gets to take on the restaurant?'

'Yes. And I can't think of anything I want more. And to prove to Giac, my grandfather, and all the men who think they're better at this just because they're men, that I can be just as good.'

'Better, if that pizza is anything to go by,' says Veronica, high-fiving me and draining her glass. 'Right! I'd better go. Your pizza is amazing. You should be very proud. I hope you get this place.'

I'm wishing our evening hadn't come to an end. But the clock in the square is striking. 'Look, Veronica,' I say, as she's zipping up her boots – I wonder if I'm being rash, but this seems like exactly the right thing. 'I need help in the kitchen.'

'Okay, well, if I hear of anyone, I'll be in touch,' she says. 'I know a lot of people.'

'No, I mean . . . if you felt you wanted to . . . if you were looking for a change of direction . . . it may not pay as well, but it would be regular.'

'What would?'

'I need help here in the kitchen. Can you cook?'

'Can I cook? Darling, I've been cooking *puttanesca* pasta all my life!'

I laugh with her.

'I'm just thinking,' I look at her sore hand, 'with those hands and arms, you'd be pretty good at kneading dough.'

She peers at her hands and then at me. 'Me? In the kitchen, here?'

'Why not? I need help. You need work. And you wouldn't have to wear such high heels all evening.'

We laugh again as she finishes zipping up her boots and winces as she puts her weight back on her feet.

'I can pay! And, of course, there's free pizza.'

She looks around as if seeing the kitchen for the first time and enjoying the idea of being here. 'But what would people say?'

'No one will say anything, because this, me becoming a *pizzaiola*, is a secret. No one will know. It's the food that will do the talking.'

'And this Giac?'

'Giac told me to get some help and that's what I'm doing. You join me here in the kitchen, helping me make pizza. You get paid. I get help . . . We take on the pizza world at its own game and earn respect.'

She nods slowly. 'I like you, Lucia. I like you a lot. You have real fire in that belly of yours.'

'As do you, Veronica.'

'I'd like to work with you. If you really think I could.'

'Of course you could. You've been cooking your whole life, probably for your family too. Now it's time to sell your food and not your—'

'Body!' she finishes.

'A change of direction,' I add.

And she beams. 'I'd like that very much,' she says. '*Grazie!*' And then she hugs me in her big, strong arms, crushing me to her.

'I won't let you down,' she says.

'I know you won't,' I say, choked. 'See you tomorrow. Use the back door. I prep the dough for the following day before lunch. Meet me here at around six, ready for the evening service. And wear sensible shoes!'

I follow her out, and see the two bright eyes between the bins.

'See you tomorrow, little one!' I say, to the cat, as I open the gate, this time looking left and right, then heading for the bright lights of the piazza at the end of the alley and on to the apartment. Home.

TWENTY-FOUR

The following morning I arrive at the restaurant just as Giacomo does. He immediately spots the wine bottle and two glasses on the table. 'A good night, I see,' he says crisply.

I scoop up the bottle and put the glasses into the sink. 'Just a friend,' I say. And that is exactly what Veronica is, I think. I just hope she turns up today.

I start to busy myself in the kitchen, scrambling into the clean whites that Nonna left out for me, then my bandanna. When I put it on, it makes me feel I am who I want to be.

'You're late this morning,' says Giacomo. 'Later than normal.'

'There was somewhere I had to be,' I say, not looking at him and not quite sure how my idea is going to pan out. But a visit to Sofia and putting my idea to her felt right. Giacomo goes out to the courtyard and we manage to ignore each other politely as we work, despite the snatched glances I take when I pass the circle of clear glass in the restaurant door, and him popping in and out more often than usual for things he says he's forgotten.

'Can I borrow some olive oil?' he says. 'I need to get more at lunchtime. I'm making pesto.'

'Pesto pizza?'

'Uh-huh,' he says, and nothing more.

'What with? Marshmallows and meringues?' I tease, feeling in high spirits.

I get the impression he's dying to ask about the bottle of wine and my friend. But doesn't.

Later, Nonna pops in with today's ingredients, and after lunch Dante arrives with Carlo, Giacomo's sous-chef. They're laughing and joking, and suddenly my earlier high spirits desert me. I feel like a complete fraud, standing in this kitchen. Am I trying to be something I'm not? Am I just making a fool of myself, and Nonno for that matter? Is he just humouring me? I slide off the bandanna, put it into my pocket and turn to stir the sauce I made to Nonna's instructions and taste it.

Giacomo's staff, Carlo and Dante, don their aprons, ready for work and I feel outnumbered. Without help in the kitchen, I'll have to throw in the towel. Giacomo was right: there's no way I can do this all on my own. What if my help doesn't turn up? I look at the clock as it nudges just past six.

'Luce, you okay?' Giacomo stops laughing with his team. 'Look, if you don't think you can do this again, it's fine. We can take over.'

I stare at him.

'Luce, you okay?' he repeats.

Suddenly the door opens and in comes Veronica, wearing high-heeled trainers. She stands at the door, and the men in the kitchen all turn to look at her.

'I am now!' I smile a smile of relief and excitement. I have no idea how this is going to work out. But she came! She walks slowly down the steps into the kitchen, as if she's wary, and stands on one side of the kitchen table, next to me, shoulder to shoulder. Giacomo and his team stand on the other.

'*Scusi*, sorry I'm late,' comes another voice. Sofia is at the door, out of breath. 'I couldn't get Rameo to let me go. He knew something was up and I was going somewhere.'

The men on the other side of the table are staring at her.

'Um . . . is everyone okay with this?' she says, coming down the two steps and facing them.

Giacomo frowns. 'Luce?'

'You told me I need help in the kitchen, Giac. You were right. I did.' I turn to Veronica and Sofia. 'This is my team.' I hold a hand out and smile. 'Veronica and Sofia.'

The men opposite stand still, mouths open.

'Oh, Lucia, you forgot these. Nonna Emilia left them for you at the apartment.' Nonna comes bustling into the kitchen waving two salamis. 'And her grandson is bringing over the mozzarella for you tomorrow.' She beams.

'Nonna? You too?' says Giacomo. 'This is how you have all these amazing ingredients?'

'So, you told them.' Nonna smiles at me. 'You have a new kitchen team? An all-women team.'

I nod and smile back.

'What does Nonno think about this?' Giacomo asks.

'Nonno is playing *bocce*. He'll never know. We all have our secrets.'

'And I have been keeping them all my life!' says Veronica again, with a mischievous look in her eye. Dante shuffles.

'These women have been cooking all their lives. We all have. It's time they had the same chance as you to make the pizzas everyone loves. It's time for them to be able to show off their skills outside the home.' Nonna looks at the men and raises an eyebrow. 'After all, isn't that where you all learnt to cook first? At your mother's or *nonna*'s table?' They shift about uneasily. 'We are the teachers, the feeders, and now it's time for us to be the restaurateurs and the *pizzaiola*s in this town as well.'

Giacomo nods slowly.

'We all deserve the chance to put out our food,' I say.

Dante smiles but it doesn't reach his eyes.

Giacomo turns to his staff. 'Right, let's get on.' Then he turns back to me and my team. 'Good luck, ladies,' he says.

I pull out my bandanna and put it back on. 'We don't need luck, Giac. We just needed a chance.'

He looks at me as if the pieces on the chessboard have shifted in my favour and he's watching my every move.

'Veronica, you're on dough. I'll show you how to tease out the base. I'll dress them and put them in the *forno*. Sofia, *dolci*, desserts. Nonna, you can help with toppings and antipasti.' And we all set about our tasks. Nonna pulls up her stool and her ingredients to top the pizzas and plate the antipasti. I show Veronica how to throw down the flour, using the heel of her hand to press out the dough, while Sofia gets acquainted with the ice-creams and starts to work out how to present them.

'Order in,' says Dante, as the first chitty comes into the kitchen.

'Veronica, dough,' I call. 'Nonna, antipasti for four,' I say reading the chitty. Sofia steps in to help Nonna. We're all working together, calling to each other.

'Antipasti is cleared, ready for pizzas!' Sofia calls, putting the plates into the sink and washing them. I put the first of the loaded pizzas into the hot *forno*.

'Order in,' calls Dante, clearly expecting us to be running around like headless chickens. Instead, we call to each other, help each other. Veronica presses out the dough, and uses the ladle to add the *sugo*, like Nonna has shown her. Like a well-oiled machine, we find our way through the rest of the busy service, as if we've been doing it all our lives.

TWENTY-FIVE

'*Salute!*' we say, each holding up a glass of red wine as we sit at the big kitchen table at the end of service.

'*Grazie*, all of you,' I say. 'I don't think that could have gone better. Sofia, your ice-cream desserts were brilliant. Veronica, you were fantastic keeping the dough coming, and, Nonna, thank you for all your help. Your sauce was amazing as usual.'

'As were you, Lucia. You made this happen. You got us here and cooking. Doing what we've done all our lives and now being recognized for it. And it was your sauce. You made it. Like you made this happen.' Nonna smiles fondly at me from her stool by the table where she has sat all service helping me put the toppings on the pizzas.

'We did it,' I say, and sip the warm, peppery wine. 'Now then, same again tomorrow?'

'Absolutely,' they all agree.

'Paolo's parents think I'm at church, saying prayers for Paolo.' Sofia looks guilty. 'It's not that I don't miss him, but it's so nice to spend a few hours not thinking about missing him,' she says, and we all understand.

'Nonno thinks I'm bottling tomato sauce with Teresa.'

Veronica looks thoughtful. 'Can't think that anyone's been wondering where I am,' she says quietly.

'Good work, ladies,' says Giacomo, as he comes into the kitchen.

Even the word 'ladies' has my hackles up. As if we've done so well, keeping up with the men!

'How are sales, Dante?' I ask, as he follows Giacomo into the kitchen.

'*Bene, bene.*' He grins. He finishes counting the receipts at the kitchen table.

'I'd say there was little in it tonight. Giac, your seafood pizza was a great seller. Lucia, your kitchen sold the most Margheritas.'

We look at each other and nod.

'I'll let Enzo have the results.' And he stuffs the receipts into an envelope and Nonna, once again, offers to take them to him.

'Can't you tell us who's in the lead, who sold the most?' I ask Dante.

'Yes, I'd like to know,' says Giacomo, folding his arms.

But Dante shakes his head. 'No, sorry. It's confidential. The winner will be announced on the final day. That's Enzo's instruction.' He puffs out his chest and runs his hand over his slicked-back hair. Dante is enjoying his role in a position of power in Nonno's absence.

'Lucia, you joining me tonight for a drink?'

'Not tonight, Dante.' I smile at his persistence.

'Don't leave it too long,' he says, teasing, but there's a hint of frustration too. After last night, I'm still feeling a little shaken and want to get back to the apartment. I'm sure Dante will understand when I get a chance to explain. But now I want to try to forget it.

'Okay, well, goodnight, ladies,' says Giacomo, interrupting my thoughts and, again, I hate the way he refers to us as 'ladies', as if we're here as a hobby. As if it's not as serious as his business idea.

He stops at the door and turns back. 'Lucia, Nonna? Can I walk you home?'

'No, thanks. We're fine!' I say breezily, waving a hand, wanting him to go.

'Might be an idea, after last night,' says Veronica, and I try to communicate with my eyes that that's a really bad idea.

She shrugs. 'I'm just saying.'

'What happened last night?' Giacomo frowns and turns back from the door.

'It was nothing.' I try to dismiss it.

Veronica raises her pencilled eyebrows.

'Well,' I say, 'it was nothing, because Veronica sorted it.' I nod gratefully at her.

'You had trouble?'

'Really, it's . . .' I wave both hands.

'Come on, I'll walk you home,' he says, and Nonna slides off her stool with an *ommpf*. And Veronica agrees with Nonna that it's a very good idea as the new friends kiss each other on the cheek.

But before I leave I put down the bowl of leftovers I kept for my little street cat friend. I can't see her, but I get the feeling she's around. A bigger cat suddenly appears from behind the bins and heads for the bowl, but before I can shoo him away, the little black cat comes out hissing and spitting, and sees him off herself.

'Good job, little one.' She's waiting for us all to leave so she can come out of her hiding place and eat in peace.

Nonna links arms with Giacomo as Sofia and Veronica walk together in the opposite direction.

'Just like old times,' I hear her say, but ignore the comment. And I know what Nonna is thinking, but it's never going to happen. Giacomo and I are over, and we're never going back there. Things will never be like the old times, thank goodness.

TWENTY-SIX

'Sorry, the customer has sent them back. They're not happy,' says Dante, standing in the kitchen doorway holding two big plates with pizzas on them.

We all look at him and the plates.

He shrugs.

'But it is what they ordered?' I look around for the order note, but can't find it.

'They've ordered from Giac's menu now,' he says, puts them down and leaves. I don't know how that can have happened. Veronica calls out the order as soon as it comes in and then it's pegged to a long piece of string in front of her at the floury dough station, where she rolls out the balls to order. I don't understand it. But I don't have time to worry about it now. I have to focus on the oven. Something isn't right tonight. It doesn't feel hot enough.

Outside I can hear the cheers as Giacomo whirls dough around and I can smell the cooking pizzas with the scent of the lemons in the pergola. There is a beautiful glow from the candles on the tables in the warm evening and it looks heavenly out there. In here, it's another matter.

The wood crackles and smokes, and trying to get the pizzas to cook evenly is a problem. I'm turning them, lifting my arms even higher to get under them. I'm hot, but the oven isn't. And the evening's service gets harder. I'm struggling. My arms and shoulders are aching. More plates are being returned by dissatisfied customers, who are deciding to choose from Giacomo's menu instead.

'I just don't understand it!' I almost cry in despair, looking at the soggy pizzas, as the fire barely warms up.

'It must be the wood,' Nonna says, as I rub aching shoulders from turning and turning the pizzas on the peel.

'Maybe it's damp,' Sofia joins in.

I stare into the *forno*. I pick up a log from the pile. 'Maybe someone has swapped my wood,' I say, staring in at the smoking, spitting and hissing fire.

'No, it couldn't happen.' Nonna shakes her head. 'Who would do that?'

But something inside me is niggling. Someone who doesn't want me to win this competition, that's who. Someone who wants me to try but fail. The evening's service is a disaster and eventually I close our kitchen and let Giacomo take the rest of the orders. I pick up the wood from the pile under the *forno*. Then again, I don't remember topping up the pile this evening and there's more there than there was yesterday.

Somebody knew what they were doing when they put that wood there, I think, as I lie in bed that night, listening to the street noise. Someone knew that the damp wood would affect the pizzas. Someone knew exactly what they were doing, says my legal head. And my heart aches, making me all the more determined to get it right tomorrow.

The following morning, I check all the wood under the *forno*. It feels denser. With more moisture in it. I show Veronica, who looks as thunderous as I feel.

'Give me your wood supplier's number. I'll ring him for you,' she says. I get it for her from Nonno and hand her the phone.

Veronica speaks quickly and lets the woodsman know about the poor quality wood. She's speaking so fast and using so much slang that even though I speak Italian, I barely understand a word of what she's saying, but I wouldn't like to be the woodsman on the receiving end. Eventually she puts down the phone.

'The order was stopped,' she says flatly.

'Stopped? By who?'

She shrugs. 'He was just told that you had a new oven and didn't need the wood.'

'Do you know who rang and told him that?'

She shakes her head. Outside the back door, I can see the little cat creeping out to her bowl as she spots another bigger cat moving in. Again, she spits and hisses and sees off the bigger cat.

'He tried to remember. But, *no*, he said his brain doesn't work so well these days.'

This time it's me who throws up my hands.

'But he will deliver wood straight away, he says. Enzo has always been a good customer. He doesn't want to do anything to affect their relationship.'

'Oh, thank goodness!' I breathe a sigh of relief.

Half an hour later, a small truck squeezes down the alleyway outside the restaurant. A small, red-faced man gets out, his hands gnarled with arthritis. He is full of apologies. He may not remember who changed the wood order, or why he misunderstood, but I have a good idea as we begin unloading wood into an unruly pile by the back door, just as Giacomo arrives.

'Here, let me help,' he says, hanging up his jacket by the back door.

'No, it's fine,' I say tightly.

'For goodness sake, Lucia! Just let someone help you once in a while,' he says, bending and picking up a log I drop and tossing it in the direction of the pile. Actually, I could do with his help right now. At least he should make up for what he's done, or tried to do.

I go to pay the woodsman, and give him something extra for the trouble he's been put to. He tries to refuse it but I tell him Enzo insists, and that he should keep the wood coming as normal. When I return to the kitchen the log pile by the back door is stacked and practically finished and Giacomo, if I'm not mistaken, is rubbing the head of the small black cat, which disappears back into the shadows when I arrive.

'There!' he says, dusting off his hands and straightening, then frowns. 'But what was wrong with the other stuff?'

'Damp!' I say.

'Ah, well, that's the beauty of the electric oven. Always the same cooking temperature every time!' He walks into the kitchen.

'Wait! You knew it was damp, didn't you? You switched the supplier.'

'Whoa!' says Giacomo, holding up his hands.

'Hello, you two!'

'Nonna,' we say.

'You won't win that way, Giac. You won't!' I say, squaring up to him.

He frowns at me, and Nonna is keeping her eye on us.

'I don't need to resort to silly tricks, Luce. And I'm surprised you could think that of me. You obviously don't know me at all.'

'No, Giac, you're right. I don't know you at all.' Because he didn't let me, I think angrily. He wouldn't tell me how he was feeling when we were getting more and more frustrated with how life wasn't going to plan, his parents' pressure and my increasing feelings of loneliness and alienation.

Nonna bustles around, getting the sauce on the stove and chiding Giacomo's sous-chef, Carlo, and Dante for bringing mud in on their shoes. It's like it's always been her kitchen, just like at home. When she has checked the sauce and that we have everything, I insist she goes home to Nonno. 'We're fine here, I promise.'

'Make sure Giac walks you back,' she says, but I have no intention of that happening again. I look out at the little black cat, slinking from the shadows behind the woodpile. She was clearly taken in by him too.

That evening's service starts smoothly. The *forno* is working well again and the orders go out without a hitch. In fact, we seem busier than ever and I wish I knew the figures and how far behind Giacomo we are.

Veronica's dough-rolling skills are getting more flamboyant as she watches and copies Giacomo through the glass in the door.

Sofia's desserts are to die for, and I can see that, like me, she has been learning her trade all her married life at the family's bakery.

'They're beautiful!' I say, admiring her rum babas.

'Thank you, Lucia, for this chance. Whatever happens at the end of the competition, I have loved this time. Just having something else to focus on has helped. I know his family mean well, and mine too . . . but I have to be able to do something for myself, not be cosseted. I've needed this!' She smiles, tears in her eyes.

'You're welcome.' I hug her. 'I couldn't do this without you.'

She puts the desserts into the refrigerated display cabinet in the restaurant and, with a spring in her step, goes to write up on the daily specials board her rum babas with fresh cream, tiramisu with cream and mascarpone, coffee and dark chocolate over soft sponge fingers.

It's only later when the dessert orders start to come in and she goes into the restaurant to take them out that she shrieks and comes back into the kitchen with bowls of melted sludge. We stop what we're doing. The display cabinet has been unplugged.

Sofia is in tears. 'I'm so sorry, Lucia.'

'It's not your fault, Sofia. Anyone could have made that mistake.'

'I thought I could do this,' she says. 'I've let you down.'

'You haven't!' I insist. 'Look, it was a simple mistake. Now go home and I'll see you tomorrow. We'll finish up here. Giac has *gelato* he can serve.'

She nods. But as she leaves, head down, I wonder if she'll come back.

Veronica and I finish up in the kitchen and I tell Veronica to go too. With no desserts to serve, we've cleared up in good time.

I go out into the backyard, and sit on the woodpile, putting some leftovers into the cat's bowl. I sit and gaze up at the night sky. I wonder if I'll ever manage to run this place smoothly. Just then a little black head appears from between the bins. Slowly but surely she steps out of the shadows, and instead of going straight for the bowl of food, she climbs up the pile and stands by me. I don't move. Then she nudges me. I reach out my hand, stroke her head and, if I'm not mistaken, there's the sound of a small purr. Slowly, slowly, I think. It looks like she might be accepting me. She stands for a while, until a Vespa revs its engine in the back alleys, and she shoots back into the shadows. I wonder whether that was the end of our time together. Then, just as I start to stand up, her little face appears at the crack between the bins, and she looks up at me. She's letting me know she'll come back, and tomorrow is another day. I smile.

'*Buona notte*, little one,' I say, and go into the kitchen to grab my bag and jacket from the hook.

'Hey, I'll walk you home!' Giacomo appears in the kitchen and, I don't know why, takes me by surprise.

Just like the cat, I feel like I'm scuttling back into the shadows so as not to trust or get hurt again.

'No need!'

'Every need. I promised Nonna.'

'I'm not a young woman any more, Giac,' I snap. 'I can take care of myself!'

'Well, I'd like to agree, but—'

'Ooof!' I throw my bag over my shoulder, turn off the lights and he follows. I look both ways out of the back door, then step out.

'Wait!' he calls.

He locks the back door as I march off. He jogs after me, catching me up in no time with his long strides.

'Giac, I told you, I'm fine!'

'Luce!' He takes my elbow as we reach the piazza under the big square streetlights. 'What is your problem?'

I can't bite my tongue any longer. 'You, Giac! You're my problem! My wood was sabotaged. Someone put damp wood on the woodpile, knowing it would ruin my chances.'

'It wasn't me, Luce, I promise you.'

'Just like you promised you'd love me for ever on our wedding day!' I could kick myself for bringing it up. He might think I care.

'Luce, we split up. That's it! No one's fault. It ended.'

'You finished it,' I retort.

'You'd left, if I remember. Gone back to Wales. It was you who said it wasn't working. I knew you weren't happy and neither was I.'

'I said it wasn't working and you agreed. It felt like you ran out on our marriage before you had a chance to be hurt. Like you were looking for a way out.'

'This has nothing to do with pizza or the woodpile. You're just still cross with me because I let you go. It was the right thing, Luce.'

'For who? We were married, Giac! Together for ever!'

'I know! I proposed! I was there!'

'*Phfffff!*' I say, throwing up my hands and marching off.

'Luce, it's all water under the bridge now. We split up. It's over. We just need to be civil for the next three weeks.'

I look at his face, his familiar face that I knew so well, and yet he's a total stranger now. 'Not yet it isn't, Giac. It's not over yet.'

'Is that why you're doing this, why you want the restaurant? So that I don't have it?'

'No, Giac, for once, this isn't about you. It's about me, just me. What I want, how I feel. And I'm saying it out loud.' Like I should have done when we agreed things weren't working. I should have done more instead of moving back to Wales and sticking my head in my law books, trying to forget him and my life out here. I should have stayed, tried harder . . . if that was what I'd wanted.

I walk across the piazza, under the streetlamps, and he follows.

'Okay, okay, you thought I didn't care enough to fight for our marriage, that I listened to my parents when they said I should let you go. But can't we at least try to get on?' he says. He stops me by taking hold of my elbow again, and I'm standing looking up at him.

'You sabotaged the wood, Giac.'

'I didn't, Luce, I promise you,' he repeats softly.

I can't help but think how it would feel the most natural thing in the world to reach up, above the dark hairs poking over the top of his open-necked linen shirt, and kiss him. He's just so damn attractive and that makes this so hard. How could the person I loved try to sabotage my best efforts? Did I ever really matter to him? Why then, did we split? Why don't I know where it went wrong?

'I think the best thing would be is if we just stayed very far apart. Keep out of my kitchen, Giac. It's not yours yet!' I shake his hand off my elbow, my heart pumping.

I run up to the apartment, go in and shut the door behind me, my lips aching and my heart breaking all over again.

TWENTY-SEVEN

The next night, Sofia is nowhere to be seen as we start to prep for service. Giacomo does exactly as I told him to and keeps his distance. He's working in the outside kitchen in the courtyard with Carlo, under the shade of the pergola.

'Any sign of her?' Veronica asks, when she arrives back after her afternoon break. There's something different about Veronica: she's cut her long purple nails and hasn't put on so much make-up, but she's still wearing her high-heeled trainers. It makes me smile, despite how sad I'm feeling about Sofia.

I shake my head.

'Shall I go and get her?' asks Veronica, ready to turn and bring her in.

'Give her time,' says Nonna, sitting on her stool preparing mushrooms.

'But desserts?' I ask Nonna. 'What shall we serve? Sofia's were just delicious.'

'We adapt. We will make them simple. Simple and fresh.'

I walk across the kitchen and peer through the circle of clear glass in the frosted-glass door into the restaurant, the covered terrace and the courtyard.

'I will speak to my friend Nonna Maria. I'll get her to pick some strawberries. She has plenty,' she tells me. 'Veronica can collect them.'

I take one last look at Giacomo, wondering what happened last night. Was the unplugged desserts cabinet an accident? It must have been. He can't be that underhand, or can he? Why can't I let it go? Why can't I just be civil, like he wants us to be? As I'm about to turn and walk away, he looks up at me, as if sensing me there. My heart pounds and I turn away, hoping he didn't spot me, thinking he might have.

I nod to Nonna. And we set to work, her on antipasti, me on the dough, and Veronica goes to collect the strawberries. Nonna and I are busier than ever getting everything prepped without Veronica.

Just before service is about to start, Veronica opens the door with a bang, carrying a basket of big, fat, ripe strawberries and wearing a smile as wide as her face. She looks beautiful. 'Look who I found outside the gate in the lane!' she announces, and steps into the kitchen, down the worn steps, expertly in her high-heeled trainers and behind her, almost meekly, follows . . .

'Sofia!' we both cry.

'I knew you'd come back! I knew you wouldn't let us down!' I shout, and run to hug her tightly.

'I was worried you wouldn't want me back, what with the refrigerator,' she says.

'Of course we do! We're in this together!'

We huddle around her and tell her how very much she's wanted and needed here. When I turn back Dante is leaning by the big kitchen stove.

'Everything okay, Dante?' I smile. 'It's fantastic, isn't it? Sofia is back. We're a full team again. Service should run without a hitch now.' I beam. If only I could get him to tell us how far apart our sales are from Giacomo's. But he won't. He just delivers them to Nonno. Well, he puts them into the envelope and Nonna delivers them to Nonno. I can only keep going and do the best I can. And now Sofia is back we'll be fine. Nonna checks all our preparations are in order.

'Let me taste the sauce before I go,' she says, as I tell her it's time for her to put her feet up.

'No, no! The sauce will be fine. It's always fine. Go on. Go home to Nonno. He'll be wondering where you are.'

I pull her cardigan around her shoulders for her and hand her her bag. 'Do you want one of us to walk you home?'

She shakes her head. 'It's light. It's fine. No one is interested in an old woman like me.'

'I am!' says a voice from the kitchen.

'Nonno!' I cry, and hug him.

'Came to see what you were doing and to find my wife.'

'I was just dropping in on Lucia, to see she's okay.' She winks at me and leaves.

'As long as that's all it was.' He gives her a stern look.

The hit from the *forno* is ferocious. The wood is dry and burning well and I know now I have a constant supply of it. I wipe my brow.

'Two more Margheritas,' I say, slipping them off the big peel and turning to see Dante standing in the kitchen with two plates.

'Sorry, the customers sent them back. They said it tastes like . . . I will not say what they said in front of ladies.'

'What?' I exclaim.

He shrugs noncommittally.

'They said it doesn't taste good. Too salty.'

I put down the plates with a bang and stalk over to where he's standing. 'What do you mean it doesn't taste good? It looks fine.'

He shrugs again. 'They said they are not the same as they used to be here.'

'Rubbish!'

The others stop what they're doing and turn to stare.

I pick up one of the slices of pizza, look at it, smell it, then bite into it and chew. I turn to the bin, lean over it and spit it out. *'Bleurgh!'*

'The sauce,' I say, slowly standing upright. 'The sauce,' I say a little louder, then turn to the pot on the stove and run to it. I dip in my finger, suck it and grimace. 'The sauce!' I cry. 'Something's happened to the sauce!' I try it again.

Veronica and Sofia stare into the big pot as if expecting it to turn green.

'It's ruined!' I say, with a crack in my voice. 'Oversalted.'

I toss the spoon into the pot. It lands with a splosh, spraying tomato sauce over the wall, like blood. Like my blood boiling over.

'But how?' says Sofia.

I shake my head. 'Maybe I did it, maybe Nonna. I should have let her taste it. She's always tasting the sauce. I was so keen to get her out before Nonno realized she'd been working here too.' I throw up my hands and let out a long, long sigh.

'What's the problem?'

Giacomo is in the kitchen and I jump. 'Dante says there's a problem in here. That you're closing your kitchen.'

'I don't remember saying that. But he's right. There's nothing I can do. I'll have to shut this kitchen down.'

'Don't beat yourself up. You tried.' Dante smiles kindly. 'Now it's time for you to relax, enjoy your holiday.'

I stare at him and frown. No one says a word. I narrow my eyes further and feel a hot rash travelling up my neck and burning my cheeks. 'I meant,' I say slowly and deliberately, 'I'd shut it down for the night. I'll be without a night's worth of orders. Not for good. I didn't say that. Neither did I say this to you before now.' I look at Giacomo.

Suddenly the mood in the kitchen becomes very tense, hot and stifling.

Giacomo looks at me, then at Dante.

'Looks like you've got a clean shirt on there, Dante,' says Veronica, walking over to his peg and rucksack by the back door.

'Hey!' he swears in Italian as she pulls out a shirt from his rucksack and holds it up.

'With tomato sauce stains.' She's holding it up like the cape of a matador to a frustrated bull about to lunge.

'I got it dirty earlier. I always keep a spare.' He reaches out and goes to snatch it back.

'Really?' she says. 'And, tell me, why were your shoes covered with mud the other day when Nonna had to shoo you and Carlo out to clean them? Perhaps you'd been collecting wood, for the *forno*.'

'Dante?' says Sofia, shocked.

'Why didn't you say anything, Veronica?' I ask.

'I needed to be sure. I have spent my life watching men covering their tracks, hiding what they get up to. I knew he would trip up sooner or later.' She glares at him as if he is the lowest of the low.

'And the dessert cabinet?' I ask.

'*Phhhf.*' He throws up an arm dismissively. 'I have work to do. I have no time for this.'

He turns back to the restaurant door, but Giacomo steps sideways and blocks his path, towering over him. 'You were asked a question,' he says, very quietly and slowly. 'The dessert cabinet?'

I want to interrupt, to tell Giacomo I can handle this, but instead I bite my tongue and let him help me.

Dante looks at Giacomo, then back over his shoulder to me, Veronica, tall and slender, and Sofia, shorter and plump. Sofia folds her arms and stares at him. Veronica and I do the same.

He turns back to Giacomo. 'You said yourself!' He raises his voice and gesticulates in our direction. 'This is ridiculous!'

'I beg your pardon!' I say, as the red-hot rash of fury runs up and around my neck again.

'This cannot be!' he says. 'We will be a laughing stock when word gets out.'

We take a sharp breath.

'Be careful, Dante,' says Giacomo.

'Someone has to say what we're all thinking.' He looks to Giacomo for support but Giacomo says nothing.

'You turned off the dessert cabinet?' asks Sofia, evenly.

'The plug came out in my hand,' he says sarcastically.

'And the wood?' says Veronica.

He sighs.

'And the sauce. It was all you!' I glare at him.

'Now, can we please get back to normal business?' he says. 'I have customers waiting and Giac needs to be out there making pizzas. It's why people come here. To see a real *pizzaiolo*!'

Nobody speaks, and then a voice comes out of me that doesn't even sound like mine. 'My great-grandfather set up this restaurant. My grandfather after that. I have known you nearly all my life, Dante, and you'd do this to me?'

'It is not your place. We do not have *pizzaiola*s. Save that for the men. Stick to helping out and waitressing.'

'Like you have,' I retort.

'I am a sought-after waiter! I have been loyal to your family. But this, this is not right. People will laugh at me.'

'What? People like your friends who hang around in the square and in alleyways, preying on women, thinking they're cool and macho?' My blood is boiling now. Why didn't I work this out sooner? It's Dante who has the problem with me and the idea of me taking over the restaurant.

'They will take their business elsewhere. The place will shut. None of us will have work!'

'Get out,' I say, in a low voice.

'What? You cannot do that,' he sneers.

'Get out, Dante. You're fired.' I fold my arms and glare at him.

'I'm not taking orders from you. Others may have indulged your idea. But that's what it is. Just a fantasy. By the *bocce* tournament, Giac will show he is the right person to take over here. And you can go back to wherever it is you come here on holiday from! This is not some holiday fun. This is our lives! I will not be made a laughing stock by working for a woman pizza chef!' he spits.

The air is full of tension. Orders are backing up.

'Giac!' his sous-chef calls, from the outside kitchen.

Dante looks at Giacomo for support.

Giacomo folds his arms, like me. 'You heard, Dante,' he says. 'You're fired.'

'What?'

'You heard what Lucia said. You're fired. Get your belongings and leave.' He looks as furious as I am and the veins in his neck are standing out.

'I will speak to Enzo about this,' Dante splutters.

'So will I,' says Giacomo, furiously. 'Lucia has fired you, and I have agreed with her decision. The restaurant has been left in our hands and you no longer work here. Now get out!' He points and steps towards Dante, squaring up to him and towering over him.

Dante hesitates, then looks at me and laughs. 'By

the way, that date I asked you on? It was a joke! A bet! See who could get the Englishwoman to go to bed first!'

Giacomo steps forward and Dante reels back.

'That's enough, Giac,' I say. 'Leave it now.' I'm worried he's going to hit Dante, he's so angry.

'You lowlife!' I say. 'Goodbye, Dante. I pity any woman who falls for your lack of charm.'

Dante catapults himself forward, grabbing his rucksack, stuffing the shirt back into it, and flings the door open, slamming it behind him before Giacomo changes his mind.

I'm shaking with fury. 'You okay?' I ask him. He nods, although his nostrils are still flaring angrily.

'You?' he asks. I nod. Still trying to take in what's happened. 'I'm sorry, Giac, really. I'm sorry I thought it was you.'

He waves a hand, dismissing it. But I was wrong. It wasn't him. 'I know you wouldn't do any of those things. I'm sorry.'

I chew my bottom lip. Dante was prepared to do all that to get rid of me! Maybe he's right. Maybe I am making Nonno's a laughing stock.

'Do you want some of my sauce? I have plenty,' says Giacomo, kindly, making me feel even worse for doubting him.

I try to smile. 'No, thank you. That wouldn't be right. It's about the food, remember? Even more so now, it needs to be about that. I can't serve your food. I'll close the kitchen. Perhaps you could explain that it's just your menu on this evening.'

'If you're sure?'

I nod. 'But thank you. People are waiting to be fed. We can't turn them away. We'll close up in here, then I'll come out and waitress. It'll be good to be out of the kitchen for a while.' Again, I try to smile. But I know that even if we keep going tomorrow, Giacomo will now be a long way ahead.

'I'm sorry,' he says. 'I didn't know. I wish I'd realized.'

'I believe you,' I say, as Veronica and Sofia clear down the kitchen and get ready to leave.

'A truce?' he says quietly, a little short of breath.

'A truce. It's all about the food, right?' I confirm.

'Right. It's all about the food on the plate.' He hesitates, then turns back to the restaurant, and to bottling up whatever's on his mind. I know how much it takes for him to open up about how he feels, and Dante almost got the full force of it, like a sudden storm that's rumbled away for the time being.

In that moment, part of me remembers the old Giacomo, when he was my favourite person in the world, always there for me, by my side.

TWENTY-EIGHT

Giacomo insists on walking me home, despite my initial inclination to tell him I'm fine. This time I let him and just say, 'Thank you.'

'It's no problem. It's on my way,' he says, as we leave the restaurant and lock up.

I place some leftovers by the back door: the little black cat comes out and lets me stroke her head as she makes for the bowl. 'I meant for tonight. With Dante.' I straighten from stroking the cat and then we head out of the back gate.

He nods, looking straight ahead, just the sound of our footsteps on the shiny cream flagstones as we walk into the piazza. The restaurants there are closing or closed by now. Giacomo waves to the waiters and restaurateurs he knows.

'You know everyone here.' I find myself smiling.

'I grew up here,' he says matter-of-factly. 'Well, between here and my town down the road.'

'And you know your customers,' I say, still wondering if what Dante said was true. Am I risking the family business by doing what I'm doing? We walk a little further in silence. 'Why now, Giac, why leave the family business? You've always wanted to be there, to take over the running of that place. It was your dream. I couldn't ever see you leaving. I was sure you wouldn't, even if I'd asked.'

He lets out a long breath. 'I suppose it's time. The right time. I want to be me. It's hard. My father is still there, and it's his place. He's been a *pizzaiolo* all his life.'

'That's how we met, through Nonno and your father.'

'And my brother is there too, and his sons are growing up and will want to get involved. It's a busy place. I have ideas I want to put in place, try out. It's just, well, it seemed like the right place to branch out on my own and the right time to do it. Sometimes you know when something feels right and you have to just go with it.'

'So you left before you were squeezed out?'

'Not really . . . Well, yes, maybe. My father, brother are great *pizzaiolo*s. I'm sure my nephews will be too. It's a new scene and I want to be part of it.'

'And if it doesn't happen?'

He shrugs. 'I don't think there's room for me at my father's place, although of course he'd insist on me going back, even though he was angry, thinking I'd deserted them, left the family business. But I'm sure he'd get used to the idea. With time. It's all about time.'

I nod. 'It can't have been easy for him, you leaving,' I say. 'Or for your mother.'

'No. He doesn't understand why I need to move on and be myself, not just the son of somebody. And she hates things not being done her way. As you probably remember!' He gives a gentle laugh and so do I. It feels like a tiny release of pressure. 'I can't explain it to my father in words. He just doesn't understand why I don't want to stay at the family business. But hopefully I'll show him why. Maybe. If I win . . . And you?' he asks, moving the conversation away from himself.

I shrug. 'Like you, I've risked it all to be here. I don't know what I'll do if I don't win. I just wanted the chance. I realized my job wasn't making me happy. I was just hiding. This is what makes me happy, this place. Nonno's. Being here. I understand that now. I just wanted a fair chance.'

He carries on in silence for a while as we cross the piazza in the lamplight. We look up at the moon and stars scattered across the dark sky.

'I'm sorry that happened tonight, Luce. Like you say, you deserve a fair shot at this.'

'Thank you,' I say again, like it's becoming a habit.

'Whatever our past is, we agreed it's about the food and nothing else. If it's any consolation, your pizzas are great,' he says, a smile pulling at the corners of his mouth.

'Really?'

'Really. Well, they look great. And the customers are loving them, from what I see in the outside kitchen. When they haven't been tampered with!' And I see the veins in his neck stand out. 'So dishonourable!' He shakes his head. 'Really, your pizzas look great.'

'I'll make you one now I'm more practised,' I say, feeling like I've got ten out of ten in my school homework. 'You can taste one for yourself.'

'I'd like that. And there's a new one I've been trying out. How about we do a swap? Cook for each other?'

'Sure,' I say, telling myself once more that it's all about the food, nothing else.

We arrive at the apartment and I suddenly realize that if Nonna was listening, she'd get completely the wrong idea. 'Just to compare. Research.'

'Absolutely!' he agrees.

'Not like—'

'Oh, no, not like a date or anything.' He looks up at the open apartment doors and says again, 'It's just about the food. And you'll be back in tomorrow, with your team?' he checks, and I'm grateful for that. I know how much getting the restaurant means to him, but he's clearly making sure it's a fair and level playing field. Unlike Nonno's *bocce* games from the sound of his complaints about his team members.

'Ready to go!' I assure him. We spin away from each other and I run upstairs to the apartment, letting myself in quietly.

Nonna is sitting up waiting for me. She smiles as she looks up from her knitting.

'Definitely not a date!' I tell her, knowing she's heard every word. She nods and follows me to bed.

But he did say my pizza was good. Tomorrow, with Dante gone, I'm going to show how good they are. And my stomach flips over in excitement.

TWENTY-NINE

I lift the spoon and sniff the sauce. I know the smell so well. Like it's a place called home. Rich, tangy, with a hint of sweetness. And all that following day at the restaurant, I taste the sauce over and over again, like a compass returning to its north. The sauce keeps returning me to why I'm here, who I am, and why I'm doing this. Service that evening goes without a hitch, although we have to double up as waitresses and cooks.

'Lucia, your bandanna!' Veronica launches herself at me as I'm about to leave the kitchen with two plates of pizza Marinara and a side salad balanced on my wrist. The smell of the fresh oregano and garlic in thick green olive oil fills my senses with joy. I'm so pleased with the pizzas on the plates that I practically forget I'm not supposed to be showing that I'm cooking.

Veronica snatches the bandanna off my head before I push through the heavy door into the restaurant, having slipped out of my whites.

'*Grazie*, Veronica.' I smile, then give a sigh of relief.

'No problem.' She smiles too. She's had my back since I first met her.

'I'll take the next ones,' says Sofia. 'My desserts are ready to go.'

'And I can help.' Nonna is back in the kitchen, unable to stay away. She sits on a stool, making up the pizzas, bored of Nonno complaining about his *bocce* team and whether they'll be ready for the tournament. Training seems to include playing in the piazza in the evening sunlight, then arguing about the rules in a bar over grappa. He's never been happier. But Nonna isn't used to him being around quite as much.

'He's in my space!' she moans, as she preps and tops the pizzas. 'Even in my kitchen! I can't wait for him to go and play *bocce*.' She plucks basil leaves from their stalks and scatters them over the pizza from a height.

With the extra effort we all put in, service runs like clockwork. At the end, when the final customers say goodnight, I open a bottle of prosecco, with a satisfying pop. I pour it bubbling into our glasses and hand them round. 'To new beginnings,' I toast, and we all raise our glasses.

As we finish up, laughing and helping each other

with the cleaning, Giacomo arrives in the kitchen with his jacket slung over his shoulder.

Wary of anyone coming in to try to catch us at work, expose the kitchen, we jump, and then relax when we see who it is.

'How was service?' he asks.

'Brilliant!' says Veronica. 'How many covers did you do?'

'Ha! That would be telling!' He seems at ease with Veronica and they slip into easy banter, as if he's known her for ever, a bit like how he and I used to be before he stopped telling me what he was thinking or how he was feeling. The atmosphere in the kitchen is really quite jolly, as if this is a normal way of doing business. But it's not, we both know that. In no time, one of us will be leaving. And if it's Giacomo, if I'm left here, how will the customers feel when they know I've been cooking all along?

'Well, goodnight all,' he says, this time not referring to us as 'ladies'. 'Goodnight, Chef!' he says to me, and I smile. I wonder whether to offer him a glass with us. I can see Nonna, Veronica and Sofia staring at me, wondering the same. Giacomo nods at us all, then heads out of the back door and I put the bottle on the table, wondering why I couldn't have invited him to sit down. He probably has somewhere to be I tell myself. But maybe, soon, I'll ask him to join us.

*

'Who's that?' Sofia asks Veronica, during the following night's service, as she rushes back in from clearing plates to check on her tiramisu in the fridge. Veronica is tall enough to see out of the clear glass circle, unlike me – I have to stretch up – and likes to keep an eye on what's going on. Sofia checks the tiramisu. We all check everything, regularly now, so nothing can go wrong.

Veronica is still peering out of the window and I stand on tiptoe to look too. A woman is sitting on her own, at a table for two, close to the outside kitchen with a front-row view of Giacomo, and she seems to like watching him work. Her face is lit by the overhead fairy lights, nestled among the greenery there and softly illuminating the lemons hanging like Christmas baubles from their trees. She is watching Giacomo closely, taking the occasional picture on her phone. She's certainly a fan of him and his cooking techniques.

'Looks like you've got competition,' says Veronica, flatly.

'What? No! Look, there is no me-and-Giac. We were over years ago. We took a break and I went back to the UK and then we spoke on the phone and ended it.' I think back to that painful phone call when I wanted him to tell me he still wanted me and we'd work it out. But maybe he wanted that from me too. Anyway, it's all in the past now.

'A break? And a phone call?' Veronica looks outraged.

'I really don't want to talk about it,' I say, my cheeks burning from the heat of the *forno* – or maybe it's the feelings I'm trying to hide from. 'Really, I'm happy for him. We've both moved on.'

'To where?' she asks. Veronica, it seems, misses nothing when it comes to relationships.

'Well, I went into law and he carried on working with his brother and father. We got on with our own lives,' I say again firmly, and I wonder who I'm trying to convince: Veronica or myself.

'And you've both ended up here.' She lifts a pencilled eyebrow.

'I promise you, Giac and I will never happen again. Now, check!' I say, holding up an order slip and taking one last glance through the round window. Giacomo throws his pizza dough into the air and catches it, passes it to the other hand, to a round of applause from the woman. I wish I didn't feel like I do, wondering if she might be catching his eye too. Then I'm cross, wishing I didn't want to know. But, infuriatingly, I do.

As service dies down, I seem to be passing the kitchen door more and more often, going the long way round the kitchen and standing on tiptoe as I pass to look out. Giacomo has joined the woman at her table and she's pouring him a glass of wine. If she isn't in his life already, it looks as if she'd like to be and could be very soon.

Sofia hands him another order and he gets up to

cook it. As he returns to his place behind the counter, beside the oven, she stands from her table, smooths down her skirt and heads straight for the kitchen.

'She's coming this way,' I hiss loudly, to Veronica and Nonna.

'Hide!' says Nonna, and I pull off my bandanna.

Despite her age and her swollen ankles, Nonna makes it off her stool and to the door, just as the woman is putting her hand to it to push it open.

'Oh!' she says, as Nonna opens it a crack and stands in her way.

'Can I help you?' Nonna asks politely but firmly.

'Toilets?' The woman is trying to see around Nonna, who isn't opening the door more than an inch or two. I have my back against the wall behind the door. Veronica has dropped to the floor behind Nonna.

I can hear Giacomo's voice and let out a sigh of relief. 'This way,' he calls, directing her to the toilets through another door at the far end of the restaurant.

'Oh, that's the kitchen. Of course,' she says. '*Scusi!* How stupid of me.' I can't help but think she's still taking her time moving away.

'In the corner, over there,' says Sofia.

Finally, as I hear her high heels totter off across the terracotta tiles, we all breathe a sigh of relief.

Giacomo pops his head in the kitchen. 'That was close,' he says to me, and watches as Veronica gets up from the floor.

'Thank you,' I say to him.

'No problem.' He swallows. 'Look, it's like Nonno says, if anyone finds out about this, the competition is off and he'd have to sell. None of us wants that to happen. I don't want our set-up revealed any more than you do.'

Of course that's why he doesn't want anyone to find out about me. It's not that he's helping me. He's the competition, and I must never, ever, forget that. Never.

THIRTY

The next couple of days pass relatively smoothly.

On Saturday morning, after a restless night when I dreamt that Giacomo and I were slinging pizza bases at each other in some kind of duel in the middle of the piazza by the *bocce* pitch, I wake to the sound of Angelo singing, reminding me to get up and be who I want to be.

Downstairs, Nonna and Nonno are bent over the kitchen table looking at something.

'*Buon giorno*,' I say brightly, and wonder what they're looking at.

'*Buon giorno*.' They straighten quickly, and I swear Nonna hides something in the kitchen-table drawer. I'm just hoping it's not bad news about Nonno, anything from the hospital.

'Is everything okay?' I ask, helping myself to coffee.

Nonna puts a plate in front of me, encouraging me to load it with a pastry, bread and jam.

'Take two,' she says, putting a second pastry on my plate despite my protests.

'You okay, Nonno?' I ask him.

'*Sì, sì*. Everything is fine,' says Nonno, sitting next to me. 'How are things at the restaurant?'

'Good, *bene!*' Everything is going well. Veronica is fantastic at helping me with the pizzas. Sofia's desserts are fantastic. And Non—' Nonna frowns at me and I stop myself saying that the customers love her antipasti. 'What about you, Nonno? What are you up to today? *Bocce?*'

'*Phhf!* If only they could decide which rules to play by! But, yes, we will play. We must be ready for the tournament in two weeks' time.'

'Looks like you'll have to make up your own and agree to stick to them,' I say. Just like we're doing in the kitchen, in the pizza community. 'Okay, I'm off to the restaurant,' I say. 'Lots of bookings today.'

'And no word from Dante?' Nonno asks. 'No more trouble?'

I shake my head.

'I'm so sorry. I am very disappointed in him. You did the right thing. If you want to run a restaurant, you have to be the boss. Sounds like that's what you did.'

'And Giac.' I nearly bite my tongue.

'Good.' He nods. 'I know the restaurant is in capable

hands. And I'm glad this is a fair competition. It wouldn't be fair to Giac if people knew my granddaughter was in the kitchen, and it wouldn't be fair to you if people like Dante favoured Giac's cooking just because of who he is. You both deserve this. I have a feeling it will be very close to call.' He frowns, as if he's got the weight of the world on his shoulders.

Nonna picks up her baskets and I know she's off to get supplies for me.

'Where are you going?' He sounds mystified.

'What did you think? That I just sat at home all day when you were in the restaurant?' She tuts and kisses the top of his head.

'I thought we could go out for coffee.'

'No time. See you later!'

'Guess I'll go and get some *bocce* practice in, then,' he says.

'Have you seen this?' I'm tasting and stirring the sauce at the restaurant after our lunchtime break and lighting the *forno*, when Veronica storms into the kitchen, waving a newspaper.

'What?' I ask, standing back from the *forno* as the smoke and flames rise. It's hot outside today, really hot, and it's going to be even hotter in here later when the *forno* heats up. I reach for my water bottle and take a swig. I run my forearm over my face and pull my bandanna further down to mop my brow.

It's the middle of August and the sun is scorching the streets. Briefly I think about the office back home, how I'd have spent all summer staring at my computer screen, hardly seeing the daylight. I wonder how the office is doing. From the terse email I had from Anthony Gwyn-Jones, having to accept that I had enough holiday leave to see out my notice period and a planned handover period, I'm guessing they may be finding out who did the lion's share of the work and that that promotion should have gone to me. But I'm so glad I'm not in that office. Instead, I'm here in the kitchen, which is getting even hotter. That's why I'm grateful we don't open at lunchtime, although if I wanted to make more sales, it's a thought.

I go over to the big wooden table where Veronica is laying out a newspaper.

'Look!' She points with a straight forefinger. I take another swig of water and nearly choke on it, spluttering over the paper. I stand and stare and cough some more.

Sofia arrives just at that moment and hangs up her jacket, taking off her bag from over her shoulder and hanging that up too. There is a blast of hot air and I don't know if it's coming from the bright sunshine outside, the lit *forno* or my cheeks, burning furiously.

'What's that?' says Sofia, coming to join us.

'A review of the restaurant,' Veronica says excitedly. 'Double page spread!'

And there, across two pages, is Giacomo, at his outside electric *forno*. 'The Changing Face of the *Pizzaiolo*' shouts the headline. The picture shows him tossing a disc of dough into the air. Around him is the outside kitchen. The lemons my great-grandmother grew are there, with the wisteria and the fairy lights I helped Nonno put up some years ago. And Giacomo, larger than life, smiling, his eyes sparkling as he watches the disc of dough in the air.

I read the article, my finger under each word. Sofia and Veronica have devoured it in no time.

The phone rings, making me jump, and the answerphone takes the message. As soon as it finishes with a *beeeep*, the phone rings again. And again. The more I read, the more I understand what's going on.

'She was a mystery diner, the woman last week.' Veronica fills in the blanks for anyone who hasn't understood. Sofia is beaming. Nonna comes in and sees us reading the paper.

'So this is what you were hiding from me earlier,' I say.

She brings the shopping to the table with an *ommph*. 'Eggs from Nonna Christina. Mozzarella. Tomatoes . . .'

'Leave the shopping,' I tell her. 'I'll unload it. Nonna, why didn't you show this to me?'

She shrugs again.

'It's amazing,' says Sofia. 'Incredible for the restaurant!'

The phone is still ringing and the answerphone still cutting in.

'Come on now, let's get the prep done,' chivvies Nonna. But I'm still looking at the article and then, as I reread it, 'Someone had better check the answerphone messages,' I say.

Veronica nods and makes her way to the high desk, where the phone is and the bookings diary.

'Sounds like the bookings are flying in,' says Sofia, cautiously.

And then I add, 'For Giac.'

And she and I both nod.

Veronica comes back into the kitchen, but the phone is still ringing.

'Lots of bookings?' I ask.

She nods.

'For Giac and his menu?'

She nods again.

' "I loved Giacomo's flair and originality," ' I reread the article. ' "In fact, I loved everything about Giacomo. One of the new breed of *pizzaiolo*s making their mark. One to look out for. Get to Nonno's if you can and order from their new range on the menu from this rising star!" '

The phone is still ringing and ringing.

'It'll be great for sales,' says Sofia.

'It'll be great for Giacomo's sales,' I say defeatedly.

'Listen to it. Table booking one after another.' I walk around the kitchen.

'What am I going to do, Nonna?' I hold my head.

'Keep doing what you're doing. You're doing it well,' she says. 'People will come. No one knows it's a competition.'

'Maybe,' I say. 'Maybe we need to rethink the menu. Do a few things differently. Mix things up a bit. Adapt. Take Giacomo on at his own game.'

Nonna shrugs, a small smile spreading across her face. 'They are all the same ingredients. It's what you do with them that makes the difference,' she says.

'Besides, Giac won't be the only one getting more customers. We will too. People want to come and eat here after this review. Not necessarily just Giac's fancy pizzas,' Veronica says.

Nonna agrees. 'She's right. Don't be too disheartened. This isn't over yet.'

'What should I do, Nonna?'

'Your best,' she says, and turns to taste the sauce. 'It's all we can do.'

THIRTY-ONE

Word has got out about Giacomo, his pizzas and his new way of cooking. People are coming from all over the area to get a taste of the new range on the menu. Customers are trying something new, choosing from his side of the menu instead of mine. The weekend was busy, and it's not looking like easing up as we go into this new week.

'I really need to work on some new dishes,' I say to the kitchen in general, at the end of a slow service for me, but Sofia, waitressing, has been run off her feet. Even Veronica has helped out.

'You want me to stay with you?' says Veronica. 'Help?'

'No, no, it's fine. You go. I'll take a bit of time here and think about things.' I get out my pen and notebook, pour a glass of red wine, leave the open bottle on the table and sit on Nonna's stool.

'*Buona notte*, Veronica, Sofia,' I call as they depart, leaving the door ajar. A welcome cooling breeze is coming in from outside.

I sit listening to the sounds of the street – youngsters laughing and joking together, a child, tired and ready for bed as its parents soothe it, singing from a balcony and families kissing each other. It's the sounds of the town. The sounds of families ending their evening, the sounds of love. Isn't that what this place is about? Love? What do I love that I can put on the menu?

I tap my teeth with my pen and take a swig of wine. As I do I hear the door hinges creak. I turn to it, then see the little black cat poking her head in. She's come to see where her dinner is. She's getting braver and braver all the time, and I think I know how she feels: little changes every day. I grab her bowl from the side with the scraps I've put into it. She looks up at me and miaows.

'Well, we're finding our manners,' I say, and smile. I put down the bowl outside and she lets me stroke her just once. I leave her to eat in peace and I can actually hear her purring with pleasure. She took a risk staying around when the other cats were here, but now she's found her own little safe place in the world.

I walk back into the kitchen, wash my hands at the sink and dry them, then pick up a ball of dough that's left over from tonight's service and look at it. What is Giac doing that's so different? He's taking what pizza always was and dressing it up differently. I toss the ball from hand to hand. That's all he's doing. Like Nonna says, it's the same ingredients. It's what you do with them that makes the difference.

I flatten the ball and try to toss it from hand to hand. I stretch it a little and toss it some more. I warm the dough in my hands to make it stretch further. Then I add more olive oil, knead it in and try again, lifting it in front of me and watching it start to grow. I attempt to spin it on one hand and pass it back to the other, the tip of my tongue poking out in concentration. Is this what you have to do to be a *pizzaiola*? Do you have to be a showwoman as well? Does it make the dough taste any different? Should I just take him on at his own game?

'Ha! How do you like that, Giac? You haven't won yet!' I say.

I toss the dough into the air, high this time, just as the kitchen door swings open and he walks in, making me jump.

The dough falls into a mess in my hands.

'I thought everyone had gone,' I stutter.

'Sorry, didn't mean to make you jump,' he says at the same time. 'It was . . . a busy night,' he says, pointing to the outside kitchen.

'The article did the trick, then,' I say, with a nod.

'I didn't know she was a mystery diner or a journalist, Luce. Otherwise I would have talked about the whole menu to her, not just my side.'

'Right.' I wish I could believe him, and wonder how she'd heard about him if not from him. 'So you didn't invite her along? Give your sales a bit of a boost. She's done a very good job in highlighting your "inventive flavours". And encouraging people to try something new.'

'I swear, Luce, I had no idea. If I had, I'd have flagged up the traditional side of the menu as well as the new at Nonno's.'

I nod, refolding the dough into a ball. 'Well, you certainly got a fan in your mystery diner,' I say, trying not to sound too hard done by.

'Yup. Are you . . . ?' He looks at the dough I'm tossing around in my hands.

'Oh, just thinking up some new ideas for the menu.'

'Right. And by the look of it, you were maybe trying some acrobatics.'

'I was just seeing if it changed the taste of the dough.'

'And did it?'

'I don't know yet. I haven't managed to make one.'

'Here, let me show you.'

'It's fine.'

'Luce.' His eyebrows rise, as if he doesn't need to point out that I'm doing it again, not letting him in, even a chink. I think about the little black cat, opening the door a crack, letting me in just a little. His hands cover mine and the ball of dough and for a second I can do nothing. That familiar touch. I'm rooted to the spot and I know that resisting would only draw out this moment. I let him take the dough from my hands, telling myself to breathe again. I can smell cooked dough on his clothes. A comforting smell. Just the woodsmoke missing to make me feel at home.

'Now, like this.' He starts with a new ball of dough and hands me one. 'Come on, follow me.' I can't help but smile.

'May I?' He points to the wine.

'Of course,' I say, and he gets himself a glass as I try to tease the dough out. He tops up my wine and pours for himself.

'Now, like this.' He shows me and I try again, but my efforts just fall to the floor.

'I was thinking of changing my menu, maybe coming up with some new ideas,' I say, not making eye contact with him as I focus on the dough disc. Somehow, concentrating on something else makes it easier to talk to Giac.

'A change?' I hear him say, a slight smile on his lips – I can hear it. He's tossing a pizza base too now.

'Well, not a change. Not a complete change. Just a few ideas to add to the menu.'

'And what does this "not a change" involve?' He tosses the pizza dough high into the air and catches it perfectly. Mine hits the deck again. I pick it up and bin it with force. He stands with his and points to the pizza peel.

'Hungry?' he says. My stomach rumbles in reply.

I pick up another ball of dough and this time dip it into the bowl of semolina flour, starting to press it out gently. The way I learnt to do it and have been doing. Then I put it onto the table and tease it into shape.

I turn to the sauce, ladle out a spoonful and, with the bottom of the ladle, spread it in circles from the centre outwards.

'May I?' Giacomo points to the sauce.

'Of course,' I say, and he helps himself to a spoonful of sauce and spreads it over his pizza base.

'I'll make one for you,' he says, opening the fridge. 'We agreed we'd cook for each other, didn't we? The other night?'

'When we agreed it wasn't a date!'

'Exactly! It's about the food.' He smiles.

'Okay, and I'll cook for you.'

'I'll cook one that says Lucia on a plate.'

I'm intrigued.

'Like the colours of the Italian flag that was made for Queen Margherita, everything she represented on a plate.'

'Okay,' I say tentatively. 'And in that case, the one I make for you may include being a little rough around the edges!' He nudges me and I smile. We're enjoying teasing each other, like he does with Veronica. It's a change from being furious with him. And right now, he's doing a great job out there in the courtyard kitchen and I may just have to face the fact that Nonno's may become Giacomo's in just a couple of weeks' time, unless I can work up some new ideas and really turn this around.

'So,' he opens the fridge and looks up and down the shelves, 'you have some lovely stuff in here.'

'Nonna gets it from her friends,' I say, without thinking.

He nods impressively. 'Ah, the Nonna Network! Wow! That mozzarella!' He smells it, then tastes it. He shuts his eyes. He opens them and looks at me. 'Where's it from?'

'I told you!' I smile. 'One of Nonna's contacts!' I shrug, just like Nonna does. It means you're not going to say any more.

'One of Nonna's contacts – she's probably trying to set you up with the woman's grandson, if I know *nonnas*!' He gives a soft, gentle laugh.

'Actually, surprisingly, she hasn't.' And she hasn't. 'But her friend with the mozzarella farm has!' I laugh. 'What about you? Your mother not trying to find you the perfect wife?' I venture, interested.

He shrugs. 'It's . . . difficult,' he finally says.

'Difficult? How? What's the problem?'

He looks at me. 'You, Luce. You're the problem.'

'Me? What have I done?'

He lets out a long sigh. 'You haven't done anything, Luce. You're just here.'

I frown.

'It's not easy dating when your ex is still in the picture. Besides, I want to work on my career right now. My pizzas are what matter to me.'

'But that's ridiculous. We've been over for years. Seven years!'

'Have we?' he says, and I'm not sure if he's questioning it being that long, or at what point we were finally over. And if I'm honest I'm not sure when that point came.

'So, no plans to settle down again yet?'

He sips his wine, staring straight ahead. 'Nope. Not yet. No plans.'

And I feel a strange sense of relief to hear it. How would I feel if he was ready to marry again?

'You? Ever tried internet dating?' he asks.

I shake my head. 'You?'

'No, me neither. Lots of people do, you know,' he says, and I'm not sure what he's getting at.

'Maybe I will, when I have time,' I say.

'Okay. So if I were describing you in a pizza, I'd put on soft mozzarella, traditional ingredients, no change in the basics. Rocket for your ambition, a little chilli, for the fire that burns in you to succeed, and anchovies for depth.' I look at him as he puts the ingredients on the plate. 'And I'd separate out the ingredients like this,' and he lays them apart from each other, 'for independence. And I'd call it the Lone Warrior.'

I look at the fridge and take out some more ingredients.

'And if I were describing you,' I say thoughtfully, feeling mischievous, and I'm not sure if it's the wine or the challenge he's thrown down, 'I'd go for something like this.' I pick up the cheese. I put in a selection of ingredients including Parma ham, soft pepperoni for his fiery temper when he finally lets rip, anchovies to bring out the flavours of the Parma ham, and onion for the layers of him that need to be peeled away. I fold the pizza over and seal the edges.

'A calzone?'

'A closed book,' I say. 'Keeping everything inside. Keeping the customer guessing. Not letting them know what's going on in your head.'

We stare at each other and something in me jolts. I snap my eyes away from him. Away from the look I remember so well and have managed to blot out for years, and from the feeling inside me right now that I thought I had long since buried. Giacomo may have been a man of few words, but his eyes always spoke to me, reassuring me, letting me know he wanted me. It was when his eyes darkened and I couldn't read him any more that we lost touch with each other and finally let go.

'Let's cook them,' I say quickly, trying to get some control back over my thoughts and feelings. Just like I have during all the years I spent in the law office, steadying my life when it felt like it was spiralling out of control, after Giac told me he thought we should have a break . . . and then when we finally split up he had sent me into sleepless nights, bouts of crying, self-doubt, before I moved back to Wales and focused on building a life and rebuilding me. But now I'm back and I know what I want. I can't get distracted.

He puts the pizza into the oven, turns it, and as the dough bubbles up and starts to turn darker in colour, he pulls it out. He lifts it to his nose and breathes it in. 'The wood,' he says thoughtfully.

'Makes a difference?' I ask, taking the peel from him and putting my own pizza in.

I pull it out and slide it onto a board he has ready for me. We pull up a stool each and he tops up the glasses while I lay out pizza cutters.

'So, this is your pizza.' He pushes towards me the one he has cooked. He cuts it and hands me a slice. 'Here, try it!' He holds it up and gently brings it closer to my mouth. I move forward and take a bite. 'That wasn't a bite. Take a bigger one!' he instructs.

I do so, taking the slice from him, trying not to touch hands, nearly dropping it in the process. I grab a napkin from the pile on the table to wipe the tomato sauce from the corners of my mouth.

Then I cut the calzone in half and hand it to him. The tips of my fingers brush his as he takes it from me, and I jolt, as if I've touched an electric cable. Why? How can he still have this effect on me, after all this time? We agreed we were over. It wasn't working. Whatever we had, whatever feelings, had gone.

He bites.

'And?' I say, watching his mouth, with its familiar outline.

'It's fabulous!' he says, after he's swallowed.

'So, should I put it on the menu?' I ask, half teasing, half serious.

'Sure. But, really, I don't think you need to change that much about what you're doing. People like it. It tastes just like Nonno's. That's what you wanted, right?'

'Yes, it is. I want it to stay just like Nonno's.'

'Just you being here is change, Lucia. I think that's all you need to do. Show them you can do this like your grandfather. You can do anything you want to if you put your mind to it. You always could.'

Is he playing a game or does he really mean I should keep it as it is?

'But maybe add something like this, a touch of Lucia. Traditional but new here.'

I smile. 'Okay!'

'It's like . . .' he takes another bite, stands up and walks around the kitchen as he eats '. . . running in the woods when we were younger, the smell of the coun-tryside around here,' he says, and bites again. 'Just like here, children playing in the streets. It's like the sing-ing in the streets, the sunshine and the smell of the coffee houses. This is . . . this makes me feel I'm at home,' he says, and his eyes sparkle with little tears. 'You're right. This is me! You know me well. It's my life, here.'

'Then why not make these pizzas?' I ask.

He stops eating and puts down the pizza, wiping his hands with a napkin. 'Because maybe you're not the only one who has spent the last few years looking to be anywhere but here,' he says quietly.

Looks like the elephant in the room has just sat right in the middle between us and is here to stay.

'Maybe I needed to prove to everyone around me that I could succeed in something, where I'd failed in others.'

He looks straight at me and my body aches for him to hold me. It takes every ounce of my self-restraint not to lean into his chest and go back to where we used to be. But I won't. I stare at him. His lips, his eyes . . .

'Come on, I'll walk you home,' he says, standing and turning away from me. And this time I don't argue. It's for the best.

'Thank you for my pizza. Thank you for the mem-ories it brought me,' he says.

And with that he holds my gaze. I can't tear myself away from his dark eyes.

Then, slowly, he reaches out a hand towards my face. I watch it as it comes towards me and suddenly flinch away, no idea what he was doing on the unknown territory we'd walked into. He doesn't drop his stare or his hand and waits for me to move back to it, waiting for me to come to him almost. I can smell him. Smell the woodsmoke on his skin. For a moment, we stare at each other, looking for signs of how the other is feeling. Then he smiles. And with his other hand he points to the corner of his mouth. 'You have some sauce,' he says slowly, making the word sound like something so much sexier and reminding me of when we first got together, how I felt as if I was on fire, excited, and with one touch he could melt my insides.

'Ah,' I say, blushing. What did I think he was going to do? He wipes at the sauce in the corner of my mouth, then licks the tips of his thumbs and wipes it again, only this time he leaves his hand there. My heart is racing and I'm really not listening to my head. I shouldn't be doing this. I really shouldn't! This is a mistake, yet it feels so right and I can't not. It's like some kind of magnetic pull, too strong for me to fight. And slowly, very slowly, not dropping each other's gaze, I turn my mouth to the palm of his hand and breathe in his familiar smell, like it's a place I've tried to forget, and missed, but never fully forgotten. I press my lips to it and close my eyes, letting time stand still. Then I feel his face move towards mine. I should stop right now. I should leave. I open my eyes, to see his close to mine, the memory of a life back then full of hope and excitement, my body feeling alive.

I can't stop. I lean in and kiss him on those lips, tasting of sauce, woodsmoke, reminding us both of happier times, of children in the street, of singing and trips to the sea. As I kiss those lips, and he returns the kiss, I can't stop, no matter how much I know I should as his familiar form wraps around mine.

THIRTY-TWO

We walk home slowly, through the piazza, my arm tucked through his, as everything closes for the evening, families and groups of friends dispersing. The warm air smells of coffee, smoke from the *forno*, and wisteria on the summer breeze. We hear music playing from one of the apartments overhead. As we reach the door to Nonno and Nonna's apartment block, Giacomo kisses me on the lips once again and my body immediately responds. I wish it didn't. I have no idea what this means to us, or the competition for that matter. No idea at all. Then, with a final touch of my cheek, he turns to leave. I watch him go, wondering what he's thinking as tears slide down my cheeks, sadness for what we lost.

I watch him, shoulders slumped. Why so sad? Why can't he tell me what he's thinking, how he's feeling?

I'm suddenly frustrated all over again, just like when we broke up. Why can't he just say what's on his mind? Did that mean nothing to him? Because it didn't feel like nothing. It felt like everything! And what did he mean when he said he'd spent years not wanting to be here either? Whatever he meant, one thing is for sure: I don't want to go home. But I have no idea if I should stay! Was that closure? Was that a final goodbye? Can he now move on and commit to somebody else?

I creep inside. Nonna is asleep on the chair, waiting up for me, and I feel bad. She wakes. 'A good night?' she asks.

'Yes, it was . . . a good night.' My cheeks are burning.

I say goodnight to her and usher her to bed, still feeling bad that I kept her up late. But it makes her happy to know I'm home and safe.

I lie in bed. My nerve endings still standing to attention. Still listening to the sounds of the street below, the occasional passers-by and the bars closing for the night. What on earth just happened there? It's like no time has passed at all. And why am I wishing it could happen all over again right now? And why do I think everything has suddenly got horribly complicated? This is the last thing either of us needed. What on earth is going to happen now?

THIRTY-THREE

'Where is your head this evening, Lucia?' asks Nonna, as I misplace the sauce spoon the following evening, forget to check the *forno* and only just save the fire as the first of the evening's diners arrive.

I'm all over the shop. That's how my mother would describe me, I think, hearing her Welsh expression said in her Italian accent. I check on the rising dough balls Veronica has pulled from the walk-in fridge to let them come up to room temperature. As I walk by the end of her work station by the pass, I peep out through the small, clear circle in the frosted-glass door and watch Giacomo as he starts to prepare his dough, laughing with Carlo. Suddenly he looks up at me and smiles. I smile briefly and blush, feeling as if I've been lit up from inside.

'So, who's on what this evening?' I ask quickly.

'We're still a waiter down so we're all going to have to pitch in again.'

'I may know of someone who needs the work,' says Veronica.

'And I could ask around,' says Sofia.

'As long as they understand that, as far as everyone's concerned, it's still Nonno in the kitchen, until we tell them otherwise, when we've had the chance to prove ourselves,' I say, more buoyed up than ever.

And then I think of Giacomo. What if I do win the restaurant? What will he do? Where will he go? This was his shot at breaking out and going it alone. Am I just stealing his dreams if I stay? And if he goes, will I want to see him again? We agreed, whoever wins, the other leaves.

I take another look at him, and sigh. Last night was . . . fabulous, amazing. But perhaps that was all it was. Just one night to get it out of our systems. The elephant in the room. But if that's the case, why do I feel the elephant is still wandering along behind me everywhere I go?

The restaurant is filling.

'I'll take orders,' says Veronica, picking up the pen and pad, whipping off her apron and dusting off any flour. She lifts her head high and walks out through the big swing door.

I check the *forno* and the sauce, of course, just as Nonna has taught me. Despite her protestations I pack her off home, telling her we'll manage. Although I'm not sure we will.

Veronica comes back into the kitchen, the door swinging violently behind her. She looks as white as a sheet, her earrings swaying and finally settling. 'What's up?' I say, as she stands there.

She shakes her head. 'Nothing, nothing,' she says, and drops her head. Then she lifts it and takes a deep breath. 'I should be used to it.'

'Used to what?'

'Seeing people.'

'What people?' I frown.

'Clients,' she says, and the penny drops for me. I don't even think about her past line of work. She's so good as a sous-chef – it's like she's done it all her life.

'Oh, Veronica,' I say, stepping forward, as does Sofia.

'It's fine, it's fine.' She sniffs. 'Like I say, I should be used to it.'

'Who is it?' asks Sofia, looking through the circle of clear glass.

'There, with his wife. Sitting at the table next to the woman who was in last week, the journalist. The one on her own in front of Giac.'

'The mystery diner!' I say, and peer through the window, forgetting about Veronica's blast from the past.

'She's back.'

'Well, in that case, we'd better make sure she orders off our menu tonight.'

'The table next to her will,' says Veronica, lifting her head. 'I'll let him know we all have secrets that we wouldn't want spilling!' She struts out towards the table where her ex-client is sitting and speaks to him quietly in his ear as we watch from behind the glass.

The single diner next to her, in front of Giacomo, looks at her and flips her menu over to read it.

Veronica stands over her, while she orders.

'I explained that the inside kitchen makes more traditional pizzas, while Giac makes the new flavours out here. I said our traditional menu was just as good as Giac's new ideas. The best. She's ordered the anti-pasti and the Margherita.'

'Yes!' I find myself high-fiving Veronica. 'If we can get publicity for Nonno's traditional pizzas, like Giac got for his, we're still in the game. She doesn't need to know it's not Nonno cooking her pizza.'

Veronica splits her time between prepping the dough for me to add the toppings and slide the piz-zas into the raging hot *forno* and taking orders. Sofia serves the food, clears tables and does desserts. It's all hands on deck and the washing-up is stacking up. But now's the time to push, and we all help each other.

Suddenly Nonna slips back into the kitchen. 'Nonno fell asleep watching the news, so I slipped out for a bit.' She starts on the washing-up. I'm so grateful, I don't even tell her to stop. The kitchen is working at full capacity. We're all focused on our jobs.

Suddenly a woman is standing at the door, holding a plate. '*Ciao*,' she says, and I freeze. We're so busy, no one has noticed her come in.

Nonna, Sofia, who is dishing up tiramisu, and I stare at her. Just as she is staring at me, by the *forno*, my bandanna low, chef's whites on, sleeves rolled up and no doubt flour all over my face.

'Um.' She breaks the silence. 'I just wanted to offer my congratulations to the chef. My pizza was fantastic!' Her eyes are dancing as she takes in the kitchen.

'*Scusi*, sorry. Sorry, Lucia, I didn't see the customer come this way. This is private back here,' says Veronica, stepping in front of her to usher her out. And if it was me I'd do what Veronica says. But the young woman attempts to stand her ground.

'It's just . . .' She looks around again, as if committing each detail of the old, worn kitchen to memory, in complete contrast to Giacomo's very modern set-up in the courtyard. 'I wanted to congratulate the chef and you were all so busy.' I stand holding the peel. I've been caught red-handed. 'I was told . . . there was something unusual about this restaurant, that I should visit.' She smiles. 'I thought it was Giacomo, the master *pizzaiolo* and his new ideas, but I can see now it's not that.'

'Sorry, but we're really busy. Chef's . . .' I struggle to make something up. 'Nonno's had to go for a lie-down.'

'From what I hear, Nonno hasn't been cooking here for some time!' she says, and raises her neat eyebrows.

'We need to get on. Sorry, out of the kitchen.' Nonna bustles over waving a tea towel at her.

There's a shout from a customer to Veronica, wondering where their food is. The pizza on my peel is burning to a crisp.

'Look, let me help. I have experience,' she says, taking the two dessert plates from Sofia, who puts up a good fight to no avail. 'Honestly, let me help. I can see what's going on here. A woman *pizzaiola*. An all-women kitchen. I like it!' Her eyes sparkle. 'I can help.'

People are starting to notice the commotion by the door and I give a quick nod to Veronica to let her through with the plates. She's drawing attention to the kitchen, which is the last thing I want. When she comes back, I say, 'Um, sorry, what was your name?'

'Maria.'

'Maria,' I say firmly. 'No one must know. Not yet.'

She nods in agreement, takes out the next plates and suddenly the backing-up orders move through the kitchen much more swiftly, with Veronica on dough again.

And as we finish service for the night, I wipe my hands, send Nonna home and agree to sit down to talk to Maria, wondering what on earth has happened tonight and who told her.

THIRTY-FOUR

'It was you, wasn't it?' I ask Giacomo, my eyes narrowing as he comes into the kitchen. I ask Maria to wait in the restaurant. I'm furious. Someone has told her about me cooking here and about the kitchen.

'I swear it wasn't, Luce.'

'Last night was all about getting me onside, wasn't it, Giac? Lulling me into a false sense of security. Getting me to let down my guard, at the same time planning to get your journalist friend to out me! How could you, Giac?' I hold my hands to the bandanna on my head.

'Lucia! I swear!' he hisses, looking back to the restaurant to make sure we're not overheard.

'I'm the one swearing, Giac. Now I have to do everything I can to stop this woman writing an article on Nonno's all-women kitchen. How could you?' I pull off my bandanna and run my hands over my unruly tied-back hair.

'If you think I'd stoop that low, you really don't know me at all!' His eyes are dark and angry.

'I think we've established, Giac, that despite my dating you for most of my young adult life, being married to you for two years, no, I still don't know you!'

'Look, I thought we were working things out,' he says gently.

'I think we can safely assume that, with a journalist sitting out in the restaurant, wanting to tell the world about me and my all-women kitchen, we are definitely not working things out.' The words catch in my throat and I pull out the tea towel I keep in the pocket of my whites and swipe it in his direction. A little sob of frustration leaps out of my mouth, but I'm determined not to cry. Determined.

Giacomo steps forward and holds out his arms. More than anything I want to fall against the big, broad chest like I did last night, when everything seemed perfect. But I can't. That was yesterday and today is a different day.

'I'll go and speak to her, put her off the scent. Offer to take her out for a drink and explain she didn't really see what she thought she saw,' he suggests.

I step back from his open arms and turn away so as not to be tempted by that embrace again. 'I think,' I say slowly, composing myself, 'it's a bit late for that.

She knows everything. She knew to come back here to find out what was going on in the kitchen. Someone tipped her off, Giac. And who would really want to do that?' I say, in my steady, legal-team voice. 'Looks like you may have got what you wanted, Giac. You win!'

I take a deep breath and turn back to him with tears in my eyes. 'It's time, Giac. We both need to move on. We need to get that divorce.' I let out a long breath. If I hadn't been so focused on dotting the is and crossing the ts on everybody else's business plans, I might not have pushed my own to the bottom of the pile and we might not still think there is some kind of attachment here. We both need a clean break – and fast. After we split, we had no contact with each other and that suited me. Maybe I was just hiding from my hurt, burying myself in work, hoping it and he would go away. It and he did. But now he's back in my life, messing with my head and my heart all over again. It's time to cut the strings between us for good.

He glares at me. 'Fine!' He picks up his jacket and storms out of the back door, leaving me standing alone. Knowing I can't put it off any longer, I open the door and call after him. 'Giac! You don't get to walk out on me again. I'm the one calling it this time. We need to talk.' But he's gone, the back gate still shaking in its frame. I sigh, hear a soft miaow and feel fur against my ankles under my chef's whites. The little black cat is weaving herself around them, her tail high.

I bend to stroke her head. She lets me, purring. I straighten and go back into the kitchen, only this time the little cat follows me, venturing bravely into the unknown, moving out of the shadows, where she's been hiding all this time. Then there's the scraping of a chair on the tiled floor in the restaurant. She flicks her tail and rushes back outside where she came from, spitting as she goes.

I turn back to the door of the restaurant and to the waiting journalist. It's over. Everything. Me, me and Giac, this place. I'm beaten.

THIRTY-FIVE

'Look, I'm not here to cause trouble,' says Maria, coming into the kitchen.

I'm staring at the back door, wondering why the floor beneath my feet seems suddenly to have turned to sand and I can't quite get my balance. But I will. It's time to move on. Last night was amazing. I have no idea why Giac makes me feel the way he does. But he does, and I know I'll never feel like that with anyone else. But it's time to move on. I want this restaurant and a new start as much as he does. And if this is how he's going to play it, I can't let him stand in my way.

'Look, thanks for your help tonight but, really, I'm not sure what you want from me. My grandfather, Nonno, it's his place. He's the chef. I'm just standing in for a bit.'

'You're not Italian, then?' She tilts her head.

'I'm . . . It's complicated,' I say.

She looks around. 'I heard Nonno's retiring and looking to hand this place on,' she says. 'Do you want to tell me about it?' She helps herself to the red wine on the table and pours us each a glass. I sigh and follow her as she takes hers to a table in the courtyard, where the wrought-iron gates are now shut and bolted for the night.

The sounds of the night in the apartments above, the windows open to the warm night air, the orange glow of the streetlights: I love this place.

'Yes,' I say, gathering my thoughts, taking a sip of wine and sitting opposite her. 'And Giacomo is here to work up new ideas . . .' I wonder how to say this '. . . with a view to taking it on.'

'Yes, and he's great, Giac, lots of brilliant ideas. You might have seen my piece in the paper.'

I nod. 'You're the mystery diner.'

'And from what I heard, there's a fantastic story in the kitchen that my readers would love to hear about.'

'I'm sorry.' I push away the glass of red wine. 'I can't help you. Like I say, I'm just helping out.'

'I've been told it's a competition, a straightforward winner past the post gets the restaurant.'

I say nothing, then pick up the glass again and take a big slug. The wine's peppery blackcurrant flavour fills my mouth and warms my throat as I swallow, hard.

I shake my head. 'I don't know what you think you know, but there's no story here. The only story is Giac,'

I say, knowing I'm handing him the baton to sprint home. But what can I do? I can't reveal the story or Nonno will be forced to sell. The very last thing he wanted to happen. 'He's the newsworthy one. He is doing some amazing new recipes. Have you seen his menu?' I look around for one. 'But of course you've seen it,' I say, waving a hand, still trying to distract her.

'And what about your kitchen crew? Is it true it's all women? That you want to be the first *pizzaiola* in these parts? Can you tell me more about your kitchen? Are you worried people will treat you or your food differently?'

'No, I'm sorry, I can't help you. I have to go now. Check on my grandfather, you understand.' It's a statement, not a question. I've learnt how to say nothing, and never to ask questions to which I don't want answers. Maybe that's why I'm scared of asking Giac how he's feeling, how he felt about me. I'm scared I won't get the answer I want.

I stand up, show her to the gates and unlock them.

She hesitates, then takes out a card and puts it on the table. 'If you change your mind, I'd love to write your story.'

I open the gates. 'There's no story, really. As I said, Giac is the big news around here.'

'Well, if you want to tell me your side of the story, I'd love to hear it.' She smiles. 'And your pizza is excellent.'

I have to smile. '*Grazie*,' I say.

'A real traditional pizza. You've learnt well.'

I thank her again. And, strangely, I can't help but like her. 'I'm sorry I can't give you what you want,' I say again, and bid her goodnight. As she dips out through the front gates I suddenly have to ask, 'Maria? How did you hear?'

She smiles. 'A friend of my second cousin. Said he'd worked here his whole life since leaving school. But things had changed. He couldn't work like that any more. Said he'd walked out.'

'Dante!' I say, and she nods.

'He knew I was working for the paper. Said he had a story I might be interested in for a small fee. I refused the fee,' she says. 'Thought I'd come and find out for myself.'

Not Giacomo. It was Dante all the time. Gah! I'm furious with myself and with Dante. 'For the record, I sacked him,' I can't stop myself saying.

She nods. 'Sounds like you do have a story to tell.'

I bite my lip. I shouldn't have said anything. I should know that.

'Especially with you and Giac being married!'

She heard us arguing, me saying I wanted a divorce. But it's been seven years since we separated.

I say goodnight, lock the gate and hold my forehead to the cool metal for a moment. This journalist knows more than I want her to. What if she writes about us anyway? Now what am I going to do?

THIRTY-SIX

Back at the apartment, Nonna is dozing in the upright chair in the soft lamplight. She wakes. 'Ah, Lucia. You're late,' she says. 'You want something to eat?' She gets up stiffly from her chair by the balcony.

'No, I'm fine, Nonna. Let me get you something,' I say.

'No, no, it's fine.' I'm beginning to see where I get it from. 'If I'm not moving and feeding others, I'll sit down and never get up again!' she says, and I realize that that may be why she's in such good health. Cooking for the family, for others, even Nonno, gives her day structure, routine, movement. It's as important to her to feed the ones she loves as it is to be fed.

'Now, what can I get you?' She ignores my refusal of food.

'Really, Nonna.'

'What about some pasta, a bit of tomato sauce with

red pepper and aubergine, and some cheese?' She smiles. It's what has kept her young and happy, just like the happiness I have found in feeding people at the restaurant.

I give in. 'That would be lovely,' I say, and I know it will. Her sauce is always lovely.

'I got the cheese from Nonna Emilia earlier today. If you like it, I can get it for the restaurant.'

I sit down at the table and she pours me wine, then lays a plate in front of me. She puts out one for herself, but I think she does that to encourage me to eat.

'Is everything okay, Lucia?' she asks, as she sits with me and pours herself just an inch of wine to keep me company.

I sigh. What can I say? That I kissed Giacomo, then accused him of telling a newspaper reporter about me, and that I feel it's time for him and me finally to say goodbye, get round to signing those divorce papers, for both our sakes. That I know he's going to win the competition because he has clearly sold far more pizzas than I have. Nonna would know: she's been keeping the tally since Dante went. Or that a journalist is about to reveal everything about the competition and I have no idea where I'll go or what I'll do, now I've discovered my vocation as a *pizzaiola*, if I can't fulfil it.

More than that, though, I'm terrified that Nonno will have to go through with his plan to sell the restaurant if anyone finds out about me and the competition. I'll have ruined everything. It was me that insisted I get the chance to prove myself. If this story comes out, he'll have to do as he said he would and sell the place. I can't bear it! It will be my fault! I feel more stressed now than I did in all my time as a business lawyer, where I worked long hours, tried to prove that I was harder-working than all my male colleagues, meeting deadlines and proving my worth. Right now, I'm about to lose everything and maybe everyone I care about. Does that include Giac?

'You have things on your mind,' she says, serving me with freshly cooked pasta, aubergines, peppers and thick tomato sauce. Suddenly I'm ravenous. I put a forkful into my mouth. It fills me with comfort and joy. 'How do you make it taste like this, Nonna?'

'Because I make it with love.' And that's it. She gets up early to cook the sauce, to make the pasta, to get the best ingredients. 'Everything you have been doing at the restaurant. That's why people love it, just like they did when Nonno was there,' she says. 'Love it like the *sugo*. Keep an eye on it. Remind it you're there and give it the attention it deserves. Never forget it and who it's for.' She smiles. 'Tell me, Lucia, what's on your mind?' She puts her old arthritic hand over mine, her wedding ring on her finger, stuck there, no way of taking it off. Mine had barely lost its shine before it had slid into the zip-up pocket in my handbag. It's been there longer than it was on my finger.

I have no idea how to tell her any of what is going on in my head.

'Have you changed your mind?' she asks.

'Not about the restaurant, no. I want it more than ever. I love being there.'

'Okay,' she says. 'And Dante has gone, so things are better.'

But for his troublemaking, I think.

'In life,' she says, 'it's good to try to see the positive in things. He may have made trouble for you,' she goes on, seeming to read my mind, 'but sometimes you have to look at turning a negative into a positive. Just like Nonno wanting to retire. I was worried I'd have him under my feet all day, but thank God for *bocce*! And for you being here.'

Tears spring to my eyes. I love her so much.

'Remember what I told you. You need to keep your friends close . . .' She gives me one of her firm stares.

'. . . and your enemies closer,' I finish.

'Take Nonna Emilia. She was after Nonno for years when we were girls growing up. If I hadn't made her my best friend, I might have ended up marrying someone else!'

I smile.

'Now . . . some tiramisu and coffee.'

I know there's no point in arguing so I sit back and sip my wine, knowing what I've got to do. Before I go to bed I text the number on the card and wait to hear back.

THIRTY-SEVEN

'I'm glad you could meet me,' I say, as Angelo, singing, delivers our coffees and *cornetto*s.

'I'm glad you rang me,' says Maria, putting her bag on the chair next to her and pulling out her notebook.

'You were going to run the story anyway, weren't you?'

She agrees. 'Yes. What can I say? It's an exciting story. A woman from Britain trying to follow in her grandfather's footsteps as a *pizzaiola*. This is groundbreaking stuff around here.' She looks up at the old apartments and the piazza at the end of the street.

'So I gather,' I say.

'I mean, the fact you're not even Italian . . .'

'I am Italian,' I correct her. 'My parents are, were, Italian.'

'Of course.' She makes a note. 'Were?'

She doesn't miss a trick. 'My father died young. My mother remarried. I grew up with my stepfather and mother in Wales. That's why I have a partly Welsh surname.'

'Ah.' She makes more notes and I feel like I'm putting all the pieces of my life onto the table, like a jigsaw, waiting for them to be slotted into place to see the bigger picture. I just can't find the missing piece or see it yet. All the colours are there but it's jumbled up.

'So, tell me about you and Giac.' Her pen is poised.

I take a moment to get my thoughts straight.

'If you want the real story of that kitchen, this competition, the restaurant, it's not just about me, or even me and Giac. It's a much bigger story.' I chew my lip. 'This is about finding your place in the world, dignity, respect. It's about all the *nonna*s who have cooked for their families, taught them to cook. It's about learning to cook with love. Learning to find and make a life for yourself from the skills we grew up with, and take for granted. It's about the soul and heart of the kitchen, not pizza acrobatics. It's about finding what you can do when you're in a corner, fight or flight.' I think suddenly of the little black cat at the restaurant, standing her ground, even though she's smaller than the other cats. 'It's what you do to survive and what you can do when you take away the fear of failure, start to believe in yourself and find out who you really are. It's the story of pizza and a *pizzaiola*.'

I take a deep breath. She's staring at me. Her pen hasn't moved.

'Wow.' She nods slowly.

'If you want the real story of the kitchen, the women of my kitchen, come and work for me as a waitress, just as a temporary thing, but so you get to understand the story and the women working there.'

'Okay, yes, of course! Look, I promise you, I can write a piece that will highlight all the things you talked about. About the rise of the *pizzaiola*.'

'Pizza-making is about tradition, the terrain and the craft,' I say, repeating my grandfather's words. 'It should not be about what sex you are or where you've come from. It's about you putting your story on the plate, wherever you've come from. It's about the love with which the food is made, and the pride that goes onto the plate. It's what you want your food to remind people of and the story it tells of where you're going in life.'

'Yes!' she says excitedly. 'I want to tell this story. The story of your kitchen and the story that is being served up on the plate.'

I'm finishing my coffee as Angelo sings to the balconies above and the young couple who have stopped calling to him to quieten down. They pick up their breakfast plates and walk inside. If they don't like it, they can always go somewhere else.

'If people don't want to hear my story or taste my

food, then so be it. But it will be my story and I do want it told. I want to inspire others to cook and take pride in making it their career and business. We'll have proved it can be done. With the kitchen staying secret, people are eating our food and enjoying it. No one knows where I came from or who I am.' Perhaps least of all me. 'But, for now, we have to let the food do the talking.'

She's scribbling again. 'I really want to write this piece.'

'Good,' I say. 'Well, I'll tell you everything you want to know about me. But, there's just one condition . . . You can write the story, about me and Giac.' I swallow. 'You can write about my food, but it mustn't be published until after the annual *bocce* tournament, here in the town, on the *bocce* court in the piazza on the thirtieth of August. It's the end of the competition. If I win or lose, it must be a fair competition. If word gets out before then, that I'm a woman, from Britain, the competition will be off. The restaurant will close and be sold.'

'Which is why Dante contacted me,' she says, putting down her pen.

'It looks that way.'

'Spite.'

'He wanted you to write about me being here so I'd lose the restaurant. He wanted to punish me for sacking him. Giac too.'

She sticks her hand out. 'You have my word. I'll write the story, and make sure it doesn't come out beforehand. I'd love to work as a waitress for you, even if it is just for the time being while I write the story.'

'Deal!' I say, and look up to Nonna, on the balcony above, hanging out the washing and smiling.

THIRTY-EIGHT

'What's she doing here?' Giacomo whispers to me that evening.

'We needed more waiting staff, and Maria's good . . . Look, Giac . . .'

He puts up a hand. 'Don't worry, I heard you. I've got it in hand. I've instructed the solicitor to raise the paperwork. You'll get your divorce. And it can't come soon enough. Now I have a kitchen to run, and a restaurant to plan when all this competition stuff is over.' He stalks off to the outdoor kitchen.

'Competition stuff!' I fume. I'll show him! I slam back into the kitchen where Maria is waiting with her apron on.

'Maria, meet the team!' I take a deep breath and introduce her. 'Now, everyone, we have pizzas to make!'

The adrenalin in the kitchen is as high as the apartment buildings around us when the first orders come in.

And I can't help but notice Giacomo, through the round glass window, watching Maria, his eyes following her around the courtyard and her smiling back at him.

'It's never too late to go for what you want in life.' Veronica cuts into my thoughts. I turn – she's watching me. 'Look at me. I was in the wilderness for a long while, but by taking a chance I got what I wanted. I'm moving apartment soon.' She smiles. 'It's not too late for you, too!'

'I know, and the restaurant is all I want,' I tell her.

She raises her eyebrows. 'If you say so,' she says, and turns back to read the next order.

'I do,' I say, with a final glance at Giacomo through the window, and then I'm back at the big work table, with the dough I'm preparing. I knead it like I've never kneaded before.

The following day I decide we should all sit and eat together, before service, just like Nonna did with Nonno, making lunch for him and the restaurant staff at the apartment. 'You cannot work on an empty stomach.' I repeat her words and insist that she and Nonno join us. Nonna makes the pasta, and I make the sauce.

'You look quite at home here,' Nonno says to Nonna, as she finds her way around the kitchen.

'I've been a part of this restaurant for as long as you have, you fool!' She laughs.

'You are right. Without you, there would be no Nonno's. I took the glory as the *pizzaiolo*, but it was you who kept me going, ran the home, the family, fed us all and let me concentrate on this place. You are the heart of this kitchen,' he says, and kisses her hand. I wish, I wish— No, I don't wish it. That ship has sailed.

I look at Giac. 'Will you join us?' I ask, as we sit down to eat at a long table on the open terrace, but he puts up his hand to decline.

Nonna tuts and shakes her head. 'He cannot just cook food. He has to remember how to eat it, too,' she says, making him up a plate and taking it to him.

All I can do is remember the night we shared the pizza, feeding each other, tasting the tangy tomato sauce, the soft, creamy mozzarella, the peppery rocket and hints of chilli. Pizza Lucia. And then the taste of his mouth on mine, his touch, as if I'd come home. He's not joining us because he's angry with me for thinking he told Maria about the kitchen. I just want to build some bridges. But I can't if he won't even come to the table and eat with us.

Maria looks out to where Giacomo is working.

'We must be catching up with him now,' says Veronica. 'Sales must be fifty–fifty.'

'I'm sure of it,' says Sofia.

'Patience, ladies,' says Nonna. 'Patience.'

I have no idea. I only know that I want this more than ever. I look out over the terrace to Giacomo at the outdoor kitchen. I want to explain that I know it wasn't him who tipped off Maria, but every time I try, he walks away, confirming the boundaries in the restaurant between us.

We finish our pasta, then return to the kitchen and our jobs for evening service. I start chopping mushrooms for the Quattro Stagioni. Maria is clearing and laying the tables. She's turning out to be an excellent waitress. She has a little more subtlety about her than Veronica, who likes to tell people what they should be eating and from which side of the menu. Maria has a great way with customers, and charms them. No wonder she's good at her job. Giacomo seems confused by her presence . . . or is it that he likes her as much as she appears to like him? It's not my business any more, who he likes or goes out with. I don't care.

If only that were true. If only I didn't care, I think, as I chop the mushrooms with ferocity – and catch the tip of my finger, just as he swings through the doors to borrow some olive oil.

'Woah!' he says, as I drop the knife with a shout and clutch my forefinger, blood seeping through my fingers.

He's in front of me before I can stop him, cupping my hands in his. 'Here.' He leads me to the sink and runs cold water over the injury, cooling my finger and calming my racing pulse – I don't know if that's down to the shock of the cut or being so close to him. I haven't been so close to him since the other night, when we kissed just like we were young and in love again.

'Hold it and hold it up,' he says, sitting me on the stool.

I am feeling lightheaded. 'What?'

'I'll get a plaster.' He turns to the first-aid kit and I watch him pull out a packet.

'Stupid mistake,' I say, cross with myself for not concentrating but instead wondering whether something is going on between him and Maria.

He nods, and I wonder if I was talking about the cut or the other night.

'It can happen to anyone,' he says, focusing on my finger, but his closeness is making me shiver. I want this to be over. I can't be this close to him, feeling as I do. And how is that? a voice asks in my head.

Now is the time to tell him, while he's wrapping my finger and can't just walk away.

'I know it wasn't you, Giac,' I say quietly, gazing at the top of his dark head.

He doesn't look up from my finger.

I clear my throat. 'I know it wasn't you who told Maria about me, about the kitchen, the competition, Nonno retiring. All of it.'

He says nothing. Finishes sticking the plaster to my finger. I look at it and, more than anything, I want him to kiss it better, like he would have done back then.

'*Bene*. Good. By the way, I've spoken to my solicitor. He's getting the paperwork together for us to sign,' he says, packing away the first-aid kit.

I have no idea what to say. This is what I wanted, isn't it?

Suddenly he turns to me, as if to say something, but I beat him to it. 'What happened, Giac? To us?'

He looks down. 'Life, Lucia. Life happened and got in the way.'

'We used to have fun,' I say.

He smiles. 'You were always fun,' he says.

'I can still be fun!' I say indignantly.

'Really? When was the last time you had fun? When you were in your office back in Cardiff working hard to climb up the legal ladder? Nonno's kept me up to date with all your news.'

I never knew. 'Nonno told you how I was?'

'Always. After your Sunday phone call.' He smiles.

'You knew what I was doing,' I repeat, my mind whirring. So, if he knew what I was doing, was it just a coincidence that he arrived the morning after I did? No. It couldn't have been.

'Sounds like it was all work and no fun.' He checks his handiwork on my finger.

'I have fun!' I say, not quite sure why I find it surprising that Nonno had kept him informed about my life back home, or why I should care.

'Sounds like you do nothing but work. Even now,

here, you're so focused on making sure nothing changes in this place, working to keep things the same. There's no room for fun,' he says.

'And you always ignored the here and now, happier to be looking at making big plans for the future.'

'But we did have fun.' He's moving away – and, I have no idea why, I don't want the moment to end.

'I told you, I can do fun!' I stand up, my head dipping and swaying – maybe it's the rush of blood. He turns slowly towards me. 'If you won't come to the staff lunch and eat with us, let me show you how sorry I am, then I'll bring it to you. Meet me here, tomorrow, lunchtime.' I shiver and feel as naked as the day I was born. What if he says no? What if he laughs? What if he doesn't turn up? What on earth am I doing?

And, slowly, he shakes his head. 'I don't think that would be a good idea, do you?'

'No,' I say quickly, 'of course it wouldn't.' He's clearly referring to the last meal we shared with each other and how that ended. Never again! I've moved on. And so has he. I feel a rush of embarrassment and disappointment, fury too, for even suggesting it when clearly it's not something Giacomo wants to repeat.

THIRTY-NINE

That night, after work, I'm determined to have some fun. What do people do for fun these days? I could watch a film on Netflix or read a magazine or a book. Nonna goes to bed, having fed me and assured herself I'm fine. I open a bottle of wine and pour a glass. I sip and run a finger along the bookshelf. There's very little I fancy, until I spot them on the bottom shelf. The photo albums! I pull them out and open them. Pictures of when I was young, with my brother, and pictures of my dad too. I pour another glass of wine and pore over them. I pull the next off the shelf and open it. I'm brought up with a jolt. It's me and Giac . . . our wedding.

I don't know how long I'm there, slowly turning the pages, not wanting to see the photos, but not wanting to look away. I top up my glass again. God, how we've changed.

*

'Lucia, wake up,' says Nonna. 'You've overslept. Everyone is looking for you!'

'What? What is it?' I look at Nonna's face. 'Is it Nonno?'

'It's the restaurant!'

Quickly I get out of bed, fuzzy-headed, eyes swollen, and bump into the furniture as I dress quickly and tell Nonna I'll meet her at the restaurant.

Everyone is there when I arrive. Sofia is wringing her hands. Veronica is sitting, her head hanging low. Maria appears to have silent tears running down her cheeks and is looking at me with huge sad eyes. Even Giacomo is there, his hands on his hips. I think of the pictures from last night. The wedding feels like it happened only yesterday, but also a lifetime ago.

'Lucia, are you okay?' he asks, as I push the dark sunglasses further onto my face and walk into the kitchen, nearly missing the step by the *forno*.

'Where have you been?' he asks. 'We've been waiting for you.'

'I was . . . out having fun,' I lie, wishing I hadn't drunk quite so much wine. I feel his body stiffen and him bristle. And he was the one who said I needed to live a little!

'What is it?' I ask, looking at everyone's sad, pinched faces.

Everyone turns to Maria.

'I'm sorry, Lucia, I really am. All of you!'

'What is it?' I say, impatient now.

Giacomo comes to stand behind me, his tall body against mine, his hand on my shoulder, and I see him look down at the paper on the table, open at a double page spread. I don't know what the words say. I can't read them through the dark glasses. But I can see the photograph and the headline, and I gasp. My head dips and sways, just like it did when I cut myself yesterday and the wound began to bleed – just like my heart is bleeding now.

FORTY

'You said. You promised,' I say quietly, whipping off my glasses and staring at the article.

'I know, I know, and I was going to keep that promise. I swear to you.'

'So?' I ask, feeling not so much shock but anger. 'Why didn't you? I trusted you! We have ten days until the *bocce* tournament.'

'What can I say?' Maria is taking short, sharp, shallow breaths. And I know you can never get any sense out of anyone when they're overanxious.

'Take a deep breath,' I say. I go to the fridge, get out the bottle of cold water, pour her a glass and hand it to her. Her hands are shaking, as are mine I notice.

'My editor asked to see the article I was working on. See how it was going. I told him there was a lot still to do on it. It was rough.' She sips the water. 'But an article was pulled at the last minute, a legal dispute featuring a big Mafia boss. So, he ran mine and told me afterwards.' She sips again. 'Sent out a junior reporter to get some more information on the kitchen team to "bulk it up a bit".'

She looks at Sofia and Veronica.

'It's not the story I wanted to write,' she says, sobbing. 'I wanted it to be a celebration of an all-woman kitchen. A celebration of the women who have grown up feeding their families and now are turning those skills into careers.'

'And what exactly is this?'

'More like a salacious piece of gossipmongering,' says Giacomo, in a low growl, behind me.

'The British Woman, the Young Widow and the Call Girl!' the headline shouts.

I look at the double page spread. The words jumble before my eyes and I can't read them. Not that I want to read any more. I know exactly what this article is. The very one I never wanted to be written. The one I tried to stop. The one that is going to ruin everything for all of us.

And then there is a furious shout and the back door is flung open.

FORTY-ONE

'So, this is where you've been when you said you were at Mass, praying for Paolo every evening!' It's Sofia's mother-in-law. 'We told you – you have no need to work. We can look after you!'

'But—' Sofia tries to get a word in. She fails.

Paolo's mother bustles in, her husband behind her.

'You have everything you need. Why do you want to hide away here, in a kitchen of all places?'

I open my mouth but Giacomo gives a little shake of his head. He's right. This is something Sofia needs to do, although the words and outrage are on the tip of my tongue. I dig my nails into my palms to stop myself stepping in.

I see Sofia take a deep breath and I'm willing her on, my fists tight. I watch her, holding my breath.

'I have everything I need, except my husband,' says

Sofia shakily at first, but getting stronger. 'You are the best parents-in-law ever, but without Paolo, well, I still need to be a family with my children. I want to provide for them. Not rely on you.'

She looks straight at them, and I want to hug her. I feel as if my chest is going to burst with pride.

'But we are your husband's family. It is what we do! We provide so you can stay at home with the children. We will look after you! You don't have to do this. People will think we cannot look after our son's widow and our own grandchildren.'

'People will think, people will think,' Nonna says, looking mutinous. 'So what will people think?' she says, her eyes flashing. 'What these women have achieved here is to be applauded. They should not be hiding away. They are brilliant cooks! Chefs! And it is the small-mindedness of this town, "what people think", that has stopped young women being happy for a long time.'

Outside, in the street, there is a catcall. My blood runs cold.

'Veronica!' I hear them call. 'Are you selling extras with the pizza?'

'It looks like what people think, no matter how hard we try to move on, will always matter,' Veronica says to Nonna. It's as if she's been hit in the stomach and all the wind knocked out of her.

She stands up and squares her shoulders, tears glinting in her eyes.

And then there is another shout from the street, a voice I recognize, sending the young men on their way and me into a sudden state of worry. Giacomo goes to the back gate and pulls it open. The young men see him and scarper by the sound of it. Then he opens the gate wide, and there, standing in the doorway, is Nonno, pale and tired. He steps into the kitchen and looks around, then at Nonna.

Then at Giacomo and me.

'This,' he holds up the paper he's carrying, and waves it crossly, ' is garbage,' he says, tossing it into the bin.

'Did you know about this?' Sofia's mother-in-law says angrily to Nonno, referring to Sofia.

'Pipe down, Angelina,' says Nonna. 'She's been working to build a life for herself and her family. You'd do the same in her shoes.'

'Yes, I knew about this. And what you've all done here is amazing. You've worked so hard, and I've been so proud of everything I've seen and heard. And, yes, Nonna, of course I knew you were working here too. Your Nonna Network is far looser-lipped than you hoped.'

And I swear Nonna blushes a little at her own duplicity.

'Lucia, you are my granddaughter and you have taken on the skills, the tradition, the craft like a true *pizzaiola*.'

Tears fill my eyes.

'And, Giac, you are like a son to me. You, too, a master *pizzaiolo*, taking the craft to a whole new level. It has been a joy to watch and hear about. Veronica – you will make a fine pizza chef one day. And, Sofia, don't stop baking and making your desserts. They are *magnifici*.'

He looks around at us and we smile. Maybe things won't be quite so bad.

He takes a deep breath. 'But you all knew how this was to work for it to be an even playing field. Word couldn't get out. In this town, people are narrow-minded. I had hoped to change that. Well, Lucia did. But now, I'm sorry, I'll have to sell. It's the only fair thing to do. None of this is fair any more. Lucia will always have to battle nonsense like this.' He points to the paper in the bin. 'How can it be fair with this kind of rubbish being written and spread around? The competition is over.' He drops his head.

There is a loud whooshing noise that sounds a lot like my dreams being smashed to pieces.

FORTY-TWO

'But, Nonno . . .' I say.

He shakes his head, his eyes wet with tears. 'What can I say, Lucia? I am a man of my word. Word is already out that I am retiring and the estate agent in town has been in touch.' He pulls his hands through his thick, white hair. 'I cannot make it fair now that this has happened.' He points to the paper. 'How can I choose who should take over?'

Maria lets out a sob. 'I'm so sorry,' she says quietly.

He pats her kindly on the shoulder.

'I wanted to write a piece celebrating your granddaughter and her team, her work here. I've done the absolute opposite and ruined your business.' She gives an even louder sob.

Angry tears fill my eyes and slide down my face. I

wipe them away quickly with the back of my hand. 'Is there nothing we can do?' I say quietly.

'Take it from me, keeping secrets never ends well,' says Veronica, shaking her head.

'How can I say who should get the restaurant? It was my only way to decide. You could both have a shot at cooking your own menus, seeing who sold the most. But now this! It's changed everything. You won't be given a fair chance, Lucia.'

I hear the back door open and shut, and distant cat-calls, and turn to see that Veronica has slid out into the street practically unnoticed. I couldn't feel any worse for her than I do. This kitchen isn't about where any of us has come from: it's about where we were going, and we were going somewhere. People loved our food, as much as Giacomo's. I'm feeling so angry. My fists tighten again.

Sofia starts gathering her belongings and is being ushered out by her in-laws.

'*Ciao*, Lucia, *e grazie*. It was great while it lasted. It made me . . . Well, it helped me. The first step is always the hardest. You made me realize there is still a life for me and my children without Paolo. I feel I'm going to be a better parent because of it.'

I can't speak or say the words I want to. I nod and hug her tightly. Then she leaves, her silent in-laws behind her, her two children waiting out in the yard, on the pile of wood, in the brilliant sunshine and, if I'm not mistaken, stroking the little black cat. I watch them through the open back door and overhear their conversation.

'Is it true, Mamma? You're a pizza chef?' says the little girl excitedly.

'Can you make tiramisu when we get home?' asks the boy.

'Of course. We can make it together,' she says, and rubs their heads, a tight smile on her lips – a bitter-sweet smile.

'Will you be working here some more?'

'No, not now,' she says, smoothing her hand round his cheek to his chin.

'You're a chef, just like Papa?' asks the girl.

'I'd like to be,' she says, 'one day, and I can show you what I make.'

'Can I be a chef like you?' says her daughter.

'I'd like that,' says Sofia.

'And me!' says her son.

'Of course,' says Sofia. 'Let's go and cook,' she says to them. 'Who fancies pasta and tiramisu for dinner? Who's cooking?'

'I am!' says the little girl, and looks back at me. 'Are you really a *pizzaiola*?' she asks me.

I have no idea how to answer. I'm right back where I started, not knowing who I am or where I'm going. 'I'd like to be,' I say.

'And me!' she says.

'Come on, let's cook,' says Sofia.

Sofia's mother-in-law stares at her, then smiles. 'And I shall stay out of the kitchen for once and lay the table.' They leave together.

Maria makes her apologies again.

'I hope you find what you want, Maria.'

'To be honest, I haven't been happier than I have been working here recently,' she says, then looks at Giacomo. He doesn't respond. He is sitting on the stool in the kitchen, looking down.

I slide off my bandanna and toss it onto the table. Maria, head down, slips out of the door.

It's just me, Nonno, Nonna and Giacomo.

'I'm sorry,' Nonno says again.

Giacomo stands up, stretching out his tense body. 'I understand,' he says sadly.

'What will you do?' I ask.

A smile tugs at the corners of his mouth. 'Go back to my family restaurant, try to carve out a space for myself there. Work alongside my brother and father.'

This was his chance to go it alone. Do what he had trained for all his life. Be the person the newspaper article showed him to be. One of the best in the area.

'*Ciao*, Nonno, Nonna.' Then he looks at me. 'Goodbye, Luce. My lawyer will be in touch with you.' He takes his jacket from the hook. 'You made a great *pizzaiola* by the way. You always did have the determination to succeed in what you set your mind to. At least now this place will stay the same in your memory for ever.'

But it's not the same. Everything has changed. And I like it. I liked Giac working in the outdoor kitchen, and I loved being here with Veronica, Sofia, Nonna and Maria. I've loved being here with Giac I realize, with a sudden shock.

He heads for the door, about to walk out of my life for the last time. The divorce lawyer will contact me.

'Wait!' I say. He stops, turns and looks at me, his eyes on mine. Nonno and Nonna turn to me and, actually, I'm not sure what I'm going to say. As if I'm being thrown a lifeline, I say, 'What about the *bocce* tournament? We can't let them down. Just let us do the tournament, Nonno. One last evening at Nonno's before you close up for good.'

He looks at Nonna, and although it may seem that he wears the trousers, I know who really does.

'One last night. We owe it to ourselves,' she says. 'One last night at Nonno's.'

But no one is in the mood to talk about a last night, and Giacomo leaves, walking out of my life for good this time.

'Giac, wait!'

'Take care of yourself, Luce.'

And I know he's just stopping himself getting any more involved, any more hurt.

We close the restaurant, turn off the lights, after a

final look around, and walk out through the courtyard to the gates, locking them behind us for what seems to be the last time.

'Let me do the *bocce* tournament, Nonno. I may not have succeeded here, but I do want to thank you for the chance. I know you were in an impossible position. But let me do the party.'

He touches my cheek with the palm of his hand. 'Cooking is in your blood. It is our craft, our tradition. Yes, do the party. It will be a wonderful way to say goodbye to the place.'

FORTY-THREE

'So, will you come back, get prepped over the next few days and help on Saturday night?'

I've spent the last week cleaning the restaurant, from top to bottom, packing away the pictures from the walls, of Nonno, his grandfather and my father. Even giving the place a lick of paint to freshen it up before the tournament, covering the stains where the pictures have been hanging, ready for the place to be sold.

Nonno couldn't bear to come in. Instead, he's focused on the tournament, on him and his team getting their game right. It's an annual event, and Nonno hopes to win back the title after a few years on the losing side. Nonna has been with me at the restaurant, and, when she wasn't cleaning and packing away utensils from the drawers that haven't seen the light of day for goodness knows how long, she has been cooking.

Huge amounts of pasta, sauce, pickling and bottling. You know things aren't good when Nonna is cooking up a storm like this one. I have a feeling I'm doing the same.

Between cleaning stints in the restaurant, I've still worked on pizza ideas and I have no idea why. I seem unable to stop myself thinking up topping combinations. And there, keeping me company, is the little black cat, strolling around the kitchen with her head and tail high, looking quite at home. And each day I keep hoping that Giacomo will come back to do the *bocce* tournament. But he doesn't. There's no word from him at all.

Now I'm in Sofia's in-laws' kitchen, Sofia looks at her mother-in-law. 'Oh, I don't know,' she says. 'The children like me being here and . . .'

'No, go! Go!' Her mother-in-law wrestles herself out of her chair. 'She's been cooking for us every day since she stopped working at Nonno's. Cakes, pastries, ice-cream. I'm getting fatter by the day! Go and cook for someone else!' She waves a tea towel in Sofia's direction.

'Well, if you're sure,' she says.

'I'm sure, I'm sure.' She shoos Sofia out.

'Yay! Mamma's a chef again!' shouts the little girl, bouncing up and down.

'And you'll be coming to the party, Angelina? You and the children?'

'That would be lovely. I shall enjoy seeing you at work, Sofia,' she says, and the children cheer.

I text Veronica and ask her to come back for one last event at Nonno's.

'Sure,' she replies, and says no more. I wonder where she is, who she's with, whether her old life is all she has right now, and my heart twists.

Back at the restaurant, a van is waiting with two men to take away the electric oven. My heart quickens. What if Giacomo is there too? But there's no sign of him and I'm disappointed.

I watch as it's bundled into the back of the van and suddenly there's a hole where that oven, Giac and his acrobatics should be.

Everything has changed.

I'm sitting in the courtyard, looking at the empty space where the outdoor oven was, then at my phone and Veronica's one-word message. Suddenly I hear the metal gates behind me squeak open. It must be the men who took away the oven, coming back for something. Or maybe Veronica, seeing how things are going.

I turn. And my heart leaps into my mouth. 'Giac!' My heart starts thundering and I feel as hot as the *forno* flames were when I worked in front of them in the kitchen.

'Hey,' he says, holding a brown envelope. 'Not interrupting, am I?'

'No, no,' I stutter. 'Just taking a moment to, well . . . taking it all in,' I say. 'Remembering.'

'They came for the oven, then?' He nods at the empty space. A space for his dreams of the future. 'Sorry I couldn't be here. Went to pick this up.' He's holding an envelope.

He joins me at the table. I don't jump up to kiss him. I have no idea how to greet him. I do the one thing Nonna would do. 'Would you like a drink? Something to eat?'

'No. I just came to drop these off,' he says, holding up the brown envelope.

My mouth goes dry.

'The divorce papers.'

But I knew that before he said it.

'Thought it would be quicker this way,' he says.

'Right.' I look at the envelope. 'I'll read them in a bit,' I say.

And neither of us knows what else to say.

'Maybe I'll take that drink,' he says, helping us over the awkward moment.

'Great. A beer?'

'That would be lovely.' He sits on the wrought-iron seat at the round table, in front of the outdoor work surface and where the oven had been.

I take the envelope with me and put it on the side,

by the packed boxes of framed photographs and pizza awards. I grab two cold beers from the bar and put them on a tray with glasses. Then I go into the kitchen, where the little black cat greets me. I put olives into a bowl and look for something else to go with the beers.

I go back out into the courtyard with the beers and a platter of antipasti.

Giac smiles. 'In true Italian style,' he says. 'A drink is never just a drink!' And he takes the beer I'm offering him and a sundried tomato from the board. I sit down and we both stare at the outside kitchen, lost in our thoughts.

Then, finally, an idea comes to me. If this is our last service at Nonno's, if these are the last pizzas that will be made, they should go out the way they started here. I sit up straight. 'Giac?'

'Sì?'

'The old *forno* out here.' I point to it. 'Could it be used still?'

He stands up and walks over to it. His familiar body, leaning against it as he looks into and up the chimney. 'It'll need a bit of cement, maybe some new tiles,' he says, peering into it now with the torch from his phone, pulling off overgrown ivy. He dusts off his hands and takes the beer I'm holding for him.

'But it can be done, right? In time for Sunday night and the *bocce* tournament? When the teams come back here for pizza afterwards?'

'Yes, I think so. But why not use the oven in the kitchen?'

'Because this time I want my team to be cooking out in the open, for everyone to see. Loud and proud,' I tell him. 'We've nothing to lose. They'll be the last pizzas served here. Why not let everyone see the faces behind them?'

A big smile grows across his face. 'And would you have room for another *pizzaiolo* on your team? One last event?'

My smile expands. 'Really?'

'Really. Neither of us won, but we should go down fighting, together,' he says.

'Here to the end? We go down together.' We chink beer bottles.

'I'm not running away this time, Luce. I'm not bailing out before the end. We may not have made it, but let's celebrate what we did.'

And we stare at each other.

'Then let's get this pizza oven up and running. Show the world how we make pizzas here at Nonno's,' I say. 'The new and the old!'

'Let's finish what we started.'

'Might even be fun?' I smile. And I feel excitement fizzing through me, like the bubbles in my beer. Giac and me, in the kitchen, one last time, and I'm looking forward to it.

FORTY-FOUR

'Everything okay with you, Veronica?'

'*Sì*, all good here,' she says, her hair piled on top of her head, big earrings swinging, kneading the dough into balls with skill and speed, pushing the heels of her hands into them as she turns them on the floury work surface and lines them up in neat rows.

'Sofia?' I ask, as I stick my head out to the covered terrace. 'All okay? Tiramisu okay?'

Maria and Sofia are busy in the courtyard. It's hot, but shaded under the pergola, and it should be a beautiful evening, as August evenings are just before August slips into September.

'*Sì, sì,*' she says, her smile as wide as can be as she lays the long table with Maria, who texted me and begged to help. 'And my own homemade *gelato*!' She beams.

Maria is working and making notes on her phone at the same time. 'I want to write a piece about Nonna, *nonnas* everywhere, their role in nurturing our love of food, and how food is love. And how this place has been run on love for years. I want to celebrate Nonno's.' Of course I agree. But this time I get to see the copy before it goes.

I walk back through the cool white-walled restaurant that is now cleared of all the photographs, framed newspaper cuttings and trophies. It looks fresh, light and inviting. I push through the big wooden door back into the busy kitchen.

Nonna is preparing antipasti, while keeping one eye on the sauce, because that's where the love comes in, she reminds me. 'Keep it close. Keep an eye on it. Remind it you're there and give it the attention it deserves. Never forget it and who it's for.'

Suddenly Nonno arrives in the kitchen, through the back door. 'Catastrophe!' he says, holding his head.

We all turn to him.

'We're a player down! *Stupido!* Not only does he not play by the right rules, now Alfonso's fallen and broken his ankle. He cannot play!'

He's talking about his teammate. Much as he argues with him, they are a team and, without him, there won't be a *bocce* competition.

Veronica straightens. 'I used to . . . see a *bocce* player,' she says.

'Really? Do you think you could get him?'

'I'll sort it out,' she says, and goes back to kneading her dough.

'I'm going to get the mozzarella,' I say to Giacomo, working beside me in the kitchen. Nonno, placated, dashes out again to tell the rest of the team his news.

I open the big walk-in refrigerator door and step inside. I love this fridge. Its chill is so refreshing compared to the heat outside and in the kitchen. I run my hands over the produce. The salads, peppery rocket, cucumbers and watercress. The aubergine for roasting as a topping, the artichokes. The big piece of ham, ready for slicing.

'Hey, Luce, pass me the Parmigiano, would you?'

Giacomo is filling the doorway.

'That one up there!' He points over my head. 'Don't worry, I've got it!' He reaches and I hold my breath.

'What's that?' he asks, picking up the cheese next to it.

'Oh, the Caerphilly!' I joke. 'Mum sent it to me in case I was missing it from home. I love cheese.' It's true. Mum really did send it to me after I phoned her about the newspaper article and how Nonno was going to sell the restaurant after all. Typical of my family. When you're happy, you celebrate with food. When you're sad, you commiserate with food. I give a small smile. 'Try it.' I break him off a piece and hand it to him. He's still reaching above me and opens his mouth for me to pop it in. I do, and shiver. And it's not just the cold in the refrigerator.

'Hmmm, good.' He sounds surprised. 'Got it,' he says, finally grabbing the cheese he's after from the top shelf. I can start to breathe again as he stops reaching over me.

'Here, try this one.' He breaks off a piece and I'm not sure whether he's going to feed it to me or I just take it. He holds it out. Neither of us says a word. Then I hear a tut. Nonna is muttering about doors being left open, and the refrigerator door slams.

'What? Wait! Nonna?' I call, and push past Giacomo to the big door and put my hands to its cold walls. 'Nonna? It's Lucia! I'm in here!'

I turn to him – and then the light goes out.

I stand, frozen to the spot.

'Giac?'

'I'm here!' he says.

'Do you have your phone?'

'No. Why would I bring my phone to the refrigerator?' he says. 'You?'

I shake my head.

'I can't see you, but I'm presuming that's a no,' he says, and I feel him next to me now. I can smell him. I'd know that smell anywhere. He bangs on the door.

'Hey, Nonna?' He bangs again, but she doesn't hear us. The others are in the courtyard.

'Someone will come soon, Luce, don't worry. They

must realize we're missing. Or someone will want something.'

'Who's worried?' I say, with a tremor in my voice. It's cold in here. Really cold. And dark.

I bang at the door again and shout. 'Oh, God! What about the party?' I start to panic.

'It's fine, we have time. Don't worry.'

'I'm not worried!' I say, then let out a long, deep sigh to calm my nerves. He's still standing right next to me and I don't know how to move away or even if I want to. It's cold in here and we're only wearing short-sleeved chef's whites.

'Sit down,' he says. 'Save your energy. Someone will come. These things have a habit of working themselves out.'

We stand and wait. And listen and wait. And wait . . .

Eventually I slide down the door. I wish I could be as optimistic as he is. All that work, and now this.

He sits down next to me. 'Cold?' he asks. I can just make out the outline of his face as my teeth start to chatter. Without asking any more, he puts his arm around me, and pulls me close. I want to argue, but I can't. Too cold.

'If I had to get stuck in here with anyone, I'm glad it was you,' he says, catching me off-guard. I still can't really see his face. I lean my head into his shoulder.

'And I'm glad it was you,' I say quietly. 'You know how much I hate keeping still.'

'You were always on the go somewhere, doing something. Redecorating or redesigning the garden.'

I shrug. 'Life's short. We shouldn't waste it. I know that from Dad dying so young.'

Suddenly the elephant snuggles in between us, and there really isn't room for him in this small space.

'What did go wrong between us, Giac?' He lets out a long sigh. I feel his warm breath on my head, down my neck, on my skin and it tingles. 'Why didn't we make the distance? Why did you let me go, Giac?'

He sighs again and at first I think he's not going to say any more. And then, to my surprise, he does.

'Because I knew I couldn't make you happy. You were unhappy here. I didn't know how to make you happy once you couldn't get work. I thought I wasn't enough for you.'

'But I could have been happy. I was like Sofia. I didn't have a place, or a role. Everything was done for me. I was shown how to clean and cook by your mother. How to iron your socks! Given instructions on the dishes you liked to eat!'

He laughs and I do too.

'I'm not even sure I liked those dishes,' he says.

'I needed to be me. The woman you fell in love with. Not just a baby-making machine, with everyone waiting for me to be pregnant as soon as we married. I wasn't ready. I just wanted it to be us for a while.'

'And you're still the same woman, Luce. I thought I

was doing it for the best. I wanted you to be happy. I thought I should let you go.'

'You said you wanted us to split up. You said we should go on a break, that I should go home for a bit. But you never asked me back.'

'Because I knew I was never going to be enough for you. This place. Us. You had a whole other life there with your law degree. I was holding you back. You weren't happy.'

'It wasn't you, it was everything. I . . . I didn't know who I was. I moved out here. Your mother did everything for us. I tried to be the best person I could be, but I didn't know who I was any more. All anyone kept doing was eyeing my stomach and asking me when we were due! Giving me tips on how to get pregnant! I wasn't ready to get pregnant. I hadn't worked out who I was.'

'And you went home, and became a big business lawyer.'

I chuckle. 'I'm not sure I found me there either.'

'And now?'

'I know where I want to be and who I want to be. I just don't think it's going to be possible. *Phhffffff.*'

'Maybe it wasn't the right time.'

And I'm not sure if he's talking about our marriage or the restaurant.

'So, it really is over,' I say. 'Us, this place. Like you say, everything changes.'

'It does. Sometimes for the better, Lucia.'

I turn to see the outline of his familiar face. I wish I could believe him. I wish this wasn't all coming to an end. But it is and I can't think of any way to change Nonno's mind. And, really, would I want to? Would I really still want to take away Giac's dream of starting a place of his own?

'You could still find somewhere, Giac. Somewhere to start up on your own.'

I can see the outline of his face as he nods slowly.

'So could you,' he says. 'But I don't have the means to start up on my own. This was it. It was one of those rare opportunities that comes your way once in a life-time. But you could.'

'I don't think so.'

'You could, Luce. You could do anything you wanted to. You've already proved that here by doing this. I've never known the kitchen work so well. You want nothing to change, Luce, but you changed everything here. You did this! You are the bravest woman I know.'

'I'm nervous.' I'm shivering again.

'Why?'

'About tonight. Us working outside. Being true to ourselves. Maybe I should stick to cooking in the kitchen.'

He laughs. 'Let them see who the real chefs are! What is there to lose now?'

'Cooks,' I say.

'Chefs,' he corrects. 'You are as good as, if not better than, many *pizzaiolo*s I've worked with. Show them!'

I think for a moment. 'You're right. What do I have to lose? I'll be going home anyway now.'

'Home?'

I give a little laugh. 'Back to Wales.'

'And do you want to?'

'No,' I say. 'I want to stay here, run this place.' With you, I find myself thinking, just as it's been these last few weeks, but there's no way I can say it. We've come too far. There's no way back. 'What about you?'

He shakes his head and I wish he'd just say what he's thinking.

'What, Giac? What would you really like to happen?' I push and hold my breath, feeling a pitter-patter of excitement inside me and trying to quash it.

'It's been good. Doing this. Together,' he finally says.

'Ha! Even if we were in different kitchens and keeping to opposite sides of the table.'

He laughs. That laugh. His laugh. His smell. His closeness. His arm around me. His neck. His skin. His jawline so close I could just touch it, or even kiss it, I think, shivering, and he pulls me even closer. My body starts to ache for him, just like the other night. If I just put up my finger to his cheek, feel his face, run the finger along his jaw, to his lips, his mouth . . .

'You'll always be one of my favourite people, even when we get divorced. Friends?' I say.

He turns to me, and I can see the outlines of his eyes, his hair, his mouth. 'No, sorry, Luce. I can't do that.'

'What?' I say, pulling away from the comfort of the crook under his arm, beside his chest. 'What do you mean? We – we— Here. Not that long ago! So, I'm good enough for that, but not to be your friend?' I'm furious. I stand up and start to bang on the big fridge door again.

'Hello! Let me out! Before I kill someone with a leg of ham!'

'Luce, stop!' He stands up next to me and takes hold of my wrists to stop me banging on the door.

'I mean it!' I glare at him. 'If I don't get out of here, I won't be responsible for my actions.'

'Luce!' he says firmly, then takes a deep breath. 'I can't be friends with you.'

'So you said.'

But he carries on: 'Because I can't watch you every day and not be with you. I can't watch you meet someone new. Because it was always you, Luce. I've loved you every day since I met you. I never stopped. I'm sorry I can't be your friend. If I can't be with you, I can only be this, the person who's looked as if he really doesn't like you. Because that's the only way I can protect myself and my fragile heart. I can't be your friend. I have plenty of friends. I don't need more.'

Suddenly the door unlocks and we stand staring at each other.

He looks at me and me at him, in utter disbelief, and as the door opens a chink, he pushes it wide. Veronica looks as if she's about to shut it on us again. He makes his way out and, by the look of it, smashes down any bridges that I thought had just been built. We can't be friends because he loves me, I think, in astonishment. We can never just be friends. If we can't be friends, we can't be anything at all.

FORTY-FIVE

Even though I'm freezing cold, my hands shaking and my head all over the place, I get straight to work in the restaurant, as does Giacomo. I start to hang more fairy lights from the pergola with Sofia, while he goes straight back into the kitchen with a tray of rolled dough for the pizzas and we work side by side, silently, until everything is ready and the sun is lowering in the sky.

'They're here!' Nonno pops his head into the courtyard, excited and nervous. 'Veronica, you have a player for us?'

'*Sì, sì!*'

We all walk down to the piazza. There, under the big olive tree, the crowds start to arrive, families greeting each other. We pour from big jugs of Aperol Spritz, as orange as the sun in the late-afternoon sky, and hand round glasses on trays to the arriving families, orange juice and lemonade for the overexcited children.

So many faces I recognize greet me, welcoming me back.

Families gather under the shade of the big olive tree where we've laid tables with the jugs of drinks, bowls of olives and fennel-seed biscuits. The teams start to gather together. Nonno is looking nervously around to see if Veronica has found them an extra member. Honour is at stake in the annual *bocce* tournament, and Nonno is desperate to win the title this year.

'So, this is Nonna Teresa who grows the tomatoes. This is Nonna Pina with the artichokes. Oh, and this is her grandson. He's single.' Nonna's eyes twinkle as she reintroduces me to all her friends. 'Oh, and Nonna Emilia with the mozzarella is here with her son, Roberto, recently divorced. He's a bit older, but all his own hair still.' She's determined to make sure I meet everyone I haven't already met and any available men. Veronica comes over to save me by offering Roberto and the *nonna*s a drink. Even Roberto pitches in to avoid the matchmaking and helps take the glasses off Veronica's tray.

'*Grazie*,' she says politely.

'Oh, little Lucia!' says one of the *nonna*s, I can't remember which one. 'Are you the one who wants to be the *pizzaiola*?'

'Are you the one from Wales?

309

'Oh, you're the one who was married to Giacomo?'

'He's a good catch.'

'But they're not married now.'

'No?'

I can hear their questions and voices like a backdrop to the gathering party, all wondering about me, where I'm from, if I'm still married, whether I'm looking for a husband – and intrigue at my culinary aspirations . . . with more than a hint of admiration in their voices.

'We've cooked for our families all our lives, why not be a *pizzaiola*?'

'In Naples, yes, but here?'

The *nonnas* debate, discuss and argue about whether I could be a *pizzaiola*. And, to be honest, I'm beginning to wonder myself.

'This town needs to catch up with the rest of the world!'

'It's true. She's doing what we've been doing all our lives, using the fresh produce, passing on our recipes and traditions, our craft,' says another. 'It's time someone noticed who really runs the kitchens and passes on the craft.'

The women raise their glasses to me, to each other, and I suddenly feel quite tearful. I mustn't let them down. Tonight will be the best food they've tasted. Even if Giacomo isn't speaking to me. I look at him. He's under the tree, holding a branch in one hand, casually sipping a bottle of beer, as Maria smiles and chats to him. He looks at me, catching my eye, and I turn away, cheeks burning, lips tingling. Something inside me shifts. It was always him. Always. No matter how many legal cases I took on to block out the hurt, it never went away.

And then I see her and I'm catapulted back to those days when we were first married. She's arriving flanked by her other son, her husband, and two nephews. It's Giacomo's mother. As the sun is dipping in the sky, she and her family walk slowly towards the *bocce* pitch. As in a Western shoot-out, they move slowly towards the pitch. The sun is in my eyes, but I'd recognize her outline anywhere. Nonno and Giacomo's father greet each other warmly, as do his brother and nephews. His mother is much less enthusiastic. She kisses him on both cheeks, then looks straight at me. I haven't seen her since I left. But I've thought about her. She looks just as I remembered, perhaps a little plumper, her hair dyed a little redder.

Giacomo stands away from the tree and goes over to her. She returns her stare to me. This time, I'm not going to be intimidated. I've been working as a lawyer since I left here, and although I may be nervous inside, I'm not going to let it show. She's probably thinking I ruined her son's life. A dreadful wife who wouldn't do things *her* way. But I couldn't just fit into their mould of new young wife, waiting to produce grandchildren for them.

I have to do this.

I grab a glass and the jug, lift my head and walk towards her. Giacomo is standing beside her.

'Isabella,' I say, pouring a glass of Aperol Spritz and holding it out to her, my hand shaking only very slightly.

She reaches for it and her face breaks into a huge smile. 'Lucia, we've missed you! We all have!' she says, and hugs me hard, the drink sloshing out of the glass. 'You look so well. Older, a little fatter, but so well.' Still the same old Isabella, saying what she thinks. And I'm trying to process what she said. She's missed me! I thought she was glad to see the back of me! Thought she couldn't stand me! The young woman from Wales who couldn't fit into life out here.

'Oh, we miss having you around. I mean, you never learnt the recipes I tried to teach you and you never could iron socks, but Giac has never been happy since you were gone. We all miss you, you and your funny Welsh ways.'

If I think about it, that's a compliment. So I thank her.

'And I hear you've been helping Giac in the kitchen here.'

Suddenly Giac is standing beside me and I shiver, despite the warm, sunny, late afternoon. 'Luce hasn't been helping, Mamma. She's been running the place.'

Her eyes widen and her eyebrows shoot up. '*Really?*'

'Really,' Giacomo says firmly, and again, I'll take it as a compliment and enjoy the moment. Because I know, after today, everything will change.

*

The church bell strikes five o'clock. The local businessman – some might say Mafia boss – announces that the competition is about to begin. The teams are introduced and Nonno is still looking nervous. Veronica walks up behind him and stands with him and his other two friends.

'Veronica!' Nonno is clearly relieved. 'So, where is he? Our extra player. When will he get here?' he whispers loudly.

'They're here!' She smiles.

'*Magnifico!* Where?'

'Here,' she says, and again, he looks around, confused.

'It's me,' she says. Head and shoulders taller than the men around her in her high-heeled sparkling trainers and huge sunglasses over her thick, dark hair.

Nonno stares at her, as do his two friends. And me. 'You said you knew someone . . .' says Nonno in disbelief.

'I did. Champion *bocce* player. Taught me everything I know.' She grins as she lifts her head high and the competition begins.

'You smashed it!' I hug Veronica, as do Nonno and his two friends. 'You did it!'

'I did,' she says, with tears in her eyes. 'You gave me the courage to be me. Loud and proud!'

'And I'm proud!' We link arms. 'Now let's go and

cook pizza!' We walk back towards the restaurant before the rest of the crowd follows.

Giacomo joins us, as does Maria. Sofia kisses her children and tells them she has to go to work and they follow her as she heads to the restaurant.

In the courtyard, we take up our positions at our stations. Sofia is bringing out boards of antipasti to put on the tables, her children helping her. Local Parma ham, olives, soft mozzarella balls, small tomatoes that burst with flavour when you bite into them, all from the families of the network of *nonna*s, each raising a glass and celebrating their own and each other's produce as they sit at the long tables, family by family. The candles on the tables in jars are lit. The fairy lights illuminate the yellow lemons hanging through the greenery in the pergola. And the air is full of the smell of woodsmoke from the old *forno* in the outside kitchen.

Giac and I take our places by the *forno*.

We look at each other and say nothing, but my knees practically give way. Veronica gets to work on the dough balls. I pull out my bandanna and tie it around my head, as does Giac, making me smile. Then we fall into work as if we've been doing it all our lives: Veronica prepping the dough, Giac preparing the discs ready for the peel, me putting on the toppings and cooking them in the high heat. We work seamlessly together until all the pizzas are ready: crispy brown crusts, deep red tomato sauce and melting cheese bubbling on top. We add basil and drizzle them with oil, some just Margheritas, or simple Marinaras, then Parma ham and rocket, mushroom and artichoke. Veronica slices them and Maria spreads them along the tables. People reach over, helping themselves to slices, stretching cheese into strings as they hold a slice above their heads, biting into the crispy base, with that hint of woodsmoke.

As the pizza is finished and children move around the tables talking to relatives, who sit and drink from jugs of wine, topped up by Maria, the tournament results are announced by the local businessman, with a special round of applause to new champion *bocce* player, Veronica.

Then as she accepts her trophy and applause, as do Nonno and his winning team, we hand around desserts: Sofia's tiramisu and *gelato*, and we make Nutella and marshmallow pizzas, much to Nonno's surprise and delight. The children's too!

Giacomo's mother looks at me in amazement. I walk out from behind the work station and top up her glass with red wine. 'I never knew . . .' she says.

'Well, Isabella, I don't think you really let me show you. You wanted me to do things your way.'

'And you needed to do things your own way. I understand that now. I'm sorry,' she says. 'I drove you away and I am ashamed.'

I put my hand on her shoulder and squeeze it. It's

over, I think. This place has changed because I let it. Everything changes, including me.

As the desserts are finished, bottles of Nonno's homemade limoncello are passed up and down the table, and Maria serves coffee. Nonno stands and raises his glass, 'To the chefs! The food here tonight has been magnificent. Everything I could have hoped to pass on when I thought about retiring. Everything I don't want to disappear,' he says, as he sits down. There is a real sadness in his eyes as he looks around the full-to-bursting restaurant, the happy, tomato-smeared faces of children and adults alike. 'Pizza brings everyone together,' he says, and the community, who have all contributed something to the plates tonight, cheer. 'And to family.' They toast and cheer again. Nonno looks at me. I know he's turning it all over in his head and I wish there was something I could do to take away his anxiety.

As the guests leave, thanking us for a wonderful evening, I put a bottle of wine on the table with glasses and call Veronica, Sofia, Maria and Giacomo to join me. Nonno appears from the kitchen, holding a bottle and glasses, with the same idea.

'It was perfect!' I say. 'Thank you!' I add to all those around the table, including Giac, most especially him.

Nonno swallows. 'I've had an offer on the place. I have to let them know if I'm to accept tomorrow. Monday morning.'

He looks pained as we finish our drinks.

Later, he locks the doors on the restaurant for the very last time.

I wish there was something I could say or do to stop this sale going ahead.

Maybe there is . . .

FORTY-SIX

'Nonna's idea?'

'Giac and I agree,' I tell Nonno, the following morning, as he waits at the restaurant for the estate agent.

'No matter who wins, we both think this is the fairest way.'

'I don't know,' says Nonno, tentatively.

'This way, you don't have to sell it out of the family, so to speak. You'll see your legacy go on. Both Giac and I want that for you.'

'It's an excellent idea,' says Nonna. 'You've seen what they can both do. Give them a chance.'

'But I did that. I'm a man of my word.'

'Everyone deserves another chance. You're cutting off your nose to spite your face, you old fool. Imagine if I hadn't given you a second chance when I caught Nonna Emilia kissing you when you were nineteen.'

He blushes and I don't know where to look.

'Nonna Emilia?' says Nonno.

'Look what you could have ended up with!' Nonna smiles.

'What you're saying is, one dish decides all?'

'Exactly! We'll cook one dish for you, and you decide which is the best. Whoever wins takes over. We'll have lunch on the covered terrace.'

He looks at me. 'And Giacomo agrees?'

'He does. He doesn't want it to be a coffee chain or pizza franchise either. None of us do.'

Nonno looks around. 'Very well. One dish and one of you takes it over.'

'Yes!' I hug him and Nonna.

'And you really don't mind if it's not you?'

'I don't, Nonno. With what you started here, carrying it on is what's important. Everything changes, and I can't think of a worthier person to take it over than Giac.' His name catches in my throat, and tears spring to my eyes. It was always Giac. But everything changes. He would be perfect here. I realize that now.

Tuesday, the first day of September. It's hot, but not as punishing as it has been. There is a gentle breeze. The back door is open and the *forno* lit. There's no team helping us today. Just Giacomo and me. One dish each. I'm going to take the inside oven and him the outside so neither of us knows what the other is

319

cooking. The little black cat is wandering around as if overseeing things and giving her approval – I need to leave a note telling Giac to look after her. She likes pizza crust, but isn't keen on mushrooms.

As my pizza dough proves, I pick up my phone. I know what I have to do now. I know what's right for this place and everyone here. I text Mum, then book a flight back to Wales and a taxi for later. My case is packed and in the corner of the kitchen. It's better I don't tell Nonna in advance. I want her to think I've given this my best shot. But I know that this is what Giacomo needs to do, to step out on his own. As for me, I have no idea what I'll do from here. But I can't go back to my old job, that's for sure. Not after leaving in such a fury . . . and after the email I sent to the senior partner. I know those bridges are burnt for good. Anyway, I don't want to go back there. I need to move on. I wonder where we'll all be this time next year, next summer when I return home – I mean, here. Whatever home means.

But I do know now what I want in my life. I want to cook. I don't have to be scared of it. I can do it. I may not have everything I wanted in my life, and I look quickly at Giac as he practises his dough-throwing moves. He catches my eye. I blush and look away. But at least I leave here knowing I'm not going back to the office. I want to cook. And I can go in the knowledge that this place will still be here this time next year. Even if everything about it and its menu will probably have changed. At least it will go to someone who has the passion for pizza, like Nonno does, like all of us do. Someone who is respecting the traditions and the craft, and will use the local products from the terrain around here. This way, I know that the town I have always loved, and the food at its heart, will still be here when I return. The menu may change, the décor may change, but the heart of the place won't. Pizzas, made for sharing, with the simplest of ingredients, cooked and served with love. That's what counts.

I look at the ingredients in front of me. One plate, one pizza that says who I am and why I want this. I wonder what Giacomo is preparing. He's had notebooks out. Spent a lot of time thinking and tossing dough. I smooth a piece and, once again, try to toss it. This time, I catch it. Yes! Finally! I toss it again and again for the sense of fun and release it brings. Finally, I know it's time. I have to make my pizza and present it to the table.

Outside in the cool of the covered terrace beside the courtyard, Nonno and Nonna have arrived.

'Everything okay?' Nonna sticks her head into the kitchen.

'Yes, yes, but you mustn't be here. I must do this on my own,' I say.

She nods. 'I'm very proud of you, Lucia. Whatever happens today, you have proved that you have a heart the size of an ox! You love this as much as anyone and are as capable as anyone.' She winks with one spark-ling eye and backs out through the door.

Nonno comes in and kisses me. 'Good luck, Lucia,' he says. 'Your father would have been proud of you here today.'

My eyes glisten and he takes two jugs of wine out to the table to share. I can hear their voices. Everyone who matters is here. Sofia and the children. Veronica, looking gorgeous, softer, very little make-up, yet glow-ing. Maria is there, delighted with her article in the paper today, the celebration of *nonna*s and their food, and, of course, Nonno and Nonna. I follow with plat-ters of antipasti.

Finally I decide on my pizza and at the stroke of one o'clock, as the church clock strikes and the sun is at its highest, I wipe the sweat from my burning face and pull out the pizza. I inspect it. It looks pretty good, even if I say so myself. I breathe it in deeply. It's every-thing I love, who I am. The smell of home.

I walk out of the swing doors onto the cool terra-cotta terrace and see Giacomo at the outside kitchen in the courtyard. He looks up at me and stares, clearly worried.

'So, Lucia, what have you got for us?' asks Nonno, breaking into my thoughts and bringing my stare away from Giacomo.

'Well.' I swallow. 'One plate that says who we are,' I say, and step forwards. My hands are shaking a little and I have no idea why. I know exactly why I'm doing this. It's the end of my journey here. It's where I find me. Even if I have to move on now. I put down the pizza in front of Nonno.

'Tell me, what's on this?'

'Well, it's pizza dough, the way you taught me. With Nonna's sauce.'

He nods and she smiles.

'And the topping?'

'Sautéed leeks, Caerphilly cheese, which Mum sent over, and basil.' I smile, watching Nonno and Nonna smile too. 'It's called the Welsh Italian. And there's some red onion on there too! Because I'm a bit Welsh, a bit Italian, and it's in the shape of a heart, because I love this place!' They all laugh and I do too. Tears stand in our eyes and we know my time here is coming to an end. There is no way I can outdo Giac. He will have something very new and inventive. And it's fine. This is me. And I'm glad finally to have found me. I know who I am. The Welsh Italian, with the food of my family at the heart of me.

'Giac?' Nonno calls. Giac's hesitant and I'm not sure why. He walks towards us carrying a plate covered with a napkin. Even I'm excited to see what he's created.

We follow the plate as he brings it towards Nonno and slowly puts it down in front of him. Nonno looks down at the plate, then up at him. Then, slowly, he slides off the napkin and we all stare in utter disbelief.

FORTY-SEVEN

'It's empty,' Nonno finally says, as we stare at the plate.

Giacomo nods slowly.

I'm confused. 'Where's your pizza? Did something happen?' I ask, looking from the plate to him.

He shakes his head. 'Nothing happened to the pizza. This is the dish I'm serving.'

'What?' Oh, for goodness sake, this time he's gone too far! 'You?' I stare at him. 'This is it? This is your plate of food?' I'm furious with him all over again. 'But you said— We agreed!' I take a deep breath but it doesn't help the surge of frustration welling up in me. 'One plate of food to say who we are! Nonno!' I look at Nonno, who shrugs.

'Look, I've gone along with your reconstructed Margheritas and your other fancy ideas but, really, you can't expect Nonno to hand you this place on some

324

kind of emperor's new clothes idea.' I point at the plate. 'What's this one called? The naked pizza!' and Sofia's children laugh.

'Why couldn't you just do it, Giac? Were you worried I was going to beat you? You'd be beaten by a woman who isn't even fully Italian? Is that it? Is this your pride – or maybe it's just your prejudice? This is what you always do! You run before you're pushed. Just like you ended our marriage because you thought I was going to leave you first.'

Everyone stares at me, then at Giac. Just like the gripping game of *bocce* yesterday and Veronica's last throw, watching to see where it would land, and what would happen.

No one else says a word.

'Or did you think I wouldn't be able to put up a pizza that described me? Did you think I'm so confused about who I am, I couldn't put it on a plate? Did you think I wasn't capable?' Tears are filling my eyes. 'Why, Giac?'

'Luce . . .'

He puts out a hand and I brush it away. 'Don't Luce me!'

Outside in the lane I can hear a car pull up and the engine running. My taxi. He's early. Unheard of.

'Or maybe you just thought I wouldn't be able to compete with you, so you let me win. Poor Lucia. Well, I did compete. You're the one who didn't. You're the one who's walked out on their future again!' I'm furious he's done this. Now what do I do? I have a taxi booked, a flight home, and I haven't even had a chance to explain to Nonno and Nonna that I'm leaving now. If Giacomo isn't going to take on this place, what will happen? Will Nonno sell it after all? This is all Giacomo's fault! 'Now what, Giac? Now what's going to happen? I was expecting you to put up something . . . amazing! One thing that described you. That's what we agreed. And because that's what you are! Amazing! I managed it. I've worked out who I am, what and where I love.'

He folds his arms over his chest and looks down.

The car engine is running in the background.

'Who's that?' Nonna asks.

'It's my taxi,' I say, on a long breath out. 'I'm sorry, Nonno, Nonna, but I booked a flight home. I figured out that I may know who I am, but I also know that this place would do best in Giac's hands. People will accept him. The restaurant will thrive. Your legacy will be passed on. People will still come and this place will go from strength to strength. They may have eaten my food, but it was me not wanting change, not thinking about what was best for this place. And what is right for this place is Giac. All you had to do was put up the dish, Giac! It was all you had to do! One dish and this would have been yours. Everyone would have been happy.'

The taxi outside beeps impatiently.

'It was the only flight time I could get,' I say. Nonno and Nonna look upset. 'I just felt I should leave as soon as possible and let Giac get on without me around.'

Nonna and Nonno are looking at me with such sadness.

Giac finally looks up and straight at me, and it's as if no one else is there except him and me.

'Everyone would be happy?' He raises an eyebrow. 'Would you have been happy, Luce? Would I?'

'Well . . .' I hesitate '. . . you'd have got what you wanted. This place.'

'It may have been what I wanted, Luce, but it wasn't what I needed. And I don't think it's what you needed either.'

'You don't know what I need, Giac!'

Still no one around us moves, and I barely know they're there.

'What I needed was for you to open up the closed book that makes you you and put your heart on the plate! Tell me how you feel.'

He chews his bottom lip. 'And,' he says, 'that is exactly what I've done.' He looks at the plate, and I wonder if something is about to appear miraculously on it.

'This dish . . . if you've finished and I can explain?' He raises an eyebrow again and brushes his long fringe from his face.

My cheeks are burning with frustration and fury. How could he do this? Now Nonno will sell for sure!

'This dish says exactly who I am,' he looks at me, 'because . . .' he swallows '. . . I am nothing without you, Lucia Rossi-Llewellyn.'

FORTY-EIGHT

I stare at him. As does everyone else. Still no one moves.

He moistens his lips nervously. 'I mean it, Lucia. In all the time we've been apart, I've never regretted that decision more. Every day. It was always you. It's always been you. And . . .' he takes a huge breath '. . . I don't want to run this place if it isn't with you. Like I say,' he gestures at the plate, 'this is me. Open book. I'm nothing without you.'

I stand there, open-mouthed.

'This is me and my heart on a plate.'

The gates to the courtyard open.

'Taxi, for the *aeroporto*,' the man says.

'Um . . .' I can't see straight, hear straight or speak straight. 'That's me,' I say weakly. 'Me!' I try to muster some sort of sense in my swirling brain and tumbling heart.

'I . . . My taxi is here,' I say.

'Case?' the taxi driver asks.

'In the kitchen,' I say, not taking my eyes off Giac, who suddenly looks like a scared young boy, teasing his lower lip with one hand, the other across his chest.

The taxi driver goes into the kitchen and comes out with my case, pulling it roughly over the courtyard to the car waiting beyond the gates.

'I . . .' I have no idea what to say.

Nonno and Nonna stand now, beside me.

'Are you sure this is what you want?' says Nonno.

I hug them both hard, barely able to speak. I can't look at anyone else.

'I wanted this for Giac,' I say quietly. 'I wanted him to have his dream.'

Then I turn quickly and run out of the courtyard, the gate slamming behind me. I lean against the car and take a huge breath. Am I really about to do this? Aren't I being a bit rash? Don't I need to take some time to think about what's just happened?

No, I know now what I'm doing is right. It feels right. I feel it in my heart and my head isn't disagreeing.

I slam down the boot of the taxi and the car speeds away.

'If you mean it, then I agree,' I say, back on the other side of the gates, in the middle of the courtyard, my suitcase behind me, looking at Giac, his head hanging.

Nonna is beside him, trying to comfort him. He lifts his head a little at first. Then all the way.

'Lucia?'

'Tell me again.' I smile.

'I mean it,' he says. 'I'm nothing without you and I don't want to run this place on my own. I want us to run it together, side by side.'

'Equal partners?'

He nods, his smile growing.

'Equal partners,' he says, slowly sliding his arms around my waist.

'And I get to keep my team.' I grin as I look up at him.

'Of course!'

'And we encourage more young women to become *pizzaiola*s?'

'Yes,' he says, pulling me closer, and Sofia's daughter cheers.

'You and me?'

'It was never not . . .' he says, lowering his lips to mine as I lift my face to him. 'If this is where you want to be.'

'With all my heart,' I say, and our lips are about to touch. 'Oh, just one thing . . .'

'Yes?' He pulls away a little.

'I think this place should be called Nonno and Nonna's because it's the *nonna*s at the heart of the kitchen.'

'I agree!' shouts Nonno. 'Now just kiss!'

And we do. A long, lingering kiss that fills my body, my soul and my heart.

'It was always you,' I say. 'You keep my heart whole.'

He holds me around my waist and everyone at the table starts to clap. We turn to them all and see them standing and clapping. My cheeks burn with embarrassment and joy at the same time. My heart is as full as it could be.

'Now, let's eat and drink. And for God's sake Giac, give us something more than this to eat,' says Nonno. We all laugh and Giacomo and I fall into place, side by side, at the outside kitchen, as if it's the most natural thing in the world. There is nowhere I'd rather be . . . ever.

We sit down to eat, together, making plans for the following week, the new suppliers of Nonna's network and the menu.

'Nonno, just out of interest, who did sell the most pizzas?' I ask, holding a slice of perfectly cooked bubbling dough, tomato and cheese.

He stops eating. 'I don't know. Dante never told me and then he left and . . . I'd have to look,' he says.

Giacomo and I turn to Nonna, who looks suitably contrite. She reaches down into her bag, pulls out the envelopes that Dante gave her for Nonno and slowly hands them to him.

Nonno takes them, then looks at Giac and me. He

stands, his eyes twinkling, walks towards the *forno* and throws the envelopes onto the embers.

'Nonno!'

'Now I can retire in peace and know the restaurant and my legacy will go on after me. None of it was in vain.'

'Peace? I'd like some peace!' says Nonna, as Nonno comes back to the table, and we all laugh.

Giacomo's eyes sparkle and he leans in to kiss me. 'Happy?'

'Never happier.'

'Just one thing left to do, then.'

He stands up, goes into the kitchen and comes out with the brown envelope I have been avoiding.

I hold my breath.

He takes my hand and follows Nonno's actions. He walks over to the old *forno* and tosses the envelope inside. We watch it catch and the flames lick up around the inside of the oven.

'For better or worse,' I say.

'Because I'm no one without you,' he says again, kissing me, and I know we have made all the promises we need to make to each other. Tomorrow is a new beginning, and just like our pizzas, Giacomo and I are a combination meant to be together. For ever.

EPILOGUE

I wake up to the sound of singing. I turn to look at Giacomo, sleeping beside me, then walk over to the big doors that lead to the balcony and open them wide. From our new apartment, opposite Nonno and Nonna's, I can look straight down on Angelo singing.

'*Buon giorno!*' I call, and the smell of coffee and warming pastries rises to meet me in the glorious September sunshine.

'*Buon giorno!*' he shouts back, and waves. 'How lovely to have you as new residents in the neighbourhood!'

'It's lovely to be here,' I say. And it is. I look up and down the street. 'We'll see you later?' I call.

'Of course! I'm bringing an orchestra!' he says, waves, and goes back to wiping down the tables.

I wander out of the bedroom and into the kitchen where I turn on the coffee machine. I'm sick with nerves – or maybe it's excitement. I turn off the coffee machine and get dressed to go to the restaurant.

At the restaurant my new young apprentice is waiting for me.

'Are you sure this is okay?' asks Sofia.

'Of course!' I say, looking at her daughter. 'It's lovely she wants to be here and join in. Now, find an apron, and I'll show you how we roll out the dough.'

'Can I learn to toss it too, like Giac does?'

'Of course,' says Giacomo, placing a bandanna on her head, just like mine, and tying it at the back.

'We need all the help we can get, with Veronica not being here.'

'But she will be coming back, won't she?' says Sofia.

'Oh, yes, she'll be back.' I smile.

Outside in the courtyard, it's all hands on deck. Nonna and her network are decorating the tables with cloths, centrepieces and candles.

And with everything ready, we make our way to the church to wait on the steps for the beautiful bride and her husband-to-be.

Veronica is beaming as she steps out of the car in a dress so flamboyant with so many layers it takes all of us to help the rest of it and her groom onto the street.

'Who'd have thought a *bocce* game could change so much?' I say to her, and kiss Roberto too. 'You look wonderful!'

'I feel wonderful,' she says. 'And now I'm going to be a mozzarella farmer's wife!'

'As long as you're still going to work at the restaurant,' I say.

'Of course!' she replies. 'And as long as I'm as happy as you and Giac, I know I have everything to look forward to.'

'For better and for worse,' I say, and we glance towards Nonna Emilia, her mother-in-law-to-be.

'I think you'll be able to handle things okay.' I smile.

And Veronica takes her groom's hand as he leads her up the steps and into the church to meet the priest there.

'Happy?' Giac asks.

'Happy,' I say, and Sofia's daughter slips her hand into mine as we make our way to our seats.

And as I sit and look up at the big stained-glass window of the Virgin Mary, holding her baby, I know that I know who I am now.

And maybe, just maybe, it's time. Time to bring a small pizza-maker of our own into the world. Time to have a family, someone to whom we can hand on the legacy. I feel the flutter in my stomach all over again and put my hand to it, as the service begins. Giacomo takes my hand and holds it in my lap, next to my stomach. It's time. Because now I know I'm ready. It's our time.

ACKNOWLEDGEMENTS

Pizza has long been a part of my family life. One pizza place in particular, Rose's. A pizzeria in the South of France where we were always welcomed back like old friends, family even. It was a family business with Rose out front, and her niece Lucy and her husband cooking the pizzas. As a family, we look back at those times with such fond memories. And even after my father was no longer with us it was somewhere we returned to, feeling the support and comfort Rose, and her family and her food, gave us.

Over the years, with the children, pizza has always been our go-to for celebrations. I remember getting my first book deal and the first thing we did was go out for pizza! There's something so warm, comforting and celebratory about getting together for pizza. It's all about simple ingredients and sharing. I have always loved making pizzas, especially as we were lucky enough to have the original bakehouse in our last house, and cooked in that. I remember the day my brother made pizzas for my children . . . Nutella and marshmallows! They loved them.

Pizza is a turn-to meal in our house when the family are getting together and we want to celebrate without too much fuss. What could be better than family, friends, wine and pizzas?!

And my brother has taken pizza to his heart and to another level, becoming a pizza chef himself – learning his skills whilst living in Italy and then setting up in business, first out of a converted horsebox and now in his restaurant at Dungeness in Kent. So, a big thank you to him for passing on his pizza skills and knowledge as I wrote this book, and for giving me the idea for Veronica!

So thank you, Rose and Rose's Place (we never knew or called it by its real name), for the happy memories we have from there, and Richard for your passing on your pizza skills and introducing us to Italy.

Thank you to Francesca Best, my editor, the team at Transworld and, as always, my fabulous agent David Headley.

*Read on for
recipes with
a taste of Italy
to try yourself*

Classic tomato sauce for pasta and pizza

A quintessential Italian staple from my editor Francesca's family.

2 tbsp sunflower oil
1 large onion, diced
3 cloves garlic, chopped
A splash of red wine (optional)
2 x 400g tins of chopped tomatoes
2 tbsp dried parsley
1 tsp mixed herbs
1 tsp dried oregano
A pinch of salt
2 tbsp powdered vegetable stock
Salt and pepper to taste

Method:

1. Start by warming the sunflower oil in a saucepan on a medium heat, then add the chopped onions. Once the onions have begun browning, add your chopped garlic. Allow the garlic and onion to simmer, and then add a dash of red wine if you choose.

2. Add the chopped tomatoes and remaining ingredients to the pan. Stir the mixture and allow to cook for 15–30 minutes, until the consistency is smooth. You may need to use a blender to ensure your sauce is even.

3. Once the desired consistency is achieved, return to medium heat (if you'd taken the pan off the heat to blend the sauce) and add additional seasoning if required.

4. You can change the quantity of the ingredients you use depending on how many you plan to serve. Once finished, serve with your favourite pasta or spread over a pizza base!

Pizza dough base

Soft and warm, just like the Italian sunset . . .

½ tsp dried yeast (not fast-action)
200ml warm water
250g plain flour, plus extra for dusting
½ tsp salt
oil, for greasing

Plus:
Tomato sauce from the previous recipe

Savoury toppings of your choice: ham, salami or crumbled cooked sausage or chicken; sliced peppers; mushrooms; artichokes; chilli slices; olives; cheese (mozzarella, cheddar, gorgonzola, or a mixture!)

Sweet toppings: Nutella or other chocolate spread, marshmallows, flaked almonds or chopped nuts, sprinkles

Method:
1. First, mix your yeast into the warm water and leave to stand for 5 minutes. Small parts of the mixture should start to rise to the top, which will indicate that the liquid is active. Once it is, put your measured-out flour and salt in a bowl and add your yeast mixture.
2. If you decide to use a standing mixer with a dough hook, turn on the motor and keep the speed on medium-high, which should bring your dough together into a ball, and knead for 5 minutes. If you're kneading entirely by hand, this should take up to 10 minutes or longer. The dough should be ready to move on once it is shiny and springs back to shape if you press you finger into it.
3. Place some oil on your hands and remove the dough from your standing mixer. Oil a separate bowl and roll the dough in this until it is lightly coated in oil. Once you're happy with the coverage, place some cling film and a tea towel tightly over the top. Keep the dough stored in a warm area until it has doubled in size. Depending on the climate, this can take between 2 and 4 hours.

4. The dough you have should create one large pizza, but you can increase the quantity of ingredients and then divide the dough to create more. Shape your dough into a ball and dust in flour to reduce stickiness. Cover the dough again with a tea towel or cling film while you prepare your toppings. You can also freeze the dough in sealed bags. Just thaw in the fridge on the day, then bring to room temperature 3 hours before using.

5. Now to make your pizza base! To create a light but crisp base, don't use a rolling pin, as this will flatten and pop the air bubbles needed. Use your fingers to gently stretch out the dough to up to 25cm wide. You can be creative and make whatever shape you want once you've mastered the stretching skill.

6. For cooking, you may want to use an outdoor gas barbecue for authentic results, or charcoal for a smoky flavour. If you're using gas, keep the flames on a medium-low heat so that the bottom of the pizza doesn't burn. If you choose to use a charcoal barbecue, let the coals turn grey before beginning to cook the pizza. Otherwise, to cook indoors, you can either preheat your oven to 220 degrees (200 if fan-assisted) and cook on a pizza stone or baking sheet, or cook on a hot (but not smoking) griddle pan.

7. If barbecuing, carefully place your pizza on a floured baking sheet or a pizza peel. Make sure to use flour and not oil, as this will make sure the pizza can slide on and off the grill without sticking. Slide your dough on to the grill, close the lid and allow the dough to rise for 3 to 4 minutes. Your base will be ready when the bottom is showing small brown stripes. If using a griddle, follow the same steps though leave your griddle uncovered. If using an oven, leave the dough on the baking sheet and cook for 3 to 4 minutes.

8. Take your pizza off the heat and assemble the cooked side with toppings of your choice – either a generous ladleful of tomato sauce, spread out almost to the edges of your base, and savoury toppings, including cheese; or, if you're making a sweet pizza for dessert, a thin layer of Nutella and whatever treats you fancy!

9. Place the pizza back on the heat, uncooked-side down (and shut the lid if barbecuing). Give it another 3 to 4 minutes for a savoury pizza: remove when the cheese is melted and the toppings are hot – or just 1 to 2 minutes for a sweet pizza. Tuck in!

Italian meatballs

Perfect as a starter or main course, and great to serve with the classic tomato sauce recipe!

A large handful of plain breadcrumbs
100ml milk
2 tbsp olive oil, plus extra for greasing
1 onion, diced
500g beef mince
500g pork mince
3 cloves garlic, crushed
2 eggs, beaten
1½ tsp salt
1 tsp ground black pepper
A handful of fresh parsley, chopped
½ tsp red chilli flakes
1 tsp dried Italian herb seasoning/mixed herbs
2 tbsp Parmesan cheese, grated

Method:

1. Start by soaking the breadcrumbs in a bowl of milk for 20 minutes. Meanwhile, cover a baking sheet with foil and drizzle lightly with olive oil, or spray with cooking spray.
2. Heat the olive oil in a frying pan over a medium heat. Add the diced onion and cook, stirring, until translucent.
3. In a large bowl, mix the beef and pork together with clean hands, then add the cooked onions, garlic, breadcrumb mixture, eggs, salt, black pepper, parsley, red chilli flakes, Italian herb/mixed herb seasoning and Parmesan cheese. Use your hands or a spoon to fully mix the ingredients until totally combined. Use cling film to cover and refrigerate for one hour.
4. When the hour is nearly over, preheat your oven to 220 degrees (200 if fan-assisted).
5. Wet your hands and begin forming the meat mixture into balls. The size can vary based on your choice, but about 4–5cm in diameter is recommended. When you're happy with the shapes/sizes, arrange the meatballs on to the baking sheet.
6. Bake in the preheated oven for 15–25 minutes, turning occasionally, until browned and thoroughly cooked.
7. Serve with spaghetti and tomato sauce.

Coming Soon

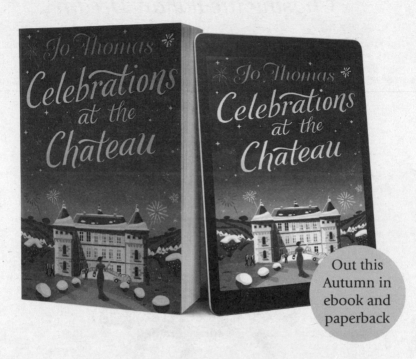

Out this Autumn in ebook and paperback

Also available

To celebrate the publication of

Chasing the Italian Dream

and the return of balmy summer nights,
we are offering one lucky reader the chance to
win a portable pizza oven from Ooni Fyra.

Ooni Fyra pizza ovens are wood-fired, easy to set up,
and light enough to carry from your back garden to
your picnic table. Perfect for relaxed evenings sharing
stories, food and drink with your loved ones!

The competition closes 15th July 2021.
For your chance to win, enter the competition
at jothomasauthor.com/pizza.